OFF LIMITS

PLAYBOYS OF NEW YORK SERIES

JA LOW

Copyright @ 2018 JA Low

Cover Design by Outlined with love

Editor by Swish Design & Editing

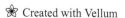 Created with Vellum

1

CHLOE

"You're getting married!" Stella raises her champagne glass in the air as my bridesmaids all cheers her.

I can't believe I'm getting married. And what's even more unbelievable, it's to Walker Randoff, the man who I initially thought was the biggest dick in the entire world. Let's face it, he has an ego the size of the football field he trains on every day. Can't blame him—star quarterback, super bowl legend, crowned football's sexiest man for three years in a row—he has women falling at his feet on a daily basis. The serial womanizer.

Personally, I wanted nothing to do with him. I mean I've had to clean up one too many of his public relations nightmares over my time —the alleged sex tapes, the girls, the partying too hard.

So, why on earth am I marrying him?

The man's relentless, and when he sets his mind on something, he goes after it. Eventually, he wore me down. Slowly but surely over the years, he showed me his softer side, cleaned up his image, stopped the womanizing, and that's the man I fell for—not the football legend but the soul underneath all that bravado and pizzazz.

Who can say no to a sexy footballer?

Feeling ever so slightly nervous about the day, I wanted to have a small intimate affair, but Walker needed this elaborate day filled with celebrities and football legends. He's invited so many people I don't even know half of them. To be honest, it's turned into a bit of a circus. He told me not to worry about a thing that he had it all covered. *Who knew Walker had a Groomzilla inside of him?* The more businesses who came to him wanting to sponsor the event, the crazier his ideas became. Honestly, if we could have eloped, I would have.

"You look a little tense. Here, have some champagne. That'll ease your nerves." Ariana shoves a glass into my hand.

"I wish I could drink." Tracey pouts while her hands rub over her protruding stomach. "This little one's doing somersaults because of all the nerves. I need him to calm down." I smile over at my oldest friend, taking in her gorgeous bump, which is wriggling under her shirt.

"He's already a handful." Watching her stomach contort, Tracey lets out a heavy sigh as Ariana hands her a glass of sparkling apple juice.

I've known Tracey all my life. We grew up together as next-door neighbors. Our moms were best friends, which meant we were too. When my parents died in my final year of high school, Tracey and her mom, Linda, took me in. My older brother, Elliot, was living overseas attending culinary school, so he couldn't take care of me. We became family.

She and my brother are all I have left in the world. As much as I love her, Tracey always gets herself into dramatic situations, especially if it involves a bad boy—bad boys are her kryptonite. That's how Tracey's found herself in the situation she's in now—pregnant and alone. The douche she was dating up and left her when he discovered she was pregnant. *Who the hell abandons the mother of your child like that?* He kicked her out of their home, which meant she was pregnant and alone.

Thankfully, I have an extraordinary fiancé, who understands the fact that Tracey and I are family and suggested she move into our guest house, so she'd have access to our staff, have security surrounding her, and most importantly, be close to us. He even flew her mother out to live with her to help Tracey prepare for the baby. *He's a keeper, that man.*

"It's so great the five of us are back together again," Emma squeals, popping another bottle of champagne.

"Um… you guys catch up all the time." Lifting the glass to my lips, I take a sip of my drink.

Emma, Ariana, and Stella all live in New York. We've known each other since college. Ariana studied architecture, and I met her on the first day as we were assigned as roommates. We then met Emma, who was sitting on a park bench on campus, crying. Ariana and I had to checked on her. She told us she'd just found out one of her sorority sisters had been sleeping with her boyfriend. That's when we took her under our wing and brought her into our little duo.

Emma's recently started her own fashion marketing agency, which has taken off quickly. Years spent modeling and working for designer brand companies has given her great connections, enough to finally launch her own agency.

And Stella, the newest member of our group, she's my brother Elliot's publicist. My brother is kind of famous—insert eye roll—he's a celebrity chef. For some reason, women like him a lot, judging from his Instagram following. Pretty sure the half-naked videos online help his popularity. But to me, he will always be stinky Elliot. He's currently based in New York where his first restaurant is located, but he's been slowly opening restaurants in other cities. He's actually working on one in Las Vegas at the moment, and I'm so proud of him.

"I'm so nervous," I state voicing my feelings to my friends. "Walker's kind of gone a little overboard… *with everything.*"

"Understatement of the year," Ariana snorts.

"It's cute that he's so into getting married," Stella, ever the romantic adds.

"Enjoy the day. You won't have another like it," Tracey states, which sounds more like a warning than a pep talk.

Maybe it's her hormones, and she doesn't realize how it sounded.

I notice Ariana and Emma looking at Tracey with frowns on their faces.

Did they hear her tone, too?

"Lucky Walker has organized a million and one cameras, so I won't forget it," I awkwardly tell her.

"Come on, let's go get pampered." Stella quickly changes the subject.

There's a knocking sound coming from outside, and Ariana stands to open the door.

"Evening, ladies."

Walker strides into the suite, confidence oozing from his every pore. "Baby." He grabs me, picking me up in his arms, and kisses me. Total Hollywood style. My friends holler and throw profanities at me.

"I just needed one last kiss before I marry the shit out of you tomorrow." He places my feet back to the floor.

I'm all giggly after one too many glasses of champagne. "I can't wait to marry you, too."

"I wish you were staying with me tonight." He nuzzles into my neck, giving me goosebumps.

"I do, too."

"It's tradition," Tracey reminds us.

I roll my eyes and suck in a deep breath of his cologne. He always smells so good.

"I'm going to miss you. My hand is a poor substitute," Walker whispers to me, sending shivers over my body.

"I promise to make it up to you on our wedding night." Shooting him a cheeky wink.

"Yeah, you will," he growls, gripping his large hand on my ass.

"Please don't make me puke, guys," Ariana jokes.

"I hate being apart from you." Walker pouts, giving me those puppy-dog eyes I can't resist.

"It's only twenty-four hours. Then you'll have me in your bed forever." That comment makes him smile.

"Can't wait." He kisses me again. "Well, ladies... I must be off. All this..." he waves his hand over his face, "... needs eight hours." His beauty regime is way more rigorous than my own. "See y'all tomorrow," he says as he heads to the door.

"Walker, wait," Tracey calls out.

I notice his shoulder tense when she says his name. *I've never seen that before,* I think to myself.

Tracey turns to us. "I'm going to head to bed, too." Her hands rub over her belly. "Otherwise I'm not going to make it all day tomorrow."

I'm surprised she's lasted as long as she has, being so heavily pregnant. Tracey says her goodbyes and walks out the door with Walker.

When I turn around, I notice Ariana's still staring at the door with a frown on her face. "Everything okay?" I question.

She shakes her head as if clearing whatever she's thinking from her mind. "Yes. Sorry. Got distracted by a work thing."

She's lying to me. I know because her right eye has the faintest of twitches, which is her tell.

"He's such a good guy," Emma moans, flopping herself backward on the sofa. "I want one of those. This being single shit is exhausting."

"What! No good men in New York?" I ask.

"Please... I've been working twenty hours a day. I don't have time to date."

"Um... what about that male model? What's his name?" Stella adds.

"Ivan?" Emma rolls her eyes.

"Yeah. That one. He's so hot." Stella practically drools.

"He was stress relief. The man's boring. Hot men don't have to try at all. They just need to show off their abs and chiseled jaw, and women drop their panties instantly."

Emma's right. But there are hot guys with great personalities out there, she just needs to make time to find them. But, starting your own business doesn't really leave much time for anything else.

"I can't walk into a meeting without some guy trying to mansplain architecture to me. Me, the person you hired to build your freaking home."

"You've met EJ, haven't you?" Stella adds.

EJ is my brother's nickname, it's short for Elliot Jones.

"The ego of a chef ... man, they're the worst." She turns to me. "No offense, Chlo."

"None taken. My brother's ego's pretty big."

"I bet that's not the only thing that's big." Emma waggles her eyebrows at Stella.

"Ew..." I curse Emma.

"Emma!" Stella squeals.

"As if you don't know," Emma goads her on.

"He's my boss," Stella argues.

"That's the best kind of sex. On the desk with the blinds shut. Late at night, or on your knees under his desk while he's on the phone." The room goes instantly silent at Emma's words. "What?" She looks at us all innocently. "Don't tell me none of you haven't done anything like that?" We all shake our heads. "I had no idea my friends were such prudes."

"No, I don't want to get fired or ruin my reputation," Ariana adds.

Emma waves her hands in the air and sings, "Whatever, guys. Let's pop some more champagne."

2

CHLOE

My bridesmaids are all snoring softly. Carefully, I pull back the covers of my bed quickly swinging my legs to the side, my toes digging into the carpet. I dare not breathe as I don't want to alert them to my defiance.

Glancing at the clock, it's just past midnight, so technically it's my wedding day, and I'm not breaking any rules or tradition.

Look, it sounds like great logic at this time of the night.

I'm simply going to sneak into Walker's room, have a quickie, and then come straight back. Spying my dress from earlier, I quickly change into it, sans the underwear.

Walker's room is on the other side of the resort, so I have to walk through the lobby to get to his tower. Silently moving through the suite, grabbing the spare key to Walker's room from beside my purse, I start tiptoeing down the hallway. Ever so slowly, I turn the door handle, praying it doesn't make a sound, which it doesn't, and sneakily I slip through.

Yes. I throw my arm up and fist pump the air.

Quietly but quickly, I make my way to the lifts before anyone notices I'm missing. The girls will kill me if they knew what I'm up to.

Eventually, I make it to Walker's penthouse. Slipping the keycard into the door, the green light flashes. Thankfully the door doesn't creak, alerting him to my presence. The room's dark, he must be asleep, but as I enter further, I can hear a woman's moan.

My heart begins to beat quickly.

Is Walker watching porn?

"Yeah, baby."

I still.

Walker's voice goes through me like ice.

I turn the corner into the living room, and there is my pregnant best friend riding my soon-to-be husband on the sofa. My mind and body go into shock, unable to comprehend what I'm seeing.

"That's it, Mama. Ride me. Ride me," Walker tells her as they both come together.

Tracey giggles, a light sheen of sweat covers her face.

Walker looks at her, and like a dagger to my heart, he wraps his hand around her neck and kisses her.

Oh, fuck! I think I'm going to be sick, but my feet are rooted to the floor.

Walker's attention is drawn to Tracey's bump. "I can't wait to meet my little man."

Wait. What did he just say?

I stumble slightly, my palm touches the hallway wall.

"He can't wait to meet his daddy, too," Tracey purrs.

"I'm glad you're living with us. It means I can spend as much time as I can with him." Walker smiles, but Tracey's face changes.

"I don't understand why you're still marrying her." There's that tone again, the one she showed me earlier today.

"Tracey…" Walker's voice is like steel. "I love Chloe."

"Yet, you've been fucking around with me for the past year."

That news sucker punches me, and I close my eyes while the pain starts to register inside me.

"You're the one who came on to me. Remember?" Walker reminds her.

"You didn't put up much of a fight," Tracey snarls.

"You told me you were happy to accept whatever I gave you."

"But, I'm having your baby. I should be the one getting married to you. Not her." I'm surprised by the venom coming from Tracey's lips.

Taking a step back, I press myself against the hallway wall hoping somehow, I can disappear like a puff of smoke from this nightmare.

"I can't afford a scandal. And this would most definitely be a scandal."

"But—" Tracey begins to argue.

"No." Walker raises his voice, "You want me to lose millions of dollars in sponsorship? You want to lose access to that credit card I gave you. The allowance. The trust fund?" There's silence. "Didn't think so."

I can't listen to anymore. Pushing my jelly-like legs to move, one in front of the other, I slowly make my way out of the hotel room.

The bell of the lift brings me back into the moment a short time later.

What the fuck!

How could they?

How fucking could they?

Tracey—she's like a sister to me.

And she's been fucking my fiancé for the past year.

And she's having his baby.

His baby!

I double over in pain, stumbling along the corridor toward my door. Sucking in shallow breaths, I realize I'm not breathing. I can't breathe. Panic engulfs me as I collapse to the floor in a flood of tears.

"Is that my sister?" a male voice echoes down the hallway.

"I don't know?" a female voice answers.

"Chloe. Chloe." I hear my brother shouting at me, his hands shaking my body. "Wake up, Chlo." The concern in his voice brings me back to the reality I don't want to be a part of. Then I hear loud banging.

"What's going on?" a female answers the door.

"Stella, something's wrong with Chlo."

"I should leave," an unrecognizable voice adds.

"Yeah, you should. This is family business," Stella says to the blurry figure beside me. Then another pair of hands are on me, shaking me, but all I want to do is curl up into the fetal position.

"We should call Walker," Stella states.

"No!" I scream, sitting up quickly. "No." The second time comes out in a wounded wail, the tears falling again as the walls close in on me. EJ picks me up in his arms and pushes his way into my suite.

"What's going on?" Ariana asks.

"I don't know. I found her outside like this," EJ tells her.

"She doesn't want us to get Walker," Stella adds.

Next thing I know, Ariana is wrapping her arms around me as we lay on the couch.

"What did he do?" she whispers in my ear.

"What the…" Emma trails off as she joins the room.

Stella and EJ fill her in.

"You saw something, didn't you?" Ariana asks.

Looking up at her, she instantly knows the answer.

"Oh, babe." She holds me tighter. "You want to go?" I agree with a simple nod. "You want to cancel the wedding?"

Inside I am yelling, screaming the word 'yes,' but I'm unable to speak the words.

Thankfully, Ariana can read me. "Okay. Sit tight. We'll pack every-thing right now." Ariana untangles herself from me. "Right, team? Walker's fucked up."

There are gasps.

"I'll fucking kill him with my bare hands," EJ snarls.

"You'll have time for that later, but for now, Chloe wants to get out of here. So, Operation Runaway Bride needs to happen, and it needs to happen now," Ariana orders everyone.

I have no idea how long it takes, but the next thing I know, I'm being whisked away from my suite with our bags in tow, EJ keeping me close as we head to the basement to get into our cars. He places me ever so gently against the leather seat and then straps me in.

"When you're ready, Chlo, I'm here for you." He kisses my forehead while everyone else slides into to car. "Where to?" EJ asks.

Somehow, I find my voice. "Home! I need to pack up my house. I have to get far, far away from *them*." I spit the words them out. The car falls silent, EJ follows my directions, and we head toward home.

After a short drive, we pull up to the large oversized gates. I mumble the passcode to EJ, who types it into the security system. We continue on through the gates and pull up in front of the tall, white columns of the front entry. Stepping over the threshold, the one that Walker was supposed to carry me over, I feel numb. Our home doesn't feel the same anymore. There's nothing here now but stark white walls and false promises.

"Please, I just need to pack up as much as I can." Telling my friends what I want to take, they understand and quickly get to work, packing up my bedroom, including all my clothes, shoes, bags, and jewelry.

"I've organized a private jet for you. We can go anywhere you like," EJ tells me as we finish the last of the packing.

"New York. I want to go to New York." EJ gives my shoulder a squeeze as he takes my bags to the car.

There is no hesitation when I shut the door to my old life. Who knew someone's life could change so much in the shortest of moments? I don't know who *that* girl is anymore, the one who lived in the white mansion on top of the hill, the one who was blissfully unaware that her life was one massive lie. That her closest ally was stabbing her in the back.

I was blinded by love.

Never again.

Once we're up in the air, I finally feel safe. I've been worried that Walker or Tracey might catch wind of what I'm doing and stop me. But now, high up in the clouds and what feels like a million miles away from them, I'm safe enough to share with everyone. Plus, there's no way any of my friends will go to jail for murder when they hear the truth.

Sipping my vodka, I clear my throat grabbing everyone's attention. "You guys really are ride or die. You've all packed up my life without hesitation or questions and got me the hell out of Dodge. How can I ever repay you guys?" Tears well in my eyes.

"Something big happened. You were in shock. We knew you needed to get out of there," Emma confesses.

Reaching out, I grab her hand giving it a thankful squeeze. "Thank you." Smiling sadly, I continue, "I snuck out of our room to visit Walker." While explaining, I look over at my friends and brother. "What I wasn't expecting was for Walker not to be alone."

"That fucker," EJ curses.

"Hope his dick falls off," Emma adds.

"Who was he with?" Ariana asks, but I think she already knows the answer.

"Tracey."

The plane falls silent.

Deathly silent.

"No..." Stella breaks the silence, "... she wouldn't?"

"I wouldn't have believed it if I hadn't seen them fucking on his sofa with my very eyes."

"That fucker," EJ curses, hurling his crystal tumbler across the plane hitting the wall and shattering it into tiny diamonds silencing everyone, the amber liquid rolling like a river down the white fuselage.

"EJ," Stella screams.

The stewardess rushes out from the back of the plane on hearing the commotion. "So sorry about that." Stella points to the wall. "We've had some bad news, and he didn't handle it well." The beautiful blonde looks over Stella's shoulder to where EJ is pacing around the cabin, almost tearing his hair out. A slight frown forms across her forehead before turning her attention back to Stella where she gives her a professional smile and quickly cleans up EJ's mess.

I'm hoping he doesn't freak out more when I tell him what else I know. Sucking in a deep breath while trying to steady the sickness rolling around in my stomach over the words I'm about to say, "The baby's his."

They all stare at me in disbelief.

Silence.

"Now, I get why you waited to tell us." Ariana adds, "You know we would have killed them both." She moves and sits beside me in the chair. I curl up into her arms.

"That's fucking messed up," Emma curses.

"It's been going on for about a year." The entire plane of people erupts into cursing and head shaking.

"And he moved her into your home," Emma states angrily.

"Fucking bastard," EJ curses.

"He's going to freak when you don't turn up." Stella smiles.

"This is the biggest 'fuck you' ever." Ariana nudges me.

"I know."

"Wait a minute…" Emma stands up abruptly, "… you leaving him at the altar isn't going to do him damage. People are going to feel sorry for him. They're going to paint *you* as the villain, Chloe."

She's ever the marketer.

"She's right," Stella agrees.

"No one knows about Tracey. They're just going to think that you're a bitch, or he's going to turn it around and say that you cheated on him."

"Would a recording of their conversation help my case?"

"You're shitting me." Emma smiles.

"I don't know what I was doing in my shock, but apparently I hit record on my phone and got it all." Years of dealing with footballers and their scandals I guess set me up for my own scandal.

"Stella. You have to send the recording to the press," EJ tells her.

"You want me, to?" Stella asks. "Once it's out, there's no going back," she advises me.

"You're right. He's going to turn this around on me. Do it!" Handing over my phone, I watch her fly into action.

3

NOAH

"This is paradise." Feeling the warmth of the sun against my skin almost gives me goosebumps but in a good way.

"We're supposed to be working," my brother and twin, Logan, reminds me.

"You told me this was an all-expenses-paid holiday. You said nothing about working," Anderson, my best friend groans beside him.

"We're supposed to be pretending to be on a guy's trip, remember?" I remind my brother. "Have another beer." Grinning at him, he rolls his eyes and lays back against his sun lounge, pulling his designer sunglasses over his eyes while a tense tick twitches across his jaw.

"I don't know how you two think this undercover mission is going to work. Everyone knows what you look like. You're the 'playboy twins of New York.'" Anderson chuckles, sipping on his beer.

Fuck, I hate that nickname the press has given us. Yes, we date. But not all the women who are seen on our arms are sleeping with us. It's good for business to be seen out and about. We are selling a luxury brand, a lifestyle—of course, my brother and I have to pretend we live the life we're selling.

"Fuck you." Flipping my friend off, he knows how much we hate that nickname. "If you're going to be a dick all week, you can get on the next plane home."

Anderson chuckles and ignores me. Pulling my own sunglasses down over my eyes, hoping the disguise will work, we all settle into our sun lounges by the pool.

Logan and I scan the resort looking at areas where we can improve —making sure the staff is doing as they're trained, checking that the guests are having a great time.

Logan and I started The Stone Group years ago. The company owns luxury boutique hotels around the world catering to the wealthy elite. People pay large amounts of money to be able to holiday in style and anonymity with us, so we have to make sure we are delivering that promise.

Anderson, as much as he's a dick, he's the one who funded our first hotel in Bali. We met him at college, the typical East Coast trust fund boy, but the difference with him was he's smart. He has a knack for numbers and business.

We were drunk one night at the bar, told him in a moment of weakness our idea, he told us he loved it, he would finance it, and the next day we were on his private jet to Bali scouting locations. The rest is history as they say.

"Please tell me you're seeing what I'm seeing." Anderson slaps me in the chest.

Logan and I look over to what's captured his attention. We fall silent. Three of the most beautiful women enter the pool area dressed in various stages of resort wear from bikini to cover up. They all have cocktails in their hands and are giggling. I think maybe they've already had one too many before visiting the pool. They move in a pack toward us, the three of us watch as they giggle their way over to where we're sitting. *Are they coming to talk to us?* Taking a quick sip of my beer to cover the fact that I can't stop staring at them, we watch in fascination as they throw their bags on the chairs right beside us. They don't break their conversations as they each grab a sun lounge and move them closer to each other.

I've noticed the other men around the pool equally as fascinated as we are with the new guests.

"Who's up for a swim?" the tall raven-haired woman asks, pulling the sarong off of her hips, exposing the tiniest white bikini.

"Fuck me," my brother curses beside me as she turns to head for the pool before suddenly stopping. Bright jade green eyes peruse us. The other girls stop their various stages of undress and follow to where her attention has been drawn.

"Well, hello there, boys." She places a manicured hand on her hip while cocking an arched brow in our direction. "Are you enjoying the view?"

"Most certainly are," Anderson calls back. The raven-haired beauty's eyes narrow in on him, and she gives him a sly smirk. Turning on her heel, she struts toward the pool, her hips swaying in a hypnotic trance. The other two girls follow suit, joining her in the pool.

"Chlo," the brunette calls out which draws my attention from them in the pool to someone else. She's waving to a beautiful blonde who's walking along the pool's edge, a towel in one arm and her cell in the other. She looks up momentarily from the screen and gives them a smile before turning back to her phone.

"Get off the phone," the raven-haired girl screams at her friend. "You know nothing good can come of it," she says, warning her.

She waves her friend's request away as she furiously types on her phone. She's so caught up in it that she doesn't notice the step, and the next thing I know, I'm jumping off of my chair as she begins to crash to earth. Lunging and stretching as far as I can, I grab her just in time before she hits the concrete, but her phone sails off and smashes onto the stone of the pool surrounds.

"Are you okay?" My arms wrap tightly around her. She looks up at me, momentarily stunned, before quickly jumping out of my arms and brushing the imaginary dust off of her.

"Oh… um… thanks." She sounds panicked. *Did I scare her?*
"Shit." She crouches down picking up her shattered phone then she closes her eyes, and I notice she's on the brink of tears.

"Told you no good would come from that phone," the raven-haired girl calls from the pool while chuckling.

Seems a little harsh of her friend to say in that moment.

The blonde picks up her phone and throws it back into her bag. She's so absorbed that it takes her a couple of moments to realize I'm still standing near her. "Sorry, I'm not myself at the moment. Thank you. Thanks for saving my ass." She gives me a small smile.

"I don't mind having a beautiful woman falling at my feet." Cracking an awful joke, she looks up at me, and the small smile disappears from her face.

"Men," she mumbles under her breath, moving away from me.

Was my pick-up line that bad?

She throws her bag down with the others and quickly strips off her sundress and joins the others in the pool.

"That was an epic strikeout." Anderson laughs, and I flip him off.

"As hot as they are, we're here to work," my brother reminds me.

"Shit!" Looking down at the red wine stain splashed across my white shirt and dripping into my lap.

"I'm so sorry, sir." The waitress looks like she's about to cry.

"It's okay," I tell her through gritted teeth. "It was an accident."

Which it was—a guest pushed passed her, which resulted in the glass ending up on my lap.

"I'll head back to my room and get changed."

Anderson, of course, doesn't stop laughing. The fucker. I roll my eyes as I exit the restaurant.

As soon as I'm on the deserted path leading back to my beach bungalow, I strip off my white shirt. I don't need the wet material sticking to me in this heat. It's going straight in the bin, I'm sure nothing can save it. I round the corner to my villa and run directly into the blonde from the pool walking along the path. She's absorbed in her phone again.

"Shit. Sorry." I reach out and grab her arms, nearly knocking her over.

"No... it's all..." She looks up and realizes who ran into her. "You again." Her tone changes dramatically.

"We've got to stop meeting like this." There I go again with the lame jokes. She doesn't smile, but she does notice the fact I don't have my shirt on. So, I flex ever so subtly. I work out when I'm home, running through Central Park every morning before work to prepare for the day. I'm confident enough to know that I look good—shirt or no shirt.

"Why do you have your shirt off?" Glaring at me, she folds her arms in front of her chest defensively.

"Waitress spilled red wine on me." Flicking the destroyed shirt up in the air, I show her the stains.

"Did you use a bad pickup line on her, too?" Her tone has a little bite to it.

What? Wonder why she's having a go at me.

"No. A guest bumped her as she was handing me my drink." Not that I owe her any sort of an explanation. "If you'll excuse me..." moving past her, "... have a good night." Making my way to my villa, I can see she has *man-hater* written right across her forehead. I don't have time for women like that.

"Hey," she calls out.

Ignoring her, I walk closer to my villa. I don't play games with women. You're either into me or not. I don't play hard to get. I don't do the whole 'treat them mean to keep them keen' routine.

Footsteps echo along the stone path behind me.

"Wait. I'm sorry."

I'm steps away from reaching the door handle of my villa when a hand touches my forearm, halting me.

"I'm not normally this much of a bitch." The words tumble out of her mouth quickly, and I smile.

"You're not interested. I get it. I'm sorry to have interfered in your holiday."

A frown falls across her face. "You were interested…" she pauses, and I watch her eyebrows squeeze together tightly, "… in me?"

Before I can answer her, she shakes her head from whatever thought had entered her mind, and she continues talking, "Sorry. I just… look at you." She points at me. Those oceanic blue eyes trail over my bare chest, a slight tint of pink falls across her cheeks. "You're all…" She waves her hand in my direction while she trails off.

"All what?" I'm slightly confused, so I want to know what she means.

"You're wanting me to say it out loud?"

"Yeah, 'cause I feel like I've missed some part of the conversation."

She rolls her eyes at me.

Why does this woman intrigue me?

"You're a good-looking man. I'm surprised at your interest, that's all." She shrugs her shoulders, looking bashful.

Is she serious? Does she not see how beautiful she is?

"You own a mirror, don't you?" I ask her.

"Yes," she hesitates.

"Then you know how beautiful you are?"

These words stop her in her tracks. I can see my compliment has stumped her.

"I'm in the middle of a breakup."

Ah, that explains a lot. Did the guy dull her shine because he couldn't handle her? By the sounds of it, he didn't compliment her a lot because she's acting as if this is the first time she's ever had any sort of flattery. "I'm actually supposed to be on my honeymoon."

Oh, shit!

"But we've turned it into a girl's holiday instead." She shrugs her shoulders, awkwardly. "So, sorry for being a bitch. I'm just—"

"Hating all men at the moment," I finish for her, which makes her chuckle.

"Yeah. I kind of am," she agrees with my comment. "You seem

lovely," she quickly adds. "And I'd totally be flirting back with you if—"

"You didn't hate men."

"I don't hate men per se," she tells me. "Just one in particular."

"That's who you were on the phone with earlier today?"

Why am I asking for more information? This chick has baggage and lots of it, far too much for me to deal with.

"Yeah. I kind of left him at the altar, and he's extremely unhappy."

My eyes widen at her response. "I guess I'd be hurt being left at the altar, too."

Humiliated actually, but I won't tell her that.

"I have my reasons," she replies quickly.

"I'm sure you do."

"What does that mean?" She tilts her head, there's a slight bite to her tone.

"Nothing. It means absolutely nothing."

Why am I still entertaining this crazy woman?

"No. Go on... tell me," she pushes.

"You really want to know?" She nods her head. "I'd be damn unhappy, too. I would also be humiliated, embarrassed, actually probably mortified being left in front of all my friends and family with no reason as to why my bride left me standing there."

"No reason?" Her voice raises. "No damn reason! How about the fact that I caught him screwing my bridesmaid and best friend?"

Okay. Well... that's a dick move.

"Who happens to be pregnant with my fiancé's baby."

Not going to lie, my jaw has dropped in this moment, and I'm all out of words.

"That's after he moved her into our home as if it were a big favor to me when, in actual fact, it was to keep her close." She catches a hitch in her throat as the words tumble out, those blue eyes glistening with unshed tears. "So yeah, I think I had a damn good reason to leave him at the altar, don't you?"

I'm speechless.

Literally dumb struck.

One—who the hell does this kind of stuff to someone they supposedly love, and two—who the hell has time to do this shit? To fuck around on your fiancée with her best friend and never think you'd get caught?

"Shit." She covers her mouth, her cheeks turn a brilliant shade of red. "I can't believe I said all that." She appears mortified. "Um... I've got to go." She turns on her heel and runs back to her villa, which is across the path from mine.

"Hey," I call out. Now it's my turn to run after her.

She's crying as she turns to face me. "I'm sorry. I'm a mess." I don't blame her. "I'm not normally this crazy. I don't have arguments with strangers in the middle of paradise."

Reaching out, I brush away her hair that keeps getting caught in her tears.

"You have every right to be upset."

"Please ignore me." She waves her hand in front of her face.

"You're kind of hard to ignore." I didn't mean for that to sound so flirty.

"Is there something wrong with you, that you keep flirting with a hot mess like me?" Those blue eyes narrow in at me.

"I... no... I don't usually flirt with women going through a life crisis, but for some reason, I can't stop with you."

We both stare at each other for an extended period.

"Are you single?" she asks me.

"Yes. I don't have time for—"

The next thing I know she's kissing me.

What the hell is happening?

Her luscious lips are pressed against mine, and my every nerve ending is on high alert. Her fingers tighten in my hair, which is one of my major turn-ons. Then she's pulling me into her villa, her hands are all over my body, almost frantic with need.

I'm so confused. It feels so good, but also doesn't feel right. Slowly, I pull myself out of her grasp. I need a goddamn gold medal for putting a stop to this. "As much as I really want to continue…" Looking down at her, I trail off. Those lips plump, ready, and willing for more. Pink cheeks. Ocean-blue eyes dilated with need.

"What if I told you, I want no strings attached sex. Right here. Right now."

My eyes widen. This is probably every man's fantasy.

"I think you're in a vulnerable place at the moment from what you've told me."

"I want to feel wanted even if it's only for a couple of minutes."

"It would be more than a couple of minutes," I reply cockily.

"My friends have been telling me the best way to get over someone is under someone else." This is a valid point. "Right now, I'm willing to do anything to get over him."

Should I be offended by this statement? I'm finding it hard to think when my dick is ready to go.

"So, how about it?" She licks her lips, teasingly.

Fuck me! Everything in me is screaming, *Yes. Yes. Yes.*

"How about this…" I start, my dick is going to hate me in two seconds. "Why don't you and your friends come and join mine for dinner tonight? We can party, have some fun, and by the end of the night if you still feel like you need to get under someone, then I'm your man."

She mulls this over for a couple of moments. "You're a good guy, aren't you?"

"I guess so."

Nooo, my dick screams at me.

"Fine," she huffs. "I think I can handle that." Giving me a small smile, she waits for my answer.

"Great. I've got to get changed. But we're in the Tropicana Bar if you want to meet us there."

"Okay." She smiles.

You've done the right thing tonight, I tell myself. It wouldn't have been the right thing to do to take advantage of a woman at her most vulnerable. Turning, I head out her door and down the path.

"Hey," she calls out, stopping me in my tracks. "What's your name?"

Shit, we haven't even exchanged names.

"Noah."

She mulls this over, tapping her fingers on the wooden door. "Chloe," she states her name. It's pretty.

"See you later, Chloe." And with that, I walk back to my villa and quickly text the guys that we will have four extras joining us for dinner.

4

CHLOE

I can't believe I just did that. *Who the hell am I?* I don't go around propositioning men. Especially after dumping all my baggage right at his feet. *You're such a loser, Chloe.*

That cheating bastard has me tied up in knots, and I'm sick of it. I'm eager to get off the Walker Randoff rollercoaster of denial.

In his texts he has vowed he would do anything and everything to destroy me after humiliating him on our wedding day. He said I should have sucked it up and married him then discreetly, in a year's time, divorced him.

Like what planet does he live on where he thinks that's okay?

He's knocked up my best friend. But true to his word, Walker's destroying me in the press with his bullshit lies, while flipping the reports of his infidelity onto me. I guess, in some ways, I saw it coming.

To add to my humiliation, all these women have come out of the woodwork and are selling their story about their 'special' night with Walker all while engaged to me. With each new story that appears, I don't know who the man I loved is anymore.

Was everything a façade? A game?

He's been telling reporters that we had an open relationship, that we both dated other people while we were engaged, and for some reason, I reneged on that deal. He even had one of his teammates vouch that he'd hooked up with me. And he retaliated and slept with Tracey.

I simply can't.

I don't want to be involved with this bullshit anymore.

This isn't my life.

I've never sought being a tabloid story, a joke that late-night talk show hosts make fun of. Honestly, I want to run away and hide, hence why I've ended up on this beautiful tropical island.

That same evening after I found them in bed, I cashed in our honeymoon and chose another destination and shouted my girlfriends to come along. *Screw you, Walker Randoff.*

Of course, Tracey or 'she who will not be named' hasn't apologized for her part in this whole sorry saga. Oh no, she's right there beside Walker agreeing to all his outlandish stories about our relationship while sending me offensive messages behind the scenes.

I'm done.

More than done.

I want nothing more to do with her.

Linda, her mother, called, apologizing on behalf of her daughter. She doesn't condone everything she's done, but she has to be there for her grandson, and I get that. I understand an innocent little baby shouldn't be punished for his parents' indiscretions, but for me, I want no part of them.

I've resigned from my position with Walker's football team. They agreed it was for the best too. Of course, they're not going to let their star quarterback go, he wins them Super Bowls, after all. Let's face it. I am definitely the replaceable one. They thought it was best that they gave me a generous parting gift—a year's salary—in exchange for me not talking about the club.

Hey, I'm okay with that. At least the money will give me something to start over with in New York. I know I can live with EJ until I land on my feet.

Forget about them, I say.

Tonight, you're going to have some fun. Get dressed up. Flirt. Drink. Stop being sad because you're the only one mourning the loss of your relationship. Enough is enough.

Pulling out my cell, I text the girls that we're having dinner with the hotties from the pool in twenty minutes. Moments later, my phone lights up with the group text going crazy.

Exactly twenty minutes later, the girls all arrive.

As Emma walks through the door, she simply stares for a few seconds with her eyebrows drawn together. "You're not wearing that."

"What? I think it's cute?"

The girls shake their head at my dress choice.

"You look like you're going to visit the damn Queen?" Emma scrunches her nose up, and her eyes narrow.

"I look classy."

"You want to look like a hooker... but a $10,000 a night one?" Emma shoves a dress in my face she's already chosen for me and brought with her.

"You need to get your groove back," Stella tells me, ironically.

"I've kind of already propositioned him. He's a sure thing." I told them about my encounter with Noah earlier via our group chat.

"This is for you," Ariana tells me. "Forget everything that's happened if only for one night."

One night to forget about how shitty my life is at the moment.

Maybe I can do that.

"You look fucking hot," Emma squeals, making me turn around for them and then do a little curtsy.

"I feel very... exposed." Pulling at the dress in an attempt to somehow make it longer, but realizing it's so short if I bent even slightly, my ass would be out on show.

Emma has lent me a gorgeous black, sheer dress with gold stars embroidered over it, and yes, it's a designer brand. It has a deep V almost to my navel which means you can't wear a bra with it—which is okay for her non-existent breasts, but mine are fighting not to have a nip slip. Thankfully, there's tape to keep them in position. The stars are strategically placed over my nipples. I roll my eyes as I look down. Emma assures me no one can tell I'm not wearing a bra. But I can. Us big-boobed ladies don't go braless. Ever. Emma adds some cute boy shorts underneath and tells me I'm done.

Damn! I'm practically naked, there's more material on my bikini than this entire outfit.

"You look amazing," Stella squeals out.

"Work it, girl," Ariana tells me as I pretend to walk the runway in my outfit, exaggeratingly moving my hips from side to side as I step.

"You look sexy but classy," Emma declares.

"This is sooo not me," I state while looking at the stranger in the mirror.

"Then it's perfect." Emma places her chin on my shoulder. "One night only, Chloe Jones. Girl gone wild."

We walk in fits of laughter all the way to the restaurant passing other people on the way also heading for a night out on the town.

"You must be Mr. Noah's guests?" the maître d acknowledges. "Please follow me." He leads us through the restaurant and past the bar. We continue down a corridor until we reach an antique-style wooden door. "This is our private dining room," the maître d informs us.

He pushes on the beautiful door, and we enter into a tropical oasis —palm trees surround the glass room, a water feature is set off to one side, and there's a long wooden table down the middle with purple orchids resting in stunning pots in the middle.

"You made it." Noah stands and greets me, placing a kiss on each of my cheeks. He looks sharp in a fresh white shirt, offsetting his tropical tan. His light brown hair is still wet from his shower earlier. And those lips? Those soft, plump lips that sent zaps of electricity directly between my legs—something I haven't felt in a long time—is something I want to try again, and again, and again.

"This is gorgeous." Looking around the luxurious private glass room, I notice greenery surrounding the outside as if we're dining directly in the forest, minus the mosquitoes. Tiki torches line the pathway outside which twinkle through the foliage like fairy lights.

"Thought it might be nicer in here." He shrugs casually. "Let me introduce you to the guys." Noah moves away from me, and that's when I notice there's another one of him. I take a double look and blink my eyes. "We're not identical," he states, noticing my reaction.

"Exactly. I'm bigger," Noah's twin cracks a joke. "I'm Logan," he introduces himself.

"And this here is…"

The tall, broad blond guy dressed in a navy polo stands up. The man has to be six foot six at the very least. He towers over us. "I'm Anderson." He holds out his hand to me, then to my girlfriends. His focus immediately zeroing in on Emma. "So, ladies, what brings you to the resort?" Anderson asks, and I can see the panicked look on Noah's face as he tries to gain his friend's attention to change the subject, which is kind of him considering he knows the reason we're here.

"Girls' trip," Ariana simply states.

"Aw… the almighty girls' trip. So, ya'll single?" Anderson's straight to the point, and I kind of like that trait.

"Yes, and ready to mingle." Emma wiggles her eyebrows at him.

"You're going to be trouble. I can see it." Anderson bursts out laughing, pointing at Emma.

"Oh, sweetie, you have no idea how much." She licks her red lips seductively.

"You look beautiful." Noah catches me off guard with his compliment. I nervously touch my dress, feeling awfully exposed, while once again trying to pull at the hem.

"Really? The girls made we wear it." Tugging at the flimsy material which leaves nothing to the imagination around my breasts, I continue, "I kind of feel a little naked. It's not normally my style."

Why did I say that?

He doesn't need to know the inner workings of my lack of confidence. I should have said 'thank you' and taken the compliment as it was meant.

"Well, I think you've pulled it off." He nudges my shoulder.

Just smile Chloe and take the compliment.

"Thank you."

The night flies by, Noah's friends and mine seem to have gotten on well. The drinks are flowing, the food is impressive, and the boys are a lot of fun, telling us stories of their time together while in college.

"I'm heading off back to my room." Stella rises from the table.

"What? No," we all whine.

"I love you, girls, but I have an early morning conference call."

"Boo," I hiss, a little tipsy. But I'm lucky Elliot let her come away with us as he's so busy, especially gearing up for the launch of his new restaurant in Vegas. Stella kisses my forehead and slips away into the night without looking back.

"I think it might be time for us to get going anyway." Noah looks over his shoulder at the waiter who keeps popping his head into our room to see if we're anywhere near ready to leave. Noah pulls out my chair for me, and we all rise from the table, a little tipsier than we started.

Tick number one—I like that he's a gentleman. Walker never did anything like pull out my chair. Actually, come to think about it, he was no gentleman.

We walk out into the night air, the chill floating around my body.

"Who's up for a party at my place?" Anderson asks. "I've rented the penthouse," he tells us.

"Does it have alcohol?" Emma asks.

"Certainly does."

"Then I'm in." She links arms with Anderson and follows after Logan and Ariana.

"What do you want to do?" Noah turns to me.

All of a sudden, my indecent proposal from earlier hits me.

Feeling slightly flustered, I answer, "Um…"

"We don't have to do a thing. I'm enjoying your company, and I'm happy to spend some more time with you if you'd like."

Seriously? Where the hell has this gentleman been hiding?

I take his hand and entwine my fingers with his. It feels strange holding another man's hand after all these years. We walk in relative silence along the winding paths until we reach the beach. The silvery moon is high in the night sky bathing the dark water and sand with its glow. Taking a seat in the cool sand, we lay back and look up at the twinkling stars.

"It's been a long time since I've taken the time to look at the stars," I tell him.

"Me, too," he agrees. "Plus, you can hardly see them in the city."

"Yeah, true. Which city do you live in?"

We haven't gotten to asking many personal questions around the dinner table.

"New York," he states, which makes me sit up quickly.

"No way."

Seriously, world, what are you doing? You send me the perfect man, who's from my city, just when I'm *not* ready for him. Typical.

"Why? Does it sound hard to believe? Do I not look like a New Yorker?"

"No. No. It's not that." I giggle. "I just moved there."

"What? No way." He looks at me with a shocked expression. "Small world, huh?"

"It is."

We look back up at the stars chatting about everything and nothing until our eyes can't stay open any longer.

5

NOAH

"What do you mean you didn't bang her?" Anderson looks at me with confusion as I stumble back into our room.

"We fell asleep on the beach."

"You fell asleep on the fucking beach? This isn't a chick flick."

"I don't have to sleep with every single woman I meet." Anderson and my brother both give me dirty but confused looks. "Well, not this time, anyway."

Why are they giving me such a hard time about this?

"Her friends were DTF," Anderson tells me.

"Well, good for you," I reply, sounding annoyed.

"Hey, don't take it out on me you didn't get laid," he jokes.

"Ignore him," Logan tells me, moving me to the side. "We're just surprised nothing happened. You two look like you hit it off last night at dinner."

"We did."

How do I tell them it was nice to simply have a conversation with an intelligent woman without sounding like a pussy?

"You like her." My twin's picking up on my vibes.

"Yeah. I kind of do."

"This is a first." He looks at me, this time the look appears more stunned than anything.

"She has a lot of baggage," I state and Logan frowns. "Did none of the girls tell you why they're here?"

Logan shakes his head.

Wow! Those girls are like a vault keeping their friend's secret, you have to give them credit.

"This was supposed to be her honeymoon." Logan's eyes widen. "She caught him with her best friend, who apparently he knocked up."

"That's a shit ton of baggage." My brother slaps me on the back as he walks past.

"I know, right? She's vulnerable. She believes having a rebound fling will help her get over him."

"But you don't want to be that rebound?"

I nod in agreement.

"That story sounds familiar," Anderson interrupts us. "Like I just read about it in the news."

"Doubt it," I say while rolling my eyes at him.

Anderson pulls out his phone and madly starts typing then stops to read. "Holy shit, man…" turning the phone toward me, "… this is your girl."

Staring back at me on his screen is Chloe. *What the fuck!*

"It says she was engaged to Walker Randoff and left him at the alter after finding her bridesmaid in bed with him." Ripping the phone from his hand, I stare at the information, reading and taking in everything that's been reported.

"That chick has waaay too much baggage," my brother warns me.

"She was engaged to Walker Randoff, dude. How can you compete with a Super Bowl legend?" Anderson questions me.

"There's no competition. He's the dick who cheated on her and knocked up her friend."

"Be careful," my brother warns me again.

"Would you both calm down? Nothing's happening between us. I think she's cute. She has a great rack, but there's way too much baggage there for anything to happen."

A throat clears behind me, so I spin around and notice Chloe, Emma, and Ariana standing in our foyer.

Oh shit! Did she just hear that?

Damn it! She did.

I watch her face fall.

She turns on her heels and walks right out of the hotel room.

"Dick," Emma mumbles under her breath as I chase after her.

"Chloe… wait." She's pressing the button to the lift over and over again probably willing it to hurry and collect her. "Chloe." She turns around abruptly, her gorgeous blue eyes glassy, and instantly I feel like shit. "I'm sorry for what you overheard."

"No. It's fine. You owe me nothing. We don't know each other. We're strangers stuck on an island together." The lift dings, and she rushes inside, and the doors begin to close.

Fuck it. I stop them with my hand, which surprises her. So, I jump in quickly, the doors closing right behind me. We're now stuck inside a confined space.

"The boys were giving me a hard time this morning, and I… just—"

"Please, Noah. You don't have to explain anything to me."

"You were engaged to Walker Randoff?" My question throws her off as an audible gasp leaves her lips.

"How… I—"

"I told them vaguely why you were here on your girls' trip, and Anderson said the story sounded familiar. He Googled it and found you. The tabloids are full of the story I'm sorry to say."

The doors to the lift open, and Chloe bolts out of them into the sunshine.

"Wait," I call after her.

She spins around and stares me down. "No." Her voice is firm. Unmoving. "Leave me alone. Like you said nothing's happening between us. We're merely acquaintances. Have a good trip but don't bother me again." And with that, she storms off into the jungle.

Maybe it's for the best, I think as I trudge back up to the penthouse where the group is still gathered.

"Guess it didn't go so well?" Anderson smirks at me.

"You're a dick!"

"I'm just going to..." glancing around, I see the four of them looking cozy, "... go to my room."

"It's probably for the best nothing happened. Chlo's going through a lot," Emma states.

I give a simple nod and disappear into my room.

6

NOAH

Three Months Later

"We've chosen the best candidate for the Director of Social and Content Marketing. She comes highly recommended with the right skill set and experience for the job. I think she will be a great asset for the team, plus I like her." Lenna, our Human Resources Director, tells us. If she can get past Lenna's icy façade and somehow thaw her, then she must be good. Extremely good. Lenna never raves about any candidate.

"She sounds great. Bring her in, Lenna," I tell her.

She nods and opens our conference room door.

"Let me introduce you to Chloe Jones."

Logan and I both stand to greet our newest employee, but I stop dead when I realize who it is walking through the door. *No fucking way.* Chloe's confident walk slows as she registers who's sitting in front of her. Somehow, she quickly schools the panic that crosses her face upon recognizing us.

"Chloe, let me introduce you to the owners of The Stone Group… Logan and Noah Stone." She points to us as she mentions our names.

Chloe holds out her hand to me and shakes it as if it's the first time I've met her and then repeats with Logan.

"It's great meeting you both. I've heard so much about the company, and I'm looking forward to working with you."

Okay, so she's going to play it like that is she?

"Really?" Raising my brow at her, I smirk.

"Yes." She smiles. "It's one of the leading luxury boutique hotel companies in the world. You have a solid customer base, especially in the VIP and celebrity area. Your ratings on Trip Advisor are strong with few low star reviews. But…"

There's a but? I sit up straighter in my chair.

"But, not many people know about your brand outside of the VIP, celebrity, socialite world, etcetera."

"Our brand is meant to be on the higher end of luxury," I argue.

"Yes. But that doesn't mean ordinary people can't aspire to it, too."

"Our resorts are open to everyone who can afford to travel to them," Logan adds.

"Yes. But it's catering more to an older clientele. What about the cashed-up millennials, who pick their next holiday destination via an influencer on Instagram, or by a celebrity showing off their latest resort photos. Your social media is nice but basic. Pretty pictures might get you likes and shares, but how much of that is converted to sales, to brand awareness, or even into cross-promotions. Why are the resorts not seen on housewives' reality shows?"

Logan and I look at each wondering the same thing.

"Most people watching can't afford to go to those places, but it's something they can aspire to. Maybe save for to be a part of the world your advertising."

Lenna has a massive grin on her face.

"And you believe you can turn this all around?" I ask her.

"Yes, of course. I have connections in the fashion, restaurant, and corporate industry that will help us reach a wider range of guests for your hotels."

"Do you think you could have a presentation with all your ideas ready for us, say… within the week?" Logan asks.

"Yes. I have one already done."

Logan smiles. "Perfect. Send it through to Lenna, and she'll forward it to us. Then we will be able to make our final decision." Chloe smiles. "It's been a pleasure, Chloe." Logan stands and shakes her hand, and I follow suit. We watch as Chloe and Lenna leave our office.

"What the fuck!" Slumping in my chair, I let out a small sigh.

"Small world," my brother jokes. "Least she was professional." I nod in agreement. "Look, I like her… she seems great at her job. But if you can't handle being around her, we don't have to hire her."

"What?" Frowning at him, I continue, "No. She's perfect." He nods in agreement. "But maybe we should catch up before she joins the team to chat and get everything that happened between us out in the open."

"You can't sleep with her," Logan warns.

"What! No. Of course, not. I didn't on our trip, and I won't now."

Logan nods once, but I can tell he's not a hundred percent agreeing with me.

"Just sort it out. I like her, and her ideas are spot on."

Fine, I think.

Getting up, I head out of the conference room. Chloe's standing by the lift, and I join her, stepping inside at the last minute.

"Are you having a strange sense of déjà vu?" Leaning against the lift wall, I gaze at her and raise an eyebrow.

"I had no idea this was your company." She quickly adds, "I totally understand you not wanting to hire me." Her shoulders slump ever so slightly as she says it.

"Why would you think we wouldn't hire you?"

"After everything that happened months ago," she replies while color rushes to her cheeks. The lift doors open and thankfully we have it to ourselves.

"That has nothing to do with you doing your job, does it?"

"No. Of course not. I just—"

"You think because my ego took a bruising that I'd hold it against you?"

"Nooo," she says slowly, but then blurts out, "Fine. Yes. I thought maybe you would be butt-hurt about it all."

"This is business. I take business seriously."

"As do I," she replies quickly.

"Good." We both stare at each other, neither one of us daring to be the first to look away. The lift stops on the way, the doors open and people pile in, pushing me up close and personal with her. "Want to grab a coffee?" I whisper in her ear.

"Sure," she replies, but she's also giving me a suspicious side-eye.

"I'm a gentleman, you know that." The lift finally makes it to the ground floor, and everyone files out. "There's a coffee shop next door."

She follows me, and we grab a booth in the back corner away from everyone. Some privacy is in order. We order our coffee from the waitress and settle in.

"How have you been?" I ask, and this makes her chuckle.

"Good and you?" she asks awkwardly.

"Good." We sit there in silence for a couple of moments. "This is awkward as all hell, isn't it?"

Chloe bursts out laughing. "It really is."

The waitress brings over our drinks and places them in front of us.

"Look. My brother and I are beyond impressed with you, and not because we semi know you, but based on your merit. Lenna, our HR Director, never talks highly about anyone. But she does you, and that speaks volumes. We want you on our team. But only if you feel comfortable."

"You want to hire me?" She seems shocked by my revelation.

"Yes. You're the best person for the job."

"I… wow… I didn't think I'd ever be able to get a job with you guys and even more so because of the whole 'Walker' thing." She uses air quotes around his name. "He's been making my life hell, sabotaging any job prospects."

"Seriously?"

What a fucking dick.

"Yeah. He and Tracey love the drama, but I don't want anything to do with any of it. I wish they'd move on with their lives and focus on the baby that's about to be born."

I reach out and touch her hand not fucking thinking to console her, but as soon as I touch it, she pulls her hand away.

"Shit! Sorry... I..."

She shakes her head. "No. It's fine. But if we're going to be working together, then that kind of thing shouldn't happen."

She's absolutely correct.

"You're right. But know I'm here for you on a professional basis and friendship level."

Chloe takes a sip of her coffee. "Friends?" She raises a brow over the lip of her mug.

"Yeah. Friends and colleagues. I enjoyed your company on the island, though."

"Yeah. I did, too." She gives me a smile. "I wasn't in a great place at that time."

"Besides your ex trying to ruin your life, everything else going well?"

Chloe gives me a genuine smile. "Yeah. I think everything's going to be just fine now. You guys are my fresh start."

"Good." Finishing my drink, I state the obvious. "Now, hurry up and send over that presentation so we can formally employ you."

She gives me a salute. "I'll get right on it, boss."

We both burst out laughing.

7

CHLOE

Three Months Later

"Vegas, baby." Emma salutes to the sun stepping off the private plane. The launch of my brother's restaurant is happening in Vegas tonight, and he's flown my friends and me in for the weekend. Ariana isn't able to make it as she has a mountain of work to get through, which is a shame.

"I've never been to Vegas before," reveals Lenna, the newest member of our squad, and the woman who hired me at The Stone Group. We've become firm friends and quickly. We're both perfectionists, workaholics, and don't do any form of bullshit at work. We watch in horror as the young girls in the office perk up and pucker their lips every time Logan and Noah enter the office. If they put more effort into their work instead of their looks, they would be climbing the corporate ladder a hell of a lot sooner.

Do they think one day they're going to get swept off their feet by a billionaire and live in a magical castle and live happily ever after?

I get that our bosses are good looking. I can't deny that fact, especially when they come in from their morning run around Central Park with their t-shirts plastered to their fit bodies. *And... um... where was*

I? I remember seeing Noah without his shirt on months before he became my boss, and his body's pretty spectacular. Not like a hot body is a good selling point, Walker had one of the best with his million-dollar underwear endorsements, but that didn't mean he wasn't a dick.

Maybe next time, I should go after a man with a dad bod, they seem safer.

We all jump into the waiting limousine and make our way to our accommodations.

"You made it," Stella greets us as we arrive at the entrance of the hotel.

"How is he?" The strained look on her face tells me everything I need to know. My brother is a perfectionist just like me. He demands exceptionally high standards from his staff, and that simple fact is what makes him the best.

"He's a lot at the moment. This is his baby. He wants perfection." Stella smiles through gritted teeth.

"Want me to see if I can calm him down?" Stella looks instantly relieved. "I'll meet you guys a little later," I tell Emma and Lenna.

"We'll be fine." Emma smiles. "I'm planning on popping Lenna's Vegas cherry this afternoon."

Lenna looks a little concerned, and she should be, Emma's a professional party girl, and Vegas is *her town.*

"Well, good luck with that." I give Lenna a thumbs up.

"I should be worried, shouldn't I?" Lenna looks to Stella and then at me.

"You'll be fine."

Emma hauls Lenna away, laughing.

"Bring me to the ogre."

Stella walks me through the vast hotel foyer and turns when we reach the eateries. There's already a lineup of people outside eager to see the celebrity clientele who will be arriving later. The security guard lets us in, and there's a hive of activity going on. I hear the distinct voice of my brother as it carries through the restaurant. We head on over to where EJ's in the kitchen barking out his orders.

"Hey," I interrupt his tirade. He stops and spins around quickly, his face like thunder before softening when he realizes who it is.

"Chloe…" pulling me into a hug, "… you made it."

"I wouldn't have missed it for the world," I tell him.

"What do you think?"

"Haven't had a chance to look around yet. Just wanted to check in and see how you were doing."

He looks over at Stella. "Let me guess. I'm being a dick, and you're here to make me stop."

"Pretty much."

"You know tonight's a big deal for me." I can see the vulnerability written all over his face.

"I know. It's going to be amazing. But you also need your staff here to help you open, too. Last thing you need is a mass walk-out due to your temper."

"They're used to it." He waves his hand in the air. "But I'll try better." He gives me a wink. "Come, let me show you around."

We head back out into the restaurant area. "We're after that cool New York loft vibe," he states as he points out the industrial styling which is made up of reclaimed wood from the old abandon New York wharves, beautiful wooden tables with soft leather chairs. If people are after a more intimate dining experience, they offer booths further toward the back of the space. The kitchen's open style, so you can see the chaos that goes into preparing your meal. Apparently, that's trendy. If you don't want to sit and eat a meal, there's the bar area where you can grab a cocktail or some tapas before rushing off to a Vegas show.

The bar's a concrete masterpiece with New York-style red bricks behind it, rusted looking pipes twisted around the bar in a sculpture. Black and glass industrial chandeliers hang from the ceiling, wrapped around old industrial cogs. It looks like a factory but way more relaxed and definitely more luxurious.

"This is so beautiful, EJ." Wrapping my arms around him again, tears well in my eyes as I say, "I'm so proud of you."

"Thanks." Kissing my head, he hugs me.

"You know Mom and Dad would be so proud."

He doesn't reply because I know he's choked up with emotion at me mentioning our parents. They would be so very proud of him, and they would be right beside him tonight celebrating his success with the widest smiles on their faces. It's times like these I really miss them. I hate that they're missing out on so much of our lives.

"Anyway. I've got to go, I have some television interviews to give," Elliot tells me.

"Fine. Mr. Celebrity Chef, I'll let you go do your thing. I'll see you tonight." He waves me goodbye as Stella ushers him to his appointment.

I take one last look around before it becomes too crowded and savor my brother's success.

8

NOAH

W e're late arriving into Vegas thanks to a meeting running overtime back in New York. We promised our good friend, EJ, that we'd be there to celebrate this momentous occasion.

I met Elliott a while ago. We had both been roped into a bachelor auction for a children's charity. We were nervously waiting out the back in the green room when he offered me a swig of his tequila. By the time they called us, we were both very, very, tipsy and the best of friends. He's a good guy, but we don't get to catch up as much as we like due to our busy schedules.

"Oh, Vegas, how I have missed thee." Anderson salutes the night sky.

"Don't involve me in any of your crap this weekend," Logan tells him.

"Me?" Anderson tries to look innocent, but we all know he's not. Somehow, he gets himself into the craziest of situations, and usually, you're dragged along with him.

"We're only here for twenty-four hours. How much trouble can he get into?" As soon as the words fall from my lips, I realize that's the stupidest statement I've ever made.

"Famous last words, brother," Logan warns.

I think he's right.

Damn! I've jinxed us.

We head to our hotel suite, quickly freshen up, then make our way to the event. There are people everywhere, standing behind a gold velvet rope watching guests arrive. The paparazzi are out in force too, standing on the other side, screaming at the celebrities posing on the step and then repeating the same out the front.

"Is there another entry?" I'm not in the mood to be photographed or harassed by them tonight.

"I don't think so. Suck it up, princess," Anderson jokes.

We head toward the entry, security ticks our name off of their list, and the paparazzi yell at us. We pose and head inside.

Wow! That's my first thought. This place is amazing. It's like we have stepped into a high-end New York loft but supersized. The place is packed with people. I search the crowd to find EJ, so I can congratulate him. A flash of red catches my attention to the side. Turning my head, I watch as a beautiful blonde passes by me. Her red dress is molded to her curvaceous body. I'm mesmerized, everything else around me ceases to exist. *Who the hell is she?* I watch her move through the crowd until she stops in front of EJ. My heart sinks as his face lights up when he sees the mysterious blonde, pulling her into his arms, and she goes willingly. *Lucky bastard.*

"There's EJ." Logan points out as he and Anderson head toward him, and I follow after them.

"EJ," Anderson shouts getting his attention.

He leaves the blonde and rushes over to us. "You made it," he greets us all.

"Man, this is fucking awesome," Logan tells him.

"Congrats, man," I add.

"Thanks, guys. And thanks so much for coming." His smile is practically lighting up the room. "Come, let me introduce you to some important people."

Suck it up, Noah.

Your fleeting crush is EJ's.

"Boys, let me introduce you to my sister, Chloe." Looking up and realizing it's Chloe Jones—the woman in red—I'm blown away.

How?

What?

I don't understand.

I'm confused.

Chloe is EJ's sister?

Chloe stills when she realizes who's standing in front of her.

"EJ." Chloe grabs his attention. "Why are my bosses here?"

EJ looks at her confused, then to us.

"Chloe works with us." Logan smiles.

"You work for them?" EJ points, then bursts out laughing. "What a small fucking world."

Yeah, you can say that again.

"You never listen to me." Chloe pouts at her brother.

"I do…" His words don't sound too convincing.

"I had no idea you guys knew my brother."

"Everyone knows EJ," I tell her.

She nods her head in agreement.

"Gotta go." EJ waves his hand in the air, and next thing he's off.

"Lenna?" Logan notices our head of HR in front of us looking very different from the structured suit-wearing woman from our office. *Who knew that body existed underneath those suits?*

"Oh, hey, boss."

She's drunk. I've never seen Lenna drunk before, she's so held together at any functions we've attended.

"First time in Vegas," Chloe tells us.

"I popped her cherry," Emma says cheerily.

"I looove Vegas," Lenna declares. "What happens in Vegas stays in Vegas. Shh." She holds up her finger to her mouth as she says it.

"What exactly has been happening?" Logan asks.

"Oh, pretty boy… wouldn't you like to know?" Lenna stumbles, pressing her finger into his chest. "Ohh… you're hard." She giggles.

"Okay, maybe that's enough drinks for tonight." Chloe places her arm around Lenna moving her away from Logan. "Come, let's grab a water."

"I'll take her," Logan adds quickly. "I'm getting a drink anyway."

Chloe hesitates.

"It's your brother's night. Enjoy," he states while he places an arm around Lenna and ushers her away.

"You better not fire her over this." Emma points the finger at me.

"Of course, not." I'm a little taken aback by her comment, to be honest.

"Good." Emma nods at me. Lenna's worked for us since day one, she's part of the Stone family, and there's no way we would fire her over having a good time.

"You're looking good, Emma." Anderson gives her a heated stare.

"I know," she tells him confidently then gives him a wink.

She's not wrong, she's dressed in a black leather dress with a dangerous V down the front.

"You'd look better spread out—"

"Okay. Well, that's me done," I cut off my friend before they start to fuck in front of us. "I'm heading to the bar."

"I'm coming with you," Chloe quickly adds.

Emma and Anderson are too lost in fuck-me eyes for them to notice we've even left. We push our way through the crowd and end up at the bar where I grab us both a glass of champagne.

"Here…" handing her a glass., "… to EJ." Holding up my glass, we cheer, then take a sip. "I had no idea you were EJ's sister."

"I had no idea you knew my brother."

"I've known him for a couple years. We're both busy, so we don't catch up as often as we would like."

Chloe nods. *I still can't believe she's EJ's little sister.*

"He didn't put you up to hiring me, did he?"

That question takes me by surprise.

"What? No. I didn't even know you existed, let alone do him a favor." This seems to reassure her.

"It's just a crazy coincidence then," she says while twisting her glass in her hand.

"Chloe…" Gaining her attention, she looks up at me with those ocean blue eyes. "You earned this job. We hired you because of how good you are at it and for no other reason."

The tension releases from her shoulders, and she smiles at me. "Thank you."

"You've earned it, okay? And all the work you're doing for us we're thrilled with, too."

"Good. I'm glad to hear that as I have a crazy idea."

"I'm up for crazy ideas." I take a sip of my drink.

"I was talking with Emma earlier, and one of her women's brands is looking at shooting their summer catalog somewhere. And I suggested Stone, in Bali."

Sounds interesting.

"They loved the idea. Not sure if you know, but Emma was a well-known model before launching her marketing business. She knows a lot of famous supermodels who'd be happy to jet set to Bali for a photoshoot."

Okay, I'm liking the sound of this.

"I think if we ran a campaign in sync with the photoshoot, it would make great content—gorgeous women on the beach, walking through the resort. We could even stock their outfits from the photoshoot in the resort's boutiques. Shop the look."

This is something we haven't done before with our resorts, but I like the idea. Showing it off to new clientele is fabulous, so I reply, "I like it."

"You do?"

I nod. "Put something together so I can show Logan next week, and yeah, let's do it."

Chloe's face lights up as she bounces up and down. "Thank you." She wraps her arms around me.

We both still.

Feeling her warm body pressed against mine is sending confusing thoughts straight to my dick.

Chloe slowly untangles herself. "I'm sorry. I…"

I wave her concerns away. "It's all good. I'm excited as well," I reassure her.

9

CHLOE

I didn't mean to hug Noah like that. It's the first time we've been close to each other in months, not since my fateful honeymoon. He was nice about it, but I could tell it made things awkward between us.

He got to talking to some people he knew, and I took that as my chance to escape. I've been searching for Emma and Lenna for some time, but they both seem to have disappeared, and Stella's busy making sure EJ talks to all the right people.

Guess it's just me and my champagne in our favorite hiding spot on the private, second-level mezzanine where I've been people-watching.

"Thought I'd find you here."

Chills run down my body. *That voice.* The one I've known so intimately for so many years.

Spinning around, "What the hell are you doing here?"

"We need to talk." Walker moves toward me, but I take a couple of steps away, which unfortunately forces my back against the railing. Panic flows over my body instantly. Shit. Looking to either side of me, I notice there's nowhere to go.

"We have nothing to talk about," I spit.

"Oh, yes, we do." His voice lowers with menace while he steps into my personal space. "You just up and left me. Then to top that shit off, you blocked me."

"Of course, I did. You knocked up my best friend."

His usually green eyes turn an almost black at the mention of Tracey.

"That was a mistake."

"Yeah. A pretty big one." Trying to shift to the side to get away from him, I realize I'm trapped.

"You need to get over it, Chloe." *What the?* "Because you're the one I love. Not her." *Is he serious right now?*

"You just had a baby together."

Does he not care?

"I'll support him. But I don't care about her." *Is he for real?* "She's not marriage material. She's happy to spread her legs for any of my teammates. I can't marry a woman like that. I don't want a woman like that. Plain and simple."

"But you can sleep with one?"

"That's all they're good for."

Oh shit! I think I'm going to be sick.

I hate Tracey with every beat of my heart for what she did to me, but she just had a baby with this man, and honestly, with the words spewing from his mouth, I'm so happy she did because I dodged the biggest bullet.

"You disgust me."

Walker lunges at me wrapping his hands around my neck. *What the hell?* Panic races through my body. My hands grab his wrists as I try to wriggle free. I've pushed him too far.

"Walker…" tears fall down my cheeks, "… you're scaring me." My heart is beating wildly inside my chest.

"Baby, I just want you to listen to me," his voice coos. "You won't listen to me."

"I'm sorry…" Trying to calm him down, I placate him by saying, "I'm listening now."

Walker's fingers release from my neck as they move to my cheek.

His rough thumb runs across my skin, sending vile goosebumps over my body.

"You humiliated me, Chloe." His voice softens. "I woke up that morning feeling on top of the world." *Yeah, because you had your mistress in your bed.* "And then..." His eyes darken as he remembers what happened next.

"I was hurt."

"Baby..." he moves closer, caging me in, "... you hurt me, too." *Is this guy delusional?* "When they told me your room was empty, and you were nowhere to be found, it crushed me. My heart broke. I never thought *my Chloe* would be capable of doing something like that to me."

Seriously, is Walker that much of egomaniac that he thinks he has the right to be upset that his fiancée bolted from the wedding after he fucked her best friend?

"I love you so much." *Not enough to not cheat.* "You're my world. My everything. I wanted to spend the rest of my life with you."

I can't.

I just can't with this man.

"But you cheated on me."

Those green eyes darken once more. "I said... it was a mistake, Chloe. You need to get over it."

"I can't." I don't know what else to say, so I try to move away from him.

"Then you better learn how because I'm never letting you go." His words chill me to my bones as he grabs my wrist. "You're mine, Chloe. Do you understand me?"

I shake my head and try to pull my arm away. Honestly, I'm scared for my life.

"Please, let me go, Walker."

"No. Not till you understand that you're mine."

"I can't. I won't," I tell him, hoping it might sink in. "What you did to me was unforgivable."

"It's going to take time, Chloe. But in the end, you *will* forgive me." His hand grips my wrist tighter.

Then out of nowhere, Walker's sideswiped by a body, and they land with a thump.

"Get your hands off her."

The sound of fists meeting flesh echoes through the mezzanine level. *What's going on?* The two men are wrestling on the floor, fists flying, and that's when I realize it's Noah. *What the...*

"Never put your hands on a woman," he curses at Walker.

"Fuck you. She's mine," Walker hisses.

"Never," Noah screams.

"Stop it," I scream, worried they're going to kill each other.

Security eventually turns up and separates them.

"This man attacked me." Walker points to Noah.

"He attacked Chloe," Noah tells them.

Security turns to me.

"Noah's right."

The look on Walker's face is what nightmares are made of. His whole demeanor changes—face red with anger, fists clenched at his sides.

"You fucking bitch," he screams while he tries to launch himself at me, but security holds him back.

"Let's take this fucker away," security mumbles.

"Get your dirty hands off me. Do you have any idea who I am?" Walker screams while trying to free himself.

"Yeah, we know who you are. We're not football fans." The two burly men haul him out of the restaurant.

"Are you okay?" Rushing to Noah, I look him over quickly. He has some bruises on his cheek and a split lip where there's a small amount of blood.

"I'm fine." He brushes himself off. "Are you?" He looks me over with concern written in his eyes.

"I am now." Wrapping my arms around him, I give him a hug. My body begins to shake as the shock of the situation hits me.

"Chloe," my brother shouts bounding up the stairs. "Are you okay?" He stops in his tracks when he sees me wrapped in Noah's arms.

"I think she's in shock," Noah tells him.

"Did he touch her?" my brother asks Noah.

"Yeah. But I took care of him."

"Thanks." Elliot gives Noah one of those man nods.

"Guys, I'm standing right here," I remind them both.

"You look a little pale." Noah runs a reassuring hand over my cheek. "And you're still shaking. Maybe we should get out of here?"

"I'm coming," Elliot states.

"No. Please. No. It's your night."

"You're more important than this." His face softens as he waves his hands around the space. "You're my family."

Shit. I burst into tears, rushing into his arms and holding him tight.

"I'm sorry, Chlo. I had no idea he was coming. He wasn't on the list. I just—"

"It's okay..." sniffling, "... it's not your fault," I say reassuring him.

How could anyone have known he'd turn up?

"I'm going to go have a drink and calm down. Then I'll be back partying away."

He doesn't seem the least bit assured by my comments.

"I've got her," Noah tells him.

Elliot slaps his friend on the back and lets us pass.

"Let's get out of here." Noah links his fingers with mine and pulls me through the crowd, security shows him to the back exit, so we don't have to run the gauntlet of the paparazzi. Noah pushes the exit door, and we're in the gaming area. The bright lights and sounds of the games hit us immediately.

"This way." Noah pulls me to the side, looking for the lifts to his floor. "Why are these hotels so fucking big?" he curses, never letting my hand go.

It feels nice. We walk all around the edge of the gaming room until we find the right lift for his floor. He swipes his keycard, and we head up to the executive suites. The doors close, forcing us into an awkward silence for a couple of beats.

I stare at him, the florescent light which is highlighting his bruises. "He did a real number on you." My fingers gently touching his skin. Noah winces ever so slightly as I come into contact with the open wound. "Your lip." My finger gently traces over his plump lips. Noah looks at me through dark lashes. "Thank you for tonight."

He doesn't say a word. His body's tense, the adrenaline from the fight still coursing through him.

Finally, we reach his floor, and Noah grabs my hand again and pulls me out of the lift. He swipes his keycard against the door and enters his room. He releases my hand and walks directly over to the built-in bar in his suite. Pouring himself a tumbler of something amber, he throws it back in one large gulp.

"Noah?" Placing my hand on his tense shoulder.

His head hangs as he places the empty tumbler back on the bar. Noah turns around, pain is etched across his face. "I couldn't get there in time, Chloe." *What's he talking about?* "I saw him with his fingers around your neck and…" The look on his face almost breaks me.

"Oh, Noah…" pulling him into my arms, "… this isn't your fault."

He wraps himself around me. "I saw you from downstairs and couldn't get there in time, Chlo. I tried. But there were too many people in my way."

Grabbing his face with my hands to stop him from blaming himself. "You're a good guy, Noah Stone. And I won't have you thinking any other way. You hear me?"

Those green eyes widen. "If anything happened to you…" Noah whispers. The air between us changes.

"Noah…" Not sure if I'm warning him away or desperately wanting him to move closer. The next thing I know he's picking me up and placing me on the bar, pressing himself between my legs. His hands resting on my hips, those green eyes looking up at me, sparkling with need, but he's hesitant.

"When he said you were his, I saw red, Chloe." Sucking in my bottom lip nervously I continue to listen. "Like you're his possession."

Reaching out, I touch his bruised cheek again. He closes his eyes as my fingers explore his face, including the small cut at the edge of his lip.

I shouldn't be doing this.

He's my boss.

My employer.

He's off-limits.

Maybe it's the adrenaline running through both of us after what happened because it's the only reason why I choose the following action. Leaning down, I press my lips against his ever so gently.

Strong fingers dig into my hips as we touch. I shouldn't be doing this, but I need something to wipe away Walker's touch from me.

"Chloe…" My name sounds pained coming from his lips.

"I know we shouldn't be doing this," I confess.

"We shouldn't," he agrees on a whisper, but he doesn't pull away.

"Just one kiss," I urge him.

"Just one," he agrees. His palm cups my cheek as his fingers dig into my hair, pulling me to him.

His lips are on mine while I'm pressed against his hardening self. This is so wrong, yet it feels so good. His lips are soft, and he's an expert kisser.

Just a little longer and then I'll put a stop to this.

Noah intensifies the kiss, pulling me closer to him, and my legs wrap around his taut hips, pressing myself against him. Hands begin to roam as we tentatively explore one another until we pull apart, both of us panting as we move away.

My lips are swollen—there's tension running across Noah's body.

"I shouldn't have done that," Noah tells me.

My stomach sinks.

I know we shouldn't have kissed, but I don't feel like it was a mistake.

Dammit! I'm such an idiot. Pushing myself away from him, I jump down from the bar. "I better go." I'm attempting to collect myself before dying of embarrassment.

"Chloe…." Noah grabs my arm. "Are we okay?"

"We're fine," I say through gritted teeth besides the fact that it was one of the hottest kisses I've ever experienced.

He lets go of me, and I move through his suite toward the door, but next thing I know Noah's blocking it. "Chloe, talk to me."

"What do you want me to say?" Throwing my hands up into the air, I'm becoming angrier by the second, not only at Noah but also myself for being so damn stupid.

"You're angry that I kissed you. I get it. I shouldn't have. I'm your boss. It goes against our contract. But I don't want to lose you. You're brilliant at your job, plus I value your friendship, too." Noah's words rush out, stopping me in my place.

"I thought you thought it was a mistake," I say quietly while letting my vulnerability show.

"What? No. We shouldn't have done it, but I wouldn't change a thing." Noah moves toward me, reaching out and pushing a stray hair away from my face. "You will never be a mistake, Chloe." His kind words hit me dead in the chest and resonate through my body.

"I know we shouldn't have done it for so many reasons… but I agree, it wasn't a mistake."

This makes him smile.

"It's going to suck going back to the office and having to watch those lips move and try not to remember how they felt against mine." His thumb runs over my bottom lip sending goosebumps all over my body.

"Did you really mean it when you said you value my friendship?" Noah's hand falls to his side.

"I did."

"I value yours, too."

He gives me a smile. "So, friends then?" he asks.

"Friends and colleagues."

"So, it won't be weird, if... um... you know..." He shrugs nervously.

"That I see you with a gaggle of supermodels?" Raising a brow at him, I ask the question which makes him laugh.

"I don't just date supermodels."

I roll my eyes because they all look like supermodels to me.

"Most of those women I don't sleep with."

"Bullshit."

"Seriously. They're just there to raise their profiles."

"So, you're doing a community service to those poor, unfortunate, supermodels who don't have enough likes on Instagram. You're such a giver, Noah." Sarcasm drips from my mouth, and it makes him laugh.

"I do what I can. I'm a man of the people."

We both burst out laughing until Noah turns serious for a couple of beats. "We're okay, aren't we? I didn't—"

"Yeah, we are." He looks relieved. "Thanks for tonight. Not for what just happened, but for saving me."

"I'd do it again." And I believe him. "Don't go," Noah tells me. "Stay." Raising my brow at him, not entirely sure what he's suggesting here. "I know I'm irresistible, so it's going to be hard for you to keep your hands to yourself." I slap him. "Ow..." He smiles. "Just stay, hang out with me."

"You don't want to go back to that party alone 'cause all your friends seem to have abandoned you," I reply, then smile.

"Please don't make me look like a lonely loser." Noah presses a hand against his chest.

"Fine. I'll stay. But it's going to cost you."

"Anything," he adds quickly.

"Don't tell my brother, but I'm starving. The stupid waitress kept missing me with the finger food."

"Consider it done."

10

NOAH

"This is so good." Chloe licks her fingers, and my thoughts go straight to all the other things she could be sucking right now. I take a deep breath and count to ten and begin to think about gross stuff to keep my dick at bay.

We've set ourselves up on the carpet in front of the floor-to-ceiling windows which look out over The Strip. It's like a mini picnic. I ordered a heap of food, and we've been slowly picking away at it while drinking champagne and chatting.

That kiss earlier was good. So good. So good that I want to do it again. My eyes are drawn to her plump lips as she talks, and I can't stop imagining them against my own, which isn't a good idea.

We've both agreed friends and colleagues—it's what's best for the company.

Never mix business and pleasure, that has always been Logan's and my motto.

But at this moment, having a picnic in my hotel room with a beautiful, intelligent, funny woman is making me question my 'no workplace romance' stance.

Chloe's relaxed. She's changed out of her red dress and into one of my t-shirts, which is riding up her tanned legs as she lays back against the sofa cushions on the floor.

"I bet you're not used to a woman enjoying food like this." She turns and looks at me.

"It does suck taking a woman to dinner, spending all that money, and all she eats is air."

Chloe laughs. "You need to stop being so shallow," she jokes.

"I'm not shallow," I argue.

"Oh, that's right, you're the community service provider for unfortunate supermodels." She chuckles, and I can't resist throwing a bread roll at her.

"Hey." She throws it back. "Have you ever dated a woman bigger than a supermodel?"

"I don't date," I tell her.

She tilts her head at me. "Why not?"

"One… I don't have time. And two… I've seen what happens when a gold digger gets her claws into someone."

Looking down at the bread roll in my hand, I draw my eyebrows together. "Wow! That's a little pessimistic."

Not many people know the story of why Logan and I are so guarded about our love lives. But I have a need to tell her, explain to her that I will never be any more than her boss, who she's had a little flirtation with.

"My father fell for his secretary. *Cliché, I know.* They had an affair for years." That tight feeling in my chest returns when I think about it. "Mom got sick."

Chloe reaches out, her hand landing on my forearm.

"She had cancer. It was quick." Sucking in a deep breath while thinking about Mom always makes me uneasy. "Dad married his mistress two months after Mom passed away. Logan and I were devastated. We thought it was totally disrespectful to Mom, who was barely cold in her grave, and he's off running around town with a woman half his age."

My anger bubbles to the surface.

"As soon as she had the ring on her finger and no pre-nuptial agreement signed, that was it, Shelly turned into a monster. She demanded my father hire staff to look after her. She, in turn, treated them like slaves. She demanded luxury holidays. The latest couture. My father worked his fingers to the bone to provide for his new wife until he got himself into a huge amount of debt while we were in college. He was bankrupt, and guess what? Shelly disappeared with his business rival when the money stopped coming in."

This next part kills me.

"My father lost everything… the love of his life, his business, everything he spent his entire life working for. Then he lost Shelly to his arch-enemy. He became a joke in his community. So, he ended it. Took the easy way out. Logan and I came home early one weekend and found him dead in his bed from an overdose. He'd been there for a couple of days."

"Oh, Noah…" Chloe moves, wrapping her arms around me, "… that's horrible."

Trying to shake away the hurt from me, I apologize, "I'm sorry. I didn't mean to dump all that on you." I don't share that story with many people.

"You don't have to apologize. It's your story." She pulls me closer. "I get it." Feeling her warmth all around me makes me feel good.

"I lost my parents, too." Looking up at her, I had no idea. "Plane crash. Faulty electrics. Bad weather." Reaching out, I take her hand in mine. "We're a pair, aren't we? Great dinner conversation," Chloe lightens the mood with a small smile.

"Do you want to talk about what happened tonight, instead?"

Chloe moves away and starts to tidy up the food. "There's nothing much to tell."

"There is a ton to tell, but I'm guessing by the way you're madly packing up you don't want to talk about it?" She stops what she's doing and sits back on the floor.

"He scared me tonight." Wrapping her arms around herself, she continues, "I've never seen him like that before. Like he's gone mad."

Chloe shivers. "He's never touched me like that. Never physically hurt me."

"I was downstairs and looked up to check on you, and that's when I saw him with his hand around your throat. I tried to get to you, but there were so many people downstairs." My heart thunders in my chest reliving that moment where I simply couldn't get through the crowd.

"It's not your fault."

"I should have gotten there sooner," I tell her, feeling guilty that she had to go through such a scary time by herself.

"Still, not your fault. Walker hates to lose, and I guess me leaving him makes him feel like he's lost."

"I think you should consider getting extra security at EJ's place." Chloe turns to me, a surprised look on her face. "I have a friend who lives in LA who runs one of the best security firms in the States. We use him for all our hotels."

"Don't you think that's a little much?"

I give her an 'is she serious' look. "The way he said 'mine' gave me the creeps," I tell her.

"You might be right…" she hesitates. "I've been looking at moving out of EJ's. Wanting my own space, but maybe I shouldn't."

"What? No. You can't let him stop you. We just need to be more vigilant."

"We?" she questions me.

"Yes, you're part of The Stone Group now. We look after our own." She nods her head, unconvincingly. "Look, I own a couple of brownstones side by side. The tenants have moved out, so it's currently unoccupied. There's a beautiful outside deck which is so rare in New York. It's close to work. There are great restaurants and shops in the area. Central Park isn't far. You'd be my neighbor. Interested?"

Probably the stupidest idea you have ever had, Noah, putting temptation right next door to you.

"So, you would be my boss and landlord, too?" She raises a brow at me.

"I guess so."

She mulls it over. "Are you going to pop in to check up on me?" Her eyes narrow.

"Not unless you invite me to."

"Are we going to carpool?"

Hadn't thought about that.

"I run in Central Park most mornings, so probably not."

She nods. "Are you sure? I don't want to cramp your style by being next door." She gives me a cheeky smile.

"Maybe it's the other way around. I don't want to cramp your style. A single, beautiful woman in New York, you're going to have men knocking down your door. Lucky you'll have extra security."

She gives me the side-eye. "After Walker, I think it's going to be a long time before I even think about dating again."

"Don't let one douchebag stop you."

Why the hell am I encouraging her?

"I think I'm just going to concentrate on me for a while. You see, I have this boss that is a real hardass." She giggles.

"Your boss sounds like a great man." Smiling at her, I don't really have female friends, and it's not because I don't think males and females can't be friends, I just never took the chance. Plus, I usually want to sleep with most females I hang out with on some level, and as much as I want to sleep with Chloe, I value her friendship more.

Man, what does that mean? Shit… am I growing up?

"He's a good guy." She gazes over at me. "I'm lucky to have him in my life."

"I think he's pretty happy to have you in his life, too."

"We're friends, aren't we?" Chloe asks.

"Yeah. I'd like to think so."

"Good. I know this might sound weird after what just happened earlier."

"When I gave you the best kiss of your life."

She rolls her eyes at me. "Okaaay," she emphasizes the word. "But, I kind of don't want to mess up this friendship that's developing," she confesses.

"Me either." I nod, agreeing.

"So, just friends?" She holds out her hand.

"Yep. Just friends." Taking it, I give it a firm shake, even though I can feel an electric undercurrent between us. I push that aside for the sake of our friendship.

"Okay. Let's be neighbors."

"Welcome to the neighborhood, Chloe."

11

CHLOE

"Are you fucking serious right now?" Emma stares at the beautiful brownstone. "And you seriously didn't suck dick for this."

"Emma," EJ shouts at her.

"Hush it, EJ. I'm sure you've had your dick sucked more than Chloe has sucked dick." That shuts my brother up but also gets us dirty looks from the people in the street.

"Would you two stop talking about dicks on the street? I don't want to get kicked out before I've even moved in."

Emma apologizes and helps by bringing in one of my bags from EJ's truck.

"This is beautiful, Chloe," Stella adds as we step inside the foyer which leads into the living room and out to a back terrace.

"Where's the kitchen? I need to check it out," EJ adds.

"Downstairs," I tell him.

We follow EJ downstairs to where the kitchen, dining, and another living room is located, which opens out to a garden area.

"Seriously, Chlo... two garden areas," Ariana moans. "This garden is the same size as my apartment."

"The kitchen's okay," EJ reports after opening and shutting everything in the kitchen.

"Lucky, there's lots of restaurants" He's not amused but my comment.

"I'll send you food, Chlo. You know it's the best anyway," he adds. I ignore his ego.

"We're going to have so many parties." Emma claps her hands together in excitement.

"Not too many, remember my landlord's just next door."

"A damn, sexy landlord at that." Emma wiggles her eyebrows, and EJ shoots her a glare that could kill.

"You can't date my friends," he adds.

"Firstly, he's my boss and now my landlord, there will be no dating. And secondly, if I want to date one of your friends, EJ..." I look at him firmly in the eyes and continue, "... I can and will."

"Hell, yeah." Emma gives me a high-five while the others snigger.

"Don't you worry, I've already warned all my friends if they touch you, they die." EJ gives me a smug look.

"You're such a cockblock, EJ," Emma tells him.

"Exactly. She's my little sister."

"This is all hypothetical. I'm not in the mood to date. Period." *Urgh, my brother is so annoying.*

"Good," EJ tells me, and I flip him off.

"So, which room is yours?" Lenna asks, steering us in another direction.

"Not sure yet. The master is on the top floor, but really, who wants to climb four flights of stairs every night to go to bed."

"True. But then you won't have to go to the gym," Lenna tells me.

"That's a good point. Come on, let's have a look."

The girls follow me up to the bedrooms which are on the top two floors. The brownstone has four bedrooms, which really is three too many, but at least I have space for a ton of sleepovers.

"This is the master," I tell them as I push open the door.

"I've died and gone to room heaven," Stella states.

The master's gorgeous. There's a king-size bed, ensuite bathroom made out of Calcutta marble with an enormous tub, bigger than anything I've ever seen, and the most gorgeous walk-in closet. I was fortunate with this home, especially as it's fully furnished. Noah had it set up for executive leasing, so everything I will need is here, and it's all top-notch.

"This closet…" Emma runs her hands over the cabinetry. "Seriously, Chloe, I wish I had a boss who looked after me like this."

"It's not like that." But as soon as the words leave my mouth, I can see my friends aren't convinced.

"What does he want? I mean he can't be doing it out of the goodness of his heart," Ariana adds.

"Noah's not like that."

"Logan and Noah do a lot for their employees," Lenna begins to back me up. "But… usually, it's free holidays," and then she drops me right in it.

"They're friends with EJ." *Why am I defending myself?* I can see on their faces they still don't believe me. "He doesn't want anything. We've agreed, friends only." The room's still silent. "Noah's not my type, anyway. I like more rugged men."

"Knock, knock," I hear someone say and close my eyes. Seriously, this can't be happening. "Sorry to interrupt…" Noah walks into the room, "… but I thought I'd pop in and see if everything's okay."

"It's perfect, thank you."

Did he just hear what I said? Fuck my life, right now.

"Okay, great," he says awkwardly. "Well, I'll leave you all to it." He spins on his heel and walks back out of the room.

"That was awkward," Emma adds.

"No, shit." I give her a death glare.

"Maybe he didn't hear what you said." Stella tries to make me feel better.

"Maybe it's for the best," Ariana adds. "He won't think you're after him."

"Maybe."

The thing is, Noah *is* my type in every single way. That kiss we had in Vegas a couple weeks ago, I haven't been able to get it out of my mind. I catch myself staring at him when he walks into the office after his morning run before heading to his executive bathroom. I've turned into one of the office groupies, swooning over my boss.

Maybe it's for the best that he thinks he's not my type.

And that there's no chance a kiss can happen between us again.

⁂

I've been in my new place for a week now, and I love it. Having my own space has been great. I've set up one of the bedrooms downstairs as an office, so I can work from home or after work on separate projects. I've even used the kitchen a couple of times to make dinner, nothing fancy just some stir fry, but I did it.

It's Friday night, and I'm curled up on my couch watching Netflix. I want to chill by myself this weekend. Explore my neighborhood. Find a farmer's market. Maybe some retail therapy at the luxury boutiques which surround my home.

What I could use right at this moment is some ice cream, but I'm so comfy on my sofa I don't want to move. I muddle over this decision, but the need for ice cream wins in the end, so I untangle myself from the blanket, grab my slides, and head on down to the corner store. I'm dressed in an old t-shirt and some track pants, with no make-up, but thankfully I do have a bra on. New York is still busy at this time of night, and that's what I love about it. There are always people around —tourists taking photos, people enjoying Friday night drinks, or some poor souls who have just finished work. Thankfully, the shop on the corner isn't far, so I hurry toward it subconsciously hoping I don't run into anyone I know while looking like a mess.

As I enter the shop, the bell rings overhead. The bright florescent lights shine, and the smell of fried food fills the air. Heading to the back area of the shop where the freezers are located, I scan the brightly colored packages until I find the one.

Then I notice the selections of wine staring at me. Calling to me. *Screw it.* I grab a bottle of rosé too.

Making my way back to the cash register, I'm distracted by some gossip magazines. Why not. Grabbing a couple, I place my haul on the counter—the cashier silently judging my selection. I'd probably judge me too, it's totally the single anti-social girl's diet. I grab a couple of chocolates and some Chex Mix to add to my collection. He rings it up, and I pay, taking my bag of goodies in my hand and head off for home. My footsteps are slow as I watch a sleek, black car pull in front of my brownstone. The driver opens the door and a gorgeous woman steps from the car, looking like a damn angel, dressed in a white evening dress, her blonde hair curled around her shoulders. Then the other door opens, and a man dressed in a tuxedo steps from the car.

He looks up and right at me.

Noah.

Shit.

He flinches for a moment upon noticing me. Those green eyes roaming over me, but a slight frown forms across his brow. The beautiful blonde says something to him, which makes him smile. He joins her on the sidewalk, linking their arms together as they stride confidently up his stairs and to his home. He holds open the door, and before he closes it behind him, his eyes meet mine, but then he's gone.

Thank fuck I bought wine, I think. *I'm going to need it.*

Not like I haven't seen Noah with other women before, just this was the first time I've seen him take one inside his home. There's a tiny bit of something gnawing away at my insides, but I know wine is going to get rid of it. As soon as I enter my home, I head downstairs to the kitchen to grab a glass from the cupboard and pour myself a large glass of rosé.

Taking my first gulp of wine—*ah, that feels better*—the crisp, dry liquid goes down smoothly. I still feel a little jittery and unsure about what to do next. *Stupid men.* I shouldn't let him get under my skin like that.

A light catches my attention—it's shining right onto the hot tub in the back garden. I haven't had a chance to enjoy it yet, so I grab my bottle of rosé and head out into the rear garden. Placing the bottle on the table, I take off the hot tub's cover, then press the button to turn it on. Slowly, the bubbles rise to the surface, and the water starts to heat. It's a beautiful night, a little on the cooler side, but still the bite of winter has passed.

Quickly looking around, I check no one can see me. Thankfully, the back garden is covered with beautiful trees. Stripping off down to my underwear, I jump in, sinking down into the bubbles, the warm water easing my tense muscles. *This is perfect.* I lean over and grab my bottle of rosé and take a sip, letting my head lay back against the edge of the tub and closing my eyes, letting the water do its magic.

Opening my eyes, the lights of the city come back into focus, the noise of the traffic, the sirens, the car horns, all sounds that I've slowly gotten used to. Feeling more relaxed, I look around my surroundings, I notice the tall buildings that dominate the skyline. Squinting my eyes to see if I can see into anyone's apartments—that's probably creepy, but still I do it. My eyes travel down until they land on the home next door.

Shit! Straight into Noah's kitchen.

There's only a couple lights on in his home, so I can't see too much, but I can most definitely see two people making out. Noah has the beautiful woman pushed up against the wall, kissing her, hands roaming all over her fully-clothed body. *Fuck, t*he rosé feeling like acid rising from my stomach.

I know I should look away.

You need to look away, Chloe.

But I don't. I can't.

Something's wrong with me.

I continue watching my boss and his date get hot and heavy in his kitchen. I don't stop watching as her hand runs down his tuxedo-clad back gripping his ass, pulling him closer to her. *I'm jealous.* Taking another sip of rosé, hoping this feeling will subside if I keep drinking, I watch her fingers dig into ass. The man has a really nice ass. If you've seen him in his suit pants, you appreciate the tight buns.

Leave, Chloe.

You need to leave now.

This is wrong. It's also creepy.

Her hand tries to disappear down the front of his trousers.

Nope. No. You need to leave now.

I stand in the tub, my eyes still focused in on them. I watch as he pulls himself away from her, and I sink back down into the water.

What just happened?

He waggles his finger at her, which she ignores and tries to grab his crotch again. He pulls himself away, which makes her mad. They have a heated conversation whereby she throws her hands in the air and storms off.

Noah doesn't follow after her.

The sound of a door being slammed echoes through the night sky. His forehead falls against the wall his fist thumps against.

What just happened?

Why would she leave after being denied the D?

Why did Noah deny her the D?

I watch as Noah moves from the kitchen to his living room where he shucks off his tuxedo jacket and throws it against a chair. He undoes his bowtie and adds it to the pile. Kicking off his shoes, he makes his way to the couch.

His living room is bathed in the faintest of light, and I can only make out an outline. I move to the other side of the hot tub to get a better look. He begins to undo his white shirt and throws it to the floor, and a belt follows soon after. He must turn the television on because I can make out his face. Looks like he flicks between a couple of channels as I can see the light change across his face then stop. Leaning back against his couch, he lets his head fall back. Actually, he looks exhausted. Scrubbing his face with his hands, I watch as his lips move as he mutters something. He stays like that for a while.

What's he thinking about?

Why does he look so stressed out?

I notice his hand move down his body and over his trousers, fisting himself. His brow crinkles in a frown. He fingers begin to unzip his pants. The steam starts to rise around me. *Am I sweating?* Because the hot tub feels like it's increased in temperature by a hundred degrees.

My heart beats wildly in my chest, the heightened beat feels loud enough that the world could hear it. I need to look away, I'm invading his personal space, but I can't.

His palm rubs his crotch again, making me bite my lower lip. I take a sip of my wine, hoping it will cool me down. It doesn't. Actually, it makes me worse.

He reaches inside his pants, readjusting himself. Must be painful. He continues this for a couple more strokes, then stops all of a sudden. His eyes pop open, his head lifts off the couch, and he looks out the window directly at me.

Fuck.

I quickly duck under the water, holding my breath. My heart's pounding loudly in my chest.

Did he see me?

I'm totally fired.

He's going to kick me out of this house. He might even go to the police and get me arrested for being some sort of creeper or something. Stupid rosé.

When I can't hold my breath any longer, I slowly lift my head out of the water and peer over the edge of the tub. His curtains are now pulled, and I can't see him anymore.

I'm relieved, but also a little disappointed. Shame, it would have been a spectacular show.

What are you saying, Chloe? No, it wouldn't have!

You can't come back from watching your boss masturbate. I think the heat is getting to me.

Stepping from the hot tub, I grab a towel and wrap it around my body. Taking my bottle, I head inside.

This has been an interesting Friday night. I think I need to get laid because what I just did in the tub isn't healthy. Maybe my hormones are getting the better of me, and I'm just projecting onto Noah because we have this little history together.

I need to find a stranger and have some fun, I think. Or I can just grab my trusty sidekick rabbit and fantasize about how that show should have ended.

12

NOAH

I was worried Chloe might be upset seeing me bring home Laurie the other night. It wasn't planned. Honestly, I thought maybe a night of fun would help me stop thinking about Chloe being so close to me. Laurie wasn't impressed when my dick wouldn't perform. Thankfully she ended up leaving.

But I'm not proud of what happened next.

While flicking through the channels on my television, my mind started thinking of Chloe and how I wished it was her that I'd brought home. Of course, my dick responded to those images, and selfishly, I decided to continue with them, jerking off to images of Chloe on my sofa on a Friday night.

Yep, I'm a creep.

Chloe isn't even interested in me, she made that perfectly clear to her girlfriends the other day. *So, why is she under my skin?* I may not be some pro athlete, but I'm still a catch.

I need to let it go. Otherwise, I'm going to drive myself insane. She's told me numerous times we're colleagues and friends, but I'm the one with the problem wanting to step over the boundaries we have in place. And that simply makes me a douche.

Walking into the office this morning after a meeting, I see Lenna and Chloe chatting away, laughing. I'm glad they get on well, they're so similar it would be a nightmare if they didn't. I notice my brother watching them intently from the corner of my eye. *What's going on there?* I head over to him to find out.

"Hey, dickhead," I greet him in the doorway.

He jumps before trying to pretend he's doing some work.

I close the door and sit in front of him. "What's going on?"

"Nothing," he says quickly.

"You seemed pretty interested in Lenna and Chloe's conversation." His head turns quickly to me, his green eyes narrow.

"What? No. I was lost in thought thinking about something..."

I'm calling bullshit on that.

"In their direction?" I question.

"That was just a coincidence."

Still bullshit, but I'll let it slide.

"How are we looking on the new The Hamptons Estate?" I ask changing the subject.

"I checked it out on the weekend, and it's coming along well. I think we might be ready for a test in a month."

Wow, that is quick. We've been pushing for our newest hotel to open in time for the summer season which is peak money-making time.

"I was thinking of taking Chloe up there, so she can finalize the marketing strategy for opening day."

My brother looks at me, suspiciously. "I'm worried about you."

"Me. Why?"

"You seem to be getting awfully close with Chloe."

"No, I'm not," I argue, but he doesn't look convinced.

"You seem to be bending over backward for her. Some might say it's leaning toward favoritism."

"Some might say or you're saying?" I question my brother.

"Me..." He arches a brow. "I'm worried that feelings are involved. You have a history with her."

"What, a kiss at a resort months ago?"

"I heard you rescued her from her ex in Vegas."

"And, where were you?" Throwing his convenient disappearance with Lenna at him. "You never came home after taking Lenna to her room."

Logan sits up in his chair—I've struck a nerve.

"Nothing's happening," he's quick to add, which totally means something has happened.

"Didn't say there was."

Logan glares at me. "You're not Dad, you know."

"I know. Because we stick to the rules."

Fuck the rules! I want to scream at him because I know he's just as lonely as I am, but I know he will never break the rules because he's always been the more disciplined twin.

"Just know I wouldn't care if something happened with Lenna," I reassure him.

Logan just glares at me. "Noah," he warns.

Urgh, he's so frustrating. I just roll my eyes at him.

"Is Chloe going to be a problem?" his tone's cutting. He couldn't be more serious if he tried.

"No," I reply through gritted teeth.

"But you like her?"

"Yes." I'm not going to lie. "Least I'm man enough to be able to acknowledge my feelings."

"You have feelings for her?" He jumps on my words straight away.

"Not like that." I'm not in love with the girl or anything, I just like hanging out with her.

"But more than friends?" he pushes. I shrug my shoulders. "Do you think taking her away to The Hamptons is a good idea?"

"It's work," I state loudly.

"I know. Just, I'm concerned after what you've just told me."

"I'm not a teenager with a crush. I know the difference between work and play," I tell him sarcastically.

"Hey, don't get pissy with me." He glares. "I'm just trying to be the voice of reason here."

"So, you didn't take Lenna to The Hamptons last weekend?"

He stills, and the room goes quiet. "It was work." Now he looks pissed. "How did you find out?"

"Anderson told me."

"Fucking loudmouth," Logan curses.

"You hid that from me."

"Because it was nothing… just work."

"And yet, you think me taking Chloe to The Hamptons is something?"

"You and Chloe have hooked up, and you just told me you like her."

"So, you don't like Lenna?" I question.

"Of course, I like Lenna… as a colleague."

We're going around and around in circles.

"You're so frustrating. I'm taking Chloe to The Hamptons this weekend for work. Nothing more," I tell him.

"Okay," he finally agrees.

"Good," I reply while standing then walking out of his office in a huff.

Stomping through the hallway back to my office before closing my door with some force, which shakes the walls when I slam it shut.

Moments later, there is a knock.

"Come in," I yell.

"You okay?" Chloe pops her head inside before closing the door behind her.

"Yeah. Just…"

Do I tell her what Logan and I spoke about? Maybe I should make sure that we're both on the same page—that it's just a work thing.

"I wanted to see if you were free to pop up to the estate in The Hamptons this weekend?"

Her eyes widen for a couple moments. "And Logan doesn't think that's a good idea?" She sounds hurt.

"Kind of… he thinks I show favoritism to you."

An awkward silence fills the room.

"It's what friends do, isn't it? I'm new to this whole being friends with the opposite sex."

"You don't have female friends?" she questions.

"I do, but…"

"Oh…" she catches my drift, "… they're more along the lines of friends with benefits." I nod my head in agreement. "Maybe Logan isn't used to you having a female friend you don't want to sleep with."

But I do.

I do want to sleep with you.

I just can't, I internally scream.

"Does he forget who my brother is?"

Fuck! EJ. I keep forgetting that she's my friend's little sister, and that's a sobering thought.

"Look, it's ridiculous, I shouldn't have said anything," she says.

"No. It's a good thing. We have a great working relationship, and I know in the past we've gotten close. I guess that would make Logan a little skittish about us. But we've put that all behind us."

"Because I'm not your type?"

A slight flush falls across Chloe's cheeks, reminding her that I overheard her conversation with her friends.

"Exactly. And I'm not yours."

Reminding me that she saw me with Laurie.

"Okay, then. Well, I'm glad we've gotten that all settled. So, you free this weekend?"

"Yes. I'm free."

"Great. I was thinking we'd leave Friday lunch to beat the rush, and be back either Saturday or Sunday, depending on how much work we can get done."

"Okay. Sounds like a plan." Chloe stands and walks toward my office door. She stops, hesitating for a moment before turning around. "I can find somewhere else to live if it makes things with your brother any better. I don't want to get in the way of your relationship with him."

"What? No," I tell her. "Honestly, I think he's projecting what's going on with him onto me." Chloe eyes narrow, and I can see she wants to say something but hesitates. "I think something's going on between him and Lenna."

"Oh, thank God you said it because I've been thinking the same thing." She rushes back to me, taking a seat.

"Has she said anything to you?"

"No. She's a vault. But I think something happened in Vegas."

"Me, too. He's so straight and narrow he won't ever do anything that's against company policy."

"Same with Lenna, but I guess that goes with the territory of HR Director." We both nod our head in agreement.

"Has she said anything about him?"

"I'm not breaking girl code." Chloe smiles.

"Fine. So, what are we going to do about them? 'Cause I think Lenna would be really great for my brother."

"Aw… you do?" She sounds surprised.

"Under this hard exterior, I'm really a romantic."

Chloe gives me a look that she thinks I just spoke utter bullshit.

"You don't get the nickname 'playboy twins' for no reason," Chloe tells me.

"Don't believe everything you read in the papers." She shrugs seemingly unconvinced. "Whatever." Rolling my eyes, I continue, "Are you going to help me play cupid, then?"

"Of course, I will," she agrees wholeheartedly. "As long as he isn't going to fire me over this?"

⁂

"I hear you're heading to The Hamptons with Chloe this weekend," Anderson questions me at lunch. *Not him too.*

"You heard correct."

Logan has a big mouth.

"Wonder what EJ thinks?"

"He probably thinks she's doing her job."

"Someone's defensive," he states. "It's obvious you have a hard-on for the girl. Not sure if you realize that."

"No, I don't." Shoving a slice of sushi in my mouth, it helps to stop any words from escaping.

"Rescuing her from her ex."

"He had his hands on her. Anyone would have done the same."

Anderson takes a sip of his beer. "True. You also asked Jackson Connolly to fit out her home with the latest security."

"It needed upgrading. She's an employee, and someone threatened her. Of course, I was going to do something about it."

Anderson's eyes narrow at me, and I can tell he's not believing a word I am saying. "You let her move into your rental at a discount."

"This sushi tastes delicious." Shoving another bite into my mouth, hoping to change the subject, I quickly grab another.

"Which happens to be next door to you." He gulps down some more beer. "I bet you've even tried to cop a look, too."

Fuck him.

He's right, though. I realize if I stand in my back garden, which I never used to do, I can see her in her living room, or I can see her from my living room in her hot tub. Most nights, she likes to relax in the tub with a glass of wine, and it's the damn highlight of my night.

I'm not a creeper.

Promise.

"I take it from your silence I'm correct?" I ignore him. "Now you're taking Miss Temptation away for the weekend."

"She's my employee. It's a work trip. Nothing more," I set him straight.

"Fine. It's a work trip. With the girl who has your balls firmly grasped in her hands."

"I'm not pining after her, I'm seeing people."

Anderson rolls his eyes. "When was the last time you had sex?"

I take a sip of my beer. "I'm not answering that... it's personal."

"Was it Laurie?" Anderson pushes. "You took her out." I keep ignoring him, but his eyes scrutinize me. "Are you serious right now, you didn't fuck Laurie? She's always up for a good time."

"I don't want to talk about it," I almost yell, trying to shut the conversation down.

"Oh, we're talking about it," Anderson pushes. "The fact that you turned down Laurie says everything. You have a thing for Chloe Jones."

"Stop trying to read more into it. You're as bad as my brother. Men and women can be friends." He gives me a look of bullshit. "I'm sorry you're unable to have a friendly relationship with a woman without wanting to fuck her."

"The difference is, Chloe's hot, and I know for a fact you want to fuck her."

"Are you saying you can only be friends with ugly women?" I question him.

"Yeah. Pretty much."

Fuck! He's such a pig.

"No wonder you're single." I finish my lunch, my appetite seems to have left me.

"This isn't about me. It's about you, and some chick who has you wrapped around her little finger."

"I've got work to do." Standing abruptly, I cut the conversation short.

"I'll be your best man at your wedding," Anderson adds.

I flip him off and head back to my office.

13

CHLOE

Being stuck in a car with Noah Stone for the next couple hours is going to be torture, especially when he takes off his suit jacket and rolls up his shirt sleeves giving me a glimpse of his tanned, toned forearms.

Not fair. Totally not fair because that's this woman's weakness. Add in his delicious cologne, the tiny bit of scruff on his jaw, and I'm done for.

We sit in silence as he pulls out of the building's underground parking garage and into Manhattan's Friday madness traffic. We spend the next few hours chatting away like we've known each other for years. Everything's so comfortable with him. We talk about anything and everything, and before we know it, hours have passed, and we're pulling up in front of the building site.

"We're here," Noah announces as we stop, the temporary fencing blocking our entrance. Noah hops out of the car and opens my door for me. Holding out his hand, he helps me from the vehicle.

"I think I'm wearing the wrong shoes?" I stare down at my heels.

"It'll be fine. The landscaping starts next week, so that's why the driveaway is unfinished. Everything else should be fine, and if not, you can jump on my back, and I'll carry you."

"Such a gentleman," I say while elbowing him. Like he could carry me, I'm twice the size of his supermodels. I'll probably break his back.

Pulling back the temporary fencing, Noah ushers me into the work-site. And, oh my goodness, the entrance is gorgeous with its white columns and gray shingles—

it's quintessential The Hamptons.

Logan and Noah purchased the historic estate and expanded it. There's the original manor house, and they have added on little bunga-lows which are dotted along the coastline nestled in the dunes surrounded by beach grass. I've seen the estate via images in presenta-tions and meetings, but never in the flesh, and honestly, the photographs don't do it justice. Stepping into the foyer of the manor house feels like I've stepped back in time, minus the mothball smell. It's light, modern, and yet they have kept all the beautiful craftmanship of yesteryear intact.

"Noah. Good to see you again." A tall beast of a man walks toward us.

"Ewan. Great to see you, too. It's looking good." Noah shakes his large hand. "This is Chloe, she runs our marketing department," he introduces me to him.

Chocolate eyes look over me. *Is that a spark of interest lying behind them?*

He extends a large hand to mine. "Nice to meet you, Chloe."

He's handsome, in a rugged, lumberjack, lost-in-the-wilderness kind of way.

"What are you doing up here?"

"Logan said you guys had progressed so quickly that he thinks we'll be ready in a month?" His words make the giant chuckle, it's deep and vibrating.

"Glad he has so much faith in us. We will try our best to accommo-date his timeline."

"You've always come through for us before." Noah slaps him on the back. *Hope he didn't break his hand against the pure muscle.*

"True. Well, I better show y'all around then." Ewan gives me a flirty wink.

He takes off in front of us, and I have to run to keep up with them both—stupid little legs and heels.

"Not sure how much you know of the history of this estate." Ewan turns to me. "It used to be the summer home of an heiress from Europe in the twenties. She lived a life of excess until she was ninety. We wanted to keep her spirit alive with her estate but give it more of a modern twist. The beautiful architecture we didn't want to lose, but let's face it, most rich city people aren't interested in ornate carvings or moldings, are they?" He chuckles. "They're more interested in if they can get Wi-Fi. Can I arrive by helicopter? Is the food gluten-free, vegan, no-calorie? Are there hot chicks in bikinis by the pool?" He laughs.

"Not all city people are like that," Noah moans.

"Really? What about that time—"

"Never mind," Noah cuts him off before Ewan can tell his story.

"Hold on, that sounded like it was going to be a good story." I look between the two of them.

"It is, but it wouldn't be very professional of me to continue with it," he says as if he's realized where he is.

"Really?" Looking over at Noah, I raise an eyebrow.

"It's not that good of a story. I promise," Noah tells me.

I continue to stare at Noah.

"Fine." He rolls his eyes. "You can tell her."

Ewan looks between Noah and me with intrigue. "Noah was dating this supermodel," Ewan starts. *Of course, he was.* "He took her to a resort in Mexico just before it opened. Anyway, she had a fit when she realized the food wasn't gluten-free, that there were bugs, and that it was a building site. She said he had promised her a luxury weekend away and brought her to a dump. She complained that they didn't arrive via helicopter and had to arrive via a car from the airport, which took an hour. Didn't help that the boys kept finding tarantulas and putting them on her bed." Ewan's bursting with laughter while telling the story.

"Best bit was she called some other rich guy she was seeing, and he picked her up down the road in his helicopter and whisked her away." Ewan's now doubled over with laughter.

"One of the worst dates of my life." Noah looks over at me, and I can't help but laugh. He's getting no sympathy from me.

"That's how Noah found out she was cheating on him."

Aw, that sucks.

"Lucky escape, I guess." Noah shrugs.

"She's onto her third husband now. So, I'd definitely agree, lucky escape," Ewan adds.

"Anyway…" Noah tries to change the subject.

"Right. Let's continue the tour," Ewan says with a smile.

We keep walking through the gorgeous estate, Ewan pointing out interesting pieces of architecture.

Ariana would love this. She adores old buildings and preserving history.

Actually, my eyes traveling over Ewan realize he would make a pretty perfect match for Ariana. She loves a big man, especially one who's good with his hands. Probably not very professional of me if I hand him my best friend's phone number.

"As you can imagine, the coastal theme has been done to death up here. The guys wanted something reminiscent of days gone by but with a modern twist. The golden, gilded glory days of The Hamptons where you might run into a Rockefeller or the Hearts. Where you can smoke a cigar and women wear diamonds."

"So, we're selling to stockbroker douchebags."

Ewan bursts out laughing, his deep chuckle vibrating right through me. "I like her. She's not from around here, is she?" he asks Noah.

"California," I tell him.

"West Coast girl, huh?" Looking me over, a flick of heat radiates from behind his chocolate eyes. "How ya finding the city?"

"Busy."

He chuckles. "Anytime you want to escape the city, just let me know. I can take you to some quieter places."

Is he flirting with me?

"Are you seriously flirting with my employee right in front of me?" Noah asks.

Ewan looks between us. "Only if she wants me to?" He gives me a wink, which makes me smile and blush all at the same time. The man's hot but not my type.

"Um..." Not knowing how to answer the question, I haven't been blatantly hit on in years. I feel my cheeks turning a bright shade of pink as I feel the intense gazes of two men bore into me. "Actually..."

Noah's phone rings at that precise moment. "I'll just get that." Noah excuses himself.

"Sorry, I didn't mean to put you on the spot like that. Especially in front of our boss."

I wave his apology away. "I'm flattered."

"But... you're not interested," he finishes for me.

"I was actually thinking you'd be kind of perfect for my best friend."

Ewan raises his eyebrows.

Pulling out my cell, I show him a picture of her, and why wouldn't he be interested in the beautiful brunette. "Ariana is an architect who loves old homes too."

"She's beautiful." Ewan gives me a smile.

"She's lovely. I think you two would be a better match."

Ewan chuckles again. "Fine. I'm not leaving brokenhearted. Here's my number if your friend would like to catch up. She's more than welcome to give me a call."

Ewan and I exchange numbers.

We chat more about the property while waiting for Noah to finish his call.

"So, are we done?" Noah steps in behind us, his tone having a slight bite to it.

Whatever happened on that phone call mustn't have been good?

"Yep, we're done," Ewan tells him. "Chloe, it was an absolute pleasure meeting you." He steps to me and kisses my cheeks. "Noah, as always, great to see ya." He reaches out and shakes his hand. "I'm off to the bar with the boys. Have a good weekend." Ewan waves and wanders off into the distance.

"You two seem to hit it off," Noah states in more of a statement than a question.

"He seems like a great guy."

"He is," he replies curtly.

"Are you okay?" I ask while we walk back through the resort.

"I'm fine."

"You don't seem fine."

Walking back to the car to grab our bags, he doesn't say anything at all. Then all of a sudden, he blurts out, "Doesn't seem very professional flirting with the workmen."

What? His comment stills me. *Is he serious?*

"You don't see me commenting on you flirting with all the younger girls in the office or having phone sex in your office where people can hear," I mouth off while stomping past him.

"Excuse me?" he raises his voice.

"You heard me. The walls between our offices are not as thick as you seem to think they are. Oh, Daphne, you make me hard. So hard. I can't wait to have those lips on my—"

"That's enough," Noah warns, his face now bright red with embarrassment.

Grabbing my bags from the trunk of his car before slamming it shut, he stomps back through the foyer and up the grand staircase. I don't have time to take it all in as he continues down the long corridor until he reaches the middle. He pushes open the door, and I follow in after him.

Oh wow, the room's gorgeous. It looks out directly over the ocean with its large bay window, but I don't have much time to enjoy it as Noah places my bag on the floor and hightails it out of my room.

"Noah," I call after him which he ignores for a couple of seconds before slowing and eventually turning around. "Did I do something wrong?"

His face softens before he speaks, "No. You did absolutely nothing wrong, Chloe." I hear the sincerity in his voice, but I'm not convinced.

"Did something happen on the phone call?"

"Yeah. Just a work thing. I'm sorry about before, I shouldn't have had a go at you about Ewan. It's none of my business."

"True. Ewan seems like a great guy."

"He is. You should give him a chance."

And that's when it dawns on me—Noah thinks I'm into Ewan.

Is he jealous? No. As if.

"Yeah, no, he's not my type. But he's definitely Ariana's type." Confusion laces his face. "I was setting up a date between them."

"Really?" he asks.

"Yeah."

Does he look relieved?

"They would be a good match," he agrees. "So, um…" looking a little embarrassed, "… do you want to meet up, in say twenty, and continue looking around?"

"Sure."

14

NOAH

I can't believe how angry I got thinking Ewan and Chloe were going to hook up. That's not right, and I shouldn't have acted like that. Fuck. Maybe Logan's right, bringing her here was not a good idea.

As soon as I got back to my room, I made a call to our maintenance guy and told him he needs to soundproof my office. The fact that Chloe heard my conversation with Daphne makes me feel like a dick. Daphne's a flirt and a fantastic phone sex talker when I need something —a release. No, I don't jerk off in my office, that's weird, gross, and probably violates so many laws. I took the call in my executive bathroom, which is connected to my office, and finished off in there, just in case someone heard. I shouldn't be doing that kind of shit at work. At the time, I just needed something, especially because Chloe had come in wearing this tight-fitting pencil skirt that was molded to her amazing curves, and it made me want to bend her over my desk and fuck her.

Those skirts of hers push me to insanity.

I've got to stop this—it's driving me crazy.

Chloe's off-limits.

I need to remember the warning EJ gave us that he would murder us, and no one would find our bodies because we would be scattered in the Vegas desert. He was pretty serious about that fact too.

I watch as she walks toward me, she's changed from her office attire and into something more casual—jeans, a white blouse, and some sandals. Her hair is out, and the breeze is blowing it around her face. The sun's beginning to set behind her—she's bathed in a golden hue and looking like a damn angel.

Stop it, Noah.

Shaking the impure thoughts from my mind, I mumble to myself, *She isn't yours and will never be yours. Forget her.*

"Hey." She smiles, which lights up her whole face. "What a view." Pointing her thumb over her shoulder toward the ocean. "You okay?" Chloe asks.

"Sorry, was a million miles away. Running through lists of things to do."

Chloe chuckles. "I do the same thing. I totally space out thinking about my internal lists, and I don't realize I've been staring at someone for like twenty minutes." She laughs. "They probably think I'm a weirdo."

Yeah, let's go with her explanation. It sounds feasible right now.

"I thought we could go for a walk along the beach. You can see the resort in all its entirety."

Chloe follows me through the sand dunes and down onto the beach. It's deserted with not a single soul in sight. We walk in silence, taking in the natural beauty.

"Wow," Chloe comments as she stops and casts her eyes over the estate.

"It's beautiful, isn't it?" Making sure I keep my eyes in front, I try not to look at her again.

"Yeah, it is." Chloe absorbs the picture-perfect vision in front of her.

"How do you think we're going to be able to market this compared to the more modern resorts?"

That's it—focus on work, Noah. Good job.

"I've been thinking about that," she muses. "We don't try and compete." She's lost me. "I was thinking in the shower earlier…"

Nope don't do it, Noah.

Do not *think of her in the shower, naked and...*

"Why don't we market this as a member's club." Shaking my lewd thoughts from my mind, I turn to her. "This estate gives me, like an old English gentleman's club vibe. Cigars on the balcony. Cognac in the library."

"The home is from that era."

"Exactly. So, why should we compete with other resorts? The Stone Group is famous for its boutique hotels. Why not make this the first members-only hotel?"

"But why would they pay to be members for only one resort?"

"That's what I thought. Only one hotel doesn't seem worth it. Unless..." her face lightening up with excitement, "... it's a members-only club during the summer."

Now I'm listening.

"People purchase a membership for the entire summer. They can use it as much or little as they want. We, of course, hope they use it all the time. It could be fully inclusive, making it cheaper than a summer house for the weekends." Interesting concept so far. "The Hamptons in summer is the place to be. So, why don't we make our little corner the most exclusive corner of the coast?"

I like the sound of where she's going with this.

"We offer them summer membership, and it includes parties all weekend long with the hottest men and women, the best DJs, the best food, and the most outrageous drinks. I bet we could even get EJ to do a summer pop up here."

"You're a genius."

She smiles proudly at my compliment.

"Emma knows enough hot people to help us out there, or we could hire hot people for the summer."

"That's brilliant. Do you think we could have this ready before opening? Logan wants it all open in eight weeks which is Memorial Day."

"As long as the resort is ready, then yeah, I think we can do it. I mean most of the marketing has been generic so far because we've been waiting on the professional photos."

"Okay, I'll talk to Ewan about maybe getting some more rooms mocked-up with the interior designer, so we can get those photos taken."

We both pull out our cells and start jotting down things on our to-do lists.

"I also know a couple of fantastic event planners, Camryn and Kimberly from Starr & Skye Events Management back in New York. We should get them to help us with the event. They know everyone we need to have here for an opening."

She nods in agreement. "Perfect. That sounds like a plan."

We decided to have dinner in town as the hotel wasn't equipped yet for us to eat there. As it's the off-season, not many places are open, so we ended up at a quaint seafood restaurant by the sea. A little romantic place with the candles and music playing in the background and couples sitting around holding hands and gazing lovingly at each other.

And there we are turning up with iPad in hand and spending most of the night on it in between courses. The maître d didn't look too impressed for most of the evening, but at least the food and wine are excellent.

Off in the distance, a storm's brewing. I've been watching it all night. The lightning illuminated the stormy sea as it rolled in closer and closer.

"We should probably go home, there's a storm coming," Chloe points out just as a crack of thunder echoes through the restaurant making everyone jump as the lights flicker.

Looking at the liquor store across the road, I ask, "Should we grab some wine first?"

"Good idea," Chloe agrees as we quickly dash across the road to purchase a couple bottles of wine before jumping into the car. The wind picks up as we head back to the resort. Leaves scatter across the road, the trees sway from side to side, the black sky lighting up under the brilliance of the strikes in the distance. Looking over, I notice Chloe gripping the seat, her knuckles are white, and her body's strung tight.

"Are you okay?" Keeping my hands on the steering wheel as the wind batters the car, I look over at her.

"Yes," she squeaks. *Is Chloe afraid of storms?*

"Chloe?" I repeat her name.

"I don't like storms." The words rush out of her mouth like a tidal wave hits the shore, fast and robust.

"I've gathered that." Chuckling, attempting to lighten the mood, but looking over at her again, she looks petrified. Reaching out, I take her hand in mine, and it's clammy. *Shit.* "You're safe," I reassure her.

"I know," she answers on barely a whisper.

My fingers link with hers tighter. "I won't let anything happen to you, okay?" Glancing over at her, her head slowly turns.

"I know you won't," she tells me, but the fear on her face is breaking my heart.

We need to hurry and get into the safety of the hotel.

Eventually, we pull into the driveway, which is filled with leaves. I hesitate to let go of her hand as I park. Quickly, I jump out and rush to her side of the car, opening the door as a massive bolt of lightning hits overhead and an almighty crack of thunder echoes around us. Then we're blanketed in darkness, the lightning strike hitting somewhere close by, cutting our power.

Chloe jumps into my arms. She's shaking, her face has paled even more.

I grab her hand again. "Come." Pulling her from the car, I slam the door after her and race inside practically dragging her behind me. As soon as we're safe inside, Chloe collapses to the floor and starts having a panic attack.

"You're safe, Chloe," I say over and over again, but it does nothing to slow down her attack. "Just breathe. Breathe, Chloe." Wrapping my arms around her as tightly as I can I cradle her on the floor. We stay like that for what feels like hours but must only be minutes. My hand strokes her hair, trying anything I can to calm her from such a severe attack of anxiety. With each flash of lightning, she jumps and shakes even more.

"Chloe, I'm going to move us." My legs are going numb against the tiled floor. "Wrap yourself around me, and I'll carry you." She does as she's told, wrapping herself around me like a monkey. Slowly, I move through the darkened foyer, with each crack of lightning slowly showing me the path upstairs. One by one, I make my way up the grand staircase and down the corridor to her bedroom.

Thankfully, the door is open, and I walk straight in. You can see the storm raging outside through the large window. I'll pull the curtains in a minute, once she's feels safe.

Gently, I place her onto the bed.

"Please don't leave me." Her words break me.

"I won't," I tell her. "I'll be right beside you."

She nods and unwraps herself from me, pulling the bedcover out as she jumps in underneath it. I move around the bed and slide in beside her, wrapping my arms around her shoulders, her head resting against my chest. Every so often, I find myself pressing a kiss to her head as if it's second nature and I have the right to.

"Would you like me to pull the curtains?"

"No. I want to watch it, so I know what's happening."

I nod my head and go back to merely holding her.

"I'm sorry. I haven't had an attack like this in long while," she confesses. "I don't know what's triggered it."

"You have nothing to apologize for."

"I never wanted you to see me like this," she confesses.

"You have nothing to be ashamed of," I tell her.

Looking up at me, tears glisten in her eyes. "I never wanted you to see me any other way than as a strong woman."

"Chloe." My hand caresses her face. "You are a strong woman. Letting me help you makes you a strong woman." A single tear falls down her cheek. Leaning forward, I press my lips against the salty tear and hope that some of my strength can absorb her fear.

"My parents died in a storm like this," she tells me. "One of Dad's clients invited him out on his private plane. He was flying them to Vegas for the night." Chloe's body tenses as she continues the story. "I remember arguing with them because I wanted to go. I'd never been to Vegas, and I wanted to go desperately. I was a senior in high school, and I thought I was old enough. They promised me they would take me for graduation, but they had a meeting with a client. I had a temper tantrum over it and refused to say goodbye to them."

Chloe's voice hitches. "They told me they loved me, then they both kissed me goodbye, even though I was being a brat. That was the last time I saw them." She breaks down in my arms, sobbing.

My heart breaks for her because I know how she feels. My father tried to call me before he passed away, and I let it go to voicemail. He left a message telling me how much he loved me and how proud he was of me. I played the what-if game for years after, wondering if I'd just taken his phone call, could I have stopped him from taking his life. Could I have talked him down from what he had planned?

I stroke Chloe's hair until there are no tears left and she's so exhausted from crying that she eventually falls asleep in my arms.

I'm not going to lie, having her here with me like this feels good. It feels right.

Gently, I place a kiss on her forehead and sink us both down into bed, pulling her tight against me as I close my eyes.

15

CHLOE

The bright sun is streaking through the window as I slowly open my puffy eyes. My mini-breakdown coming back to me like a sucker punch to the stomach. It's been years since I had a breakdown over a storm. *Shit.*

Quickly, sitting up on my bed, I remember falling asleep in Noah's arms last night.

"Morning," Noah's deep voice surprises me.

Turning, I see his smiling face.

"You look a little freaked out. Nothing happened."

Feeling slightly relieved, but a small portion of me is quite disappointed, I start to apologize, "About last night—"

But Noah stops me. "Chloe." His voice is stern. "I'm glad I was here to help."

Sitting up on the bed beside me, thankfully he's fully clothed.

"Thank you," I state feeling awfully sheepish. *How does he look so good first thing in the morning?* "I should go have a shower, I probably look like shit." Jumping out of bed, I head for the bathroom.

"You don't." Noah's voice stops me in my tracks.

"Is this going to be weird now?" Moving my hand between us, I state the obvious.

"Because we slept together?" Noah finishes for me.

"No, we didn't..." I quickly add which makes him burst out laughing.

"I know, but you're freaking out, and it's kind of funny to watch." Noah continues laughing at me.

I pick up the pillow and throw it at him, which makes him laugh even harder. I curse him, "Fuck you."

"It's all good on my end," he tells me.

"Okay. Good." Walking over to my bag, I start to grab things I will need for my shower.

"I liked it, though," Noah tells me.

"Liked what?" I still, immediately.

"Being your person."

Turning around, his answer surprises me. "My person?" I question.

"Yeah. I liked that you confided in me." Seeing as he was the only person here, I didn't have much of a choice. "I know it was by default, but still."

I walk back over to him and sit beside him. "I can't thank you enough for what you did for me last night, Noah." Grabbing his hand in mine. "You were a real friend to me."

The faintest of flinches forms across his face at the word 'friend.'

"Anytime, Chlo. I do think I deserve a reward for being such a brilliant *friend,* though." He smiles at me.

"A reward?"

"Yep." He nods, a huge grin forming on his face. "How about a friendly kiss, then?" Wiggling his eyebrows at me, he's laughing. I slap him on his arm, playfully.

"You were doing so well till then." Now I'm laughing along with him.

"Hey, I'm new to all of this friend business. Just thought I'd try my luck."

"I'm going to take a shower." I head off, walking away from him.

"There won't be much hot water as the power went out last night.

Maybe we should shower together." His words make him howl with laughter.

"You're such a dick."

Smiling, the awkwardness of last night lifts between us.

"Thanks for a great weekend." Jumping out of Noah's car as he parks out the front of our homes.

"No, thank you. I'm so excited to pitch your idea to Logan tomorrow. I think it's a great innovative strategy." Seeing him just as enthusiastic about my idea as I am fills me with pride. "Did you want to come over and finish it off tonight?"

"I'd love to, but I have plans with the girls. They're coming over to help me organize my thirtieth birthday party."

"Oh, okay, well, have fun," he says cheerily while grabbing his bag and heading to his home.

I do the same, quickly jumping into the shower and getting everything ready for the girls to come over.

A few hours later, one by one, the girls arrive filling up my quiet home.

"I love this place so much," Emma muses sipping her glass of bubbly while sitting in the living room.

"Can't wait till the weather heats up and we can use the outside patio," I tell them.

"You do realize you're hosting all our parties from now on," Stella informs me.

"I have the space." Waving my arms around, and the girls laugh.

"So, how was your weekend away?" Lenna asks once we've all settled down with drinks and food.

"It was really good. I have so much to tell you, I don't know where to start," I say excitedly.

"I knew it. You banged your boss." Emma squeals jumping up and down in her seat. The rest of the girls excitedly chatter in agreement.

"No." Silencing them, I continue, "I did not sleep with Noah."

"Seriously?" Emma groans. "It was the perfect moment. No one would know."

"Except you want me to tell you all," I remind her of her question.

"We don't count. It's a given you tell us everything," she jokes.

I roll my eyes at her.

"So, what did happen?" Ariana asks.

"Well, firstly, I found your dream man." I point to Ariana. "I have his phone number here if you're interested."

"Wait! What?" Ariana asks, confused.

"Did you get to meet Ewan?" I ask Lenna who has been up there too.

"Oh my God, yes," she swoons. "He's so hot."

"Yes, he is. He has this whole lumberjack, man of the wild, thing going on. Plus, he loves old houses and could talk for hours about the historic moldings of The Hamptons Estate."

"Do you have a photo?" Ariana asks.

"No. I forgot to get that, but he is cute."

"Hold on, it's probably on his website," Lenna adds. Pulling out her phone, she madly types away then thrusts her cell into Ariana's face. "That's him."

Ariana takes her phone and peruses it.

"Show me," Emma says, looking over her shoulder. "That man is fine." She elbows Ariana. "I wouldn't mind climbing that man mountain." Emma licks her lips.

"Back off, sister. He's for Ariana." I wiggle my finger at her, and Emma throws her hands up laughing.

"He's cute," Ariana finally answers. "I just don't have time for dating."

"Who said anything about dating. You have time for fucking, right?" Emma nudges her.

"Emma!" Ariana squeals at her.

"Please, we all know you're not a prude. But it's been a while since you've been laid," Emma points out.

"That's because I have a demanding job."

"And running my own business isn't demanding?" Emma argues back.

Ariana is stumped. She's got nothing to say because Emma's right, nothing is busier than running your own business.

"Why don't you invite him to your party? It will be less set up and more casual," Lenna tells the group.

"Good idea," Stella adds.

"Want me to invite him?" I ask Ariana.

"Fine. If it will get you all off my back. Invite him."

We all squeal with delight.

"So, back to your weekend away. What happened?" Stella asks.

"Something weird happened." The group quietens waiting for me tell them my story. "A storm hit, and I had a panic attack."

"Shit," Emma states.

"Are you okay?" Ariana asks.

"I don't know. I was so embarrassed Noah had to help me. He stayed with me all night."

"When you say… all night… you mean in the same bed?" Emma asks.

"Yes."

The girls squeal again.

"Nothing happened," I state dampening their spirits. "He just held me and calmed me down."

"That's romantic." Stella sighs.

"Why do you think you're having the attacks again?" Ariana asks.

"Noah seems to think Walker's attack triggered me somehow."

"I wouldn't be surprised," Ariana adds.

"Fuck! I wish I could have cock-punched him that night," Emma curses.

"It is what it is, guys. I'm going to see someone again to help me because it was a severe attack."

"I'm sorry." Ariana rubs my leg.

"Anyway, something else exciting happened." Changing the

subject, the girls are all ears. "I'm going to need your help, Emma." She raises her brows at me. "We came up with an idea of making The Hamptons Estate 'members-only' for the summer. Membership includes all food, drink, and all the partying you desire. We will get in international DJs, the hottest models...." I look over at Emma.

"Oh... I like it." Emma grins. "That's such a great idea. I know so many people who would be into this."

"I'm so happy you said that because I'm going to need your little black book of awesomeness to help fill the pool area with hot people." Emma smiles. "We have eight weeks to pull this off."

"Sweetie, consider it done." Emma waves her champagne glass in my direction.

"Great. We will tee up a meeting for next week." She nods in agreement.

Yes. Killing it.

We chat a little bit more about what everyone else has been up to before diving into my birthday party.

"What's the theme?" Lenna asks.

"I have no idea."

"It needs to be something sexy as you're moving into your prime sexual years," Emma tells us.

"Where will it be? That might dictate a theme," Ariana suggests.

"Um... hello. You have this huge house with all this space, you should have it here," Emma states.

I'm not so convinced about that idea.

"EJ said you could use the restaurant," Stella suggests.

That's so sweet of my brother, but I'm not letting him close his restaurant on a Friday night, which is his biggest night for him.

"Tell him he can do the food."

Stella writes it down.

"Still think you should do it here," Emma pushes.

"I'm sure the boys would let you borrow one of the resorts if you want to go away?" Lenna advises.

"There are too many decisions, and I can't make one." Damn, I'm feeling slightly overwhelmed.

"Fine. You twisted my arm. I'll organize it," Emma chimes in.

"No," Ariana quickly adds. "Don't give her the power, she won't be able to stop herself."

"You're such a bitch." Emma throws a cushion at Ariana, which makes them both burst out laughing.

"Do I seriously *need* a party?"

"Yes," the room erupts.

"Wow! Okay. Fine. I'll have a party." Bowing to peer pressure, I add, "Can I trust you?" Pointing to Emma who nods her head eagerly. "Fine, then you can organize it."

"Yes." Emma fist pumps the air.

16

CHLOE

Three weeks later

Seriously, this can't be happening. I struggle to free myself from the stupid, stretchy lycra fabric. This is what I get for trying to be healthy on my thirtieth birthday. I'm a curvy woman—Marilyn Monroe curves. I have a butt and boobs, unlike all these stick-thin women of Manhattan. Now, these curves have me tied up like a damn pretzel. The skin-tight sports shirt I bought in a bout of enthusiasm to get fit, might actually be the death of me. The peppy, blonde, flat-chested saleswoman insisted that this top was technologically advanced for larger-chested women with its built-in sports bra. I call bullshit because now the stupid thing is currently stuck against my sweaty, oversized chest. I'm adding to the problem with my huge head which is covered in masses of blonde curls.

I knew I shouldn't have skipped straightening my hair this morning, but I wanted those precious extra thirty minutes in bed. I mean, I was already getting up at ass-o'clock, and I didn't want to get up even earlier. Now, I see my mistake.

I try tugging at the sticky material again, but it's still stuck like glue to my skin. I'm probably going to end up suffocating, entombed in lycra. My death making some BuzzFeed article's top ten stupid ways to die.

I'll be number three—*Girl Suffocates Trying to Escape Sports Bra.*

It's Darwinism at its best, and my poor brother will be stigmatized for all eternity. *Yes, I'm being dramatic.* Borderline hysterical, but it's my birthday, and this is not at all how I thought I'd be celebrating it.

"Motherfucker," I yell, stubbing my toe on the edge of the desk. Frustration is getting the better of me as I jump around the room. If anyone sees me, they'll probably think I've escaped a mental institution and am trying to free myself from my straitjacket. I'm at work early, and there's no one here to witness this.

If Noah saw me tied up like this, he'd never let me live it down. I'd be the butt of all his jokes for the next year, especially as he has been bugging me to come running in Central Park with him and his brother in the mornings.

That's pushing the friendship, I think.

Plus, I'm not fit *at all* and would probably end up having a heart attack on the side of the path while Noah and Logan do laps around me. No thanks. I have some dignity. Even if it's not obvious right at this very moment.

Thankfully, he has a breakfast meeting this morning, which means he misses my total and utter humiliation. *Thank you, birthday gods.*

Why doesn't he look like a sweaty pig when he arrives in the office?

Tugging at my shirt again, I bet he doesn't get stuck in his skintight t-shirt each morning. It probably slips right off him. He always looks like he's stepped off a photoshoot for a men's health magazine, his face glowing from the endorphins. The man doesn't even stink of sweat. Somehow, he smells fresh and manly. And yet, here I am practically suffocating.

Tugging frantically again, I let out a scream as I begin to panic.

How the hell did I get myself in a situation like this? Because you wanted to start being healthy, that's why. Stupid idea. *Next time, ignore that inner voice inside your head, Chloe.*

So, here I am, stuck in my boss's office because hello, he has a private bathroom and I thought I'd sneak in after my morning run, have a quick shower, and no one would be the wiser. Then I could walk around with a gorgeous workout glow on my face, and people would compliment me saying thirty looks good on me. Instead, I'm going to be passed out, maybe even dead, and people are just going to shake their heads and say, 'Well, at least she tried.' I struggle again trying to get this stupid shirt off because I'm not going out like this.

"Um, Chloe... what the..."

My body stills.

No, no, no. I did not just hear his voice.

I wriggle a little more, but I'm stuck.

Shit! No!

17

NOAH

Holy shit, her breasts are amazing. Perfect size. More than a handful, but not too much. I bite my bottom lip, trying to stifle a groan that has worked its way up my throat all the way from my dick. This is not what I thought I'd be seeing walking into my office this morning.

I was in a foul mood, stomping down the empty halls of The Stone Group, my morning appointment canceling on me at the last moment. But now... now my morning is looking up.

It's not the only thing up either. Goddammit, Chloe Jones.

Since the Hamptons, I've been working really hard at disguising my feelings for her, going out on dates with other women, and I've even stopped flirting with her. I tried being the friend I kept saying I was and not the man who wants nothing more than to jump her at any moment.

"Are you okay?" I'm looking at her tied up in knots.

"Does it look like I'm okay?" she growls, wriggling again against the lycra top. I try not to laugh because she really is stuck. "Stop looking at my breasts," she mumbles through the fabric. Even in a humiliating scenario she's still sassing me.

"Chloe, you're the one bouncing around my office with your tits out. It's kind of hard not to look." I hear her groan. "What happens if I tell you I think they're spectacular, and you have made my morning."

She stops moving. "I'm glad this is funny to you, Noah. But seriously, the last thing I want to do on my birthday is flash my boss." She wriggles again, my attention following her movements.

Shit, it's her birthday.

"I'm sorry, Chloe." She lets out a sigh. "What if I told you this is exactly what I wanted for my birthday. Will that help?"

Chloe stomps her feet in anger at my comment. "Never going to happen," she says through gritted teeth. "This isn't funny, Noah. Would you fucking help me, please? I think I've suffered enough public humiliation for one day. No, for one lifetime."

I can hear it in her voice she's embarrassed, so I stop with the jokes. "It would be my pleasure to help."

"Noah. Put your sex voice away, you dirty perv," she yells, trying to squirm but gets herself even more stuck.

"How do you know what my sex voice sounds like?" I question her.

"Um... hello, I've overheard your conversations with your bimbo of the month."

"Bimbo of the month?"

She stomps her feet again. "Seriously, do you want to have a conversation about your sex voice, right now?" she screeches.

"Okay, I guess you're right." I take a couple of steps toward her, trying to work out how the hell I'm going to get her free from this mess she's created. "Would it be a bad time to tell you, I'm a boob guy?"

"Noah," she yells my name.

"You're right, not the right time. But one more thing..." She groans. "I'm a connoisseur of breasts, and yours are the best I've ever seen."

"Shut up, Noah. Just shut up. I'm not in the mood for your flirting. Would you please just help me."

I hear the panic in her voice and feel a tiny bit bad for flirting with her at her most vulnerable moment, but if I'm honest, it's the only time

I can probably ever tell her the things I've always wanted to say to her. Because once this shirt comes off, that's it, we're back to boss and employee, and there will be no flirting, there will be no admiration of her boobs. Nothing.

So, I grab the tight material and try to pull, but nothing happens. I try again and realize it's really jammed on her body. "Shit, Chloe, you're stuck."

"No shit, Captain Obvious," she yells at me.

"Hold on." I walk to my desk in search of some scissors. "How attached are you to this top?" I ask.

"Fucking get it off me," she screams.

Okay, so she doesn't care. That's good, at least.

"Stay still, I'm going to cut it off you." She stiffens. "I promise I'll be gentle." My voice drops to a calm, soothing level.

"Sex voice again," she mumbles, which makes me laugh.

She holds still. The scissors glide effortlessly through the material until it's cut all the way through. She's facing me, her face is red, sweaty and puffy. Tears glisten in her eyes.

"You're free," I say as we both stare at each other for a moment too long.

"Thank you," she mouths as she launches herself into my arms, hugging me tightly.

Goddammit, her naked, heated skin is pressing against the fabric of my suit, and my dick twitches to life. This is not good. Then as quickly as she hugs me, she's running from my arms and locking herself in my ensuite, leaving me standing there trying to calm my body's physical reaction to her.

I need to get out of my office.

I need to get my desire for her under control.

"I'll head out and grab us some breakfast."

"Thank you," she yells back through the door. I hear the shower turn on.

Now I'm picturing her naked.

I definitely need to get out of here because those images are not helping me with the problem that's currently digging at the zipper in my pants. I rush out of my office and pull my cell from my pocket and hit AK.

"Why are you calling me so early," Anderson moans into the phone.

"I have a fucking emergency." There's silence on the other end of the phone. "A personal one, not a business one." I hear the sigh of relief through the phone.

"Can't you talk to your brother about this or EJ?"

My stomach flips, there's no way I am talking to EJ, he's Chloe's brother.

"Fuck no," I yell down the phone in a panic. "I can't talk to them about this problem." I duck and weave through the morning rush hour along the sidewalks.

"Then what's the problem?" I can almost see the eye roll through the phone.

"Chloe just flashed me her boobs."

Silence.

"I'm sorry, what did you say?" Anderson asks. "Back up a minute. I don't think I heard you right."

"You heard me right, man. Chloe flashed me her boobs in my office, and they are spectacular."

More silence.

"How the hell did that happen? I thought you were firmly in the friendzone?"

I rake my fingers through my hair. "No, shit. Hence, I have a problem. She got—"

"She got what?" Anderson raises his voice.

"She got stuck in her sports shirt."

He bursts out laughing. "You fucking liar."

"No, I'm serious. I was pissed because my breakfast meeting was canceled. So, I went back to my office, and there she was bouncing around in all her naked glory. I honestly thought I'd died and gone to heaven."

"I always suspected she had great tits." His voice fades away.

"Focus, man. What the hell do I do? Because I can't forget about what I saw. I mean... shit... I've always wanted to see her naked, and now... fuck."

"Told you, you should have fucked her months ago when you had the chance." Anderson chuckles.

"Fuck you. I'm serious. It's her birthday, and I know she's been feeling weird about turning thirty." Silence fills the phone. "Anderson!"

"Sorry, my mind was wandering."

"She feels humiliated," I tell him.

"Then you need to do something to humiliate yourself, so you're even."

That's the stupidest—actually, maybe he's onto something.

"Like what? 'Cause I'm all out of ideas. "

"She showed you her boobs, so why don't you show her your dick."

Is he fucking stupid?

"I'm pretty sure that's sexual harassment, and Lenna would cut my balls off. So would Logan."

"Out of context, yes it would be. But she flashed you first, and I think this will make her humiliation not so... you know... bad."

Maybe seeing Chloe's boobs has short-circuited my addled brain because I'm seeing his logic.

"So, what, I just whip it out?"

"Yeah."

"This could end horribly. You know that, right?"

Anderson bursts out laughing again. "I know. But only you could get yourself into a situation like this."

"Fuck you."

"Have fun. I'll see ya tonight." Then he hangs up on me.

Is flashing my cock really a good idea?

Flashing my chest isn't the same.

Nothing else is the equivalent on a guy as boobs is to a girl. I distract myself at the bakery grabbing all her favorite food items as well as a cake. She's always told me cake makes things better. Lastly, I grab her a coffee and head up to my office where things could go one of two ways.

She will either chop my dick off or laugh?

I'm hoping she doesn't laugh because that gives a guy a complex. Not that I have anything to worry about because I think I have a pretty good dick, but this is about Chloe and trying to make her feel better.

18

CHLOE

The hot water rushes over my body, I can't believe I flashed Noah my boobs. It's not like I did it on purpose.

How am I going to look at him again?

How is he going to take me seriously after this?

He did say I had the best boobs. *Focus Chloe.*

That is not important.

But there is a little portion of me that's kind of a giddy because he told me he thinks I have the best boobs he's ever seen, and Noah Stone has seen many a boob. Not to mention, he gave me his sex voice. I wasn't lying when I told him that I've overheard him using his sex voice. It gives me the chills, the way he drops it low, his dirty words vibrate through you.

But we're friends. Only friends. We have agreed on this so many times, especially anytime we have come close to crossing over into something more.

I let my forehead hit the tiled wall. Last year, I thought I would be celebrating my thirtieth birthday differently, that I would be enjoying it with my husband. Instead, I'm starting a new chapter of my life. Single. I should be thankful because I'm much happier now. I have a job where I get to travel the world, the most fantastic home I could only ever have dreamed of, and I'm with my friends living in a new city where I'm close to my brother again. I have so much to be thankful for. Maybe I do need to get laid. I haven't been with anyone since walking out on my wedding day six months ago.

Maybe I need to start my thirties with a bang.

Yes. That's exactly it.

No more feeling sorry for myself. No more pining after Noah Stone. Chloe Jones is thirty and fabulous. I will not let this one humiliating moment derail my birthday. I square my shoulders, giving myself one last pep talk and walk out into Noah's office.

"Happy birthday," he sings, standing before me with a cake in his hands and his pants around his legs. My eyes widen. Holy shit! He's flashing me his dick.

Have I blacked out or something?

This seriously cannot be happening right at this moment.

"What the h-hell are you d-doing?" I stutter my words, my eyes transfixed on his dick, and they don't move. His gloriously perfect dick. Now that I know what he's packing under those ten-thousand-dollar suits, I kind of wish I had jumped on it months ago. No wonder he has women lining up to be with him. I wouldn't want to be giving up that D for anyone.

"I thought it was only fair that I show you mine, seeing as you've showed me yours."

"This isn't elementary school, Noah."

"I simply wanted you to feel comfortable, you know, after exposing yourself to me."

My heart blooms. He's trying to take away my humiliation by humiliating himself.

"I'm guessing it isn't the right time to tell you, I'm a dick-liking kind of gal."

These few words make him burst out laughing. I still haven't taken my eyes off the D. I'm soaking it all in as much as I can before it vanishes forever.

"Noah, pull up your pants."

"You sure?" His voice dips low, making me raise an eyebrow.

No, I'm not sure, but if anyone walked into the office at this moment, it wouldn't look good for him or me.

"Yes, I'm sure." He places my gorgeous cake on the side of the table and pulls up his pants. I watch in fascination as he tries and wrangles that thing back into his underwear. My cheeks heat up with the thoughts running around in my head that are not G rated, at all.

Urgh. I'm supposed to be getting over him, not making my infatuation worse.

"There we go, it's as if nothing happened." He gives me a wink as he straightens his tie.

"We will never speak of this again."

Noah pretends to lock his mouth up and throw away the key.

"Can I have some cake now? I feel like I kind of deserve cake." I eye off the beautiful pink masterpiece.

"Your wish is my command."

He hands me a knife, and I carve into the stunning creation. I cut a slice for each of us, and we take a seat in his chairs. The first bite of the vanilla bean cake is delicious, and I can't help but moan at the glorious burst of flavor in my mouth.

"Seriously?" Noah glares at me.

"What? It's delicious."

"For the next ten minutes, I do not want to hear anything that resembles a moan, especially coming from you."

Frowning at him as I lick my spoon, his green eyes flare as they concentrate on my spoon.

"And don't do that either." He points his spoon directly at me.

"So, I can't enjoy this cake. Is that what you're saying?"

Noah lets out a heavy sigh. "No. But after seeing some of the best boobs in my entire life, then the body attached to the said boobs is moaning and licking a spoon wickedly, it's a little hard."

"A little hard to concentrate." I giggle, my cheeks flushing from his compliment.

"No. Literally. It's a little hard."

My jaw drops at what he's saying. Then I burst out laughing because, in all honesty, this morning has been crazy.

"Please tell me you're not laughing at my dick?"

"No. I'm laughing at how messed up this morning has been."

Noah smiles.

"Definitely different to how I saw my morning going," I say then take a bite of his delicious cake. "I'm really sorry about this morning, though," I tell him.

"Honestly, I'm not complaining." He smirks over his plate. "But may I ask why you were stuck in that shirt in the first place."

"I was thinking maybe it's time I got back out onto the dating scene." Noah pauses, his spoon halfway to his mouth. "But New York is filled with all these beautiful, skinny women, and I guess I thought I needed to lose some weight."

"You what?" Noah exclaims.

"I've put on a couple of pounds since leaving California, mainly because I've been doing a lot of comfort eating." I'm feeling a little weird telling him this fact.

"There's nothing wrong with you." Noah looks me over. "You're a beautiful woman." My heart skips a beat at his comment.

"You're just saying that cause it's my birthday." Awkwardly, I shrug it off.

"No, I'm not." Putting his slice of cake down on the table, he says, "You have no idea how beautiful you are. And I know I shouldn't be saying this, especially at work, but you're stunning."

I give him a nervous smile. "That's sweet of you. But I haven't seen you date anyone my size."

"That's not fair. You know I don't date. And the women who are seen on my arm are there for exposure, most definitely not for me."

"Doesn't matter." Putting down the plate, I stand. "Thanks for the cake, it was delicious and sorry about before." Turning on my heel, I start heading for the door, but Noah rushes past, stopping me.

"No. You don't get to drop that statement on me and walk away." Folding his arms across his chest.

"I have nothing to say."

"Yes, you do," he argues back. "Has someone said something to you?" Concern flitters across his face. It's stupid, so fucking stupid, and I shouldn't have done it, but I did, and I can't look at him. He'll probably think I'm still hung up on Walker.

"Noah. Please." His arms fall down to his sides.

"Talk to me, Chlo. We just saw each other's bits this morning, nothing could be more embarrassing than that." He attempts to make a joke.

"It's stupid," I confess.

"I won't judge. I promise." His voice softens.

"I don't want to talk about it here," I tell him as I begin to hear the sounds of the office starting to come to life.

"Okay. Grab your coffee, and we'll head across to the park."

He leads me out of the office with his hand on the small of my back, and we had down and outside. Taking the short route, we begin walking through the park, the morning commuters rushing past us. I take a sip of my second cup of coffee for the morning.

"Ready to tell me now?" Noah pushes.

"It's foolish, idiotic, and I can't believe I dragged you all the way out here for you to hear it."

"Well, I'm here. So, you might as well tell me now."

It's true. Just like a Band-Aid, I need to rip this off.

"Fine." Rolling my eyes. "Last night I was sitting by myself and thinking how this is the last night in my twenties."

"Was wine involved?"

"Yes." Of course, wine's involved because I was grieving the loss of my youth. "Anyway, I was thinking about how much my life has changed in the past six months. I thought I'd be married by the time I was thirty. Well, I was supposed to be." Shrugging my shoulders, I continue, "And now I'm living in New York. Single. Starting over again."

The panic that I felt last night returns with a vengeance. "It's stupid because men don't have to worry about their biological clock ticking."

Noah wisely doesn't say anything to that. "Walker and I spoke about having kids after I turned thirty." My stomach turns merely thinking about that man. "And now... I have no idea if that's even going to happen for me."

"Chloe, you have years before you have to worry about a family."

"Not really. What happens if the next guy I date lasts a year or two and then fizzles out? I'm two years older, and in the same place. What happens if we end up dating for five years and then nothing? My window of opportunity keeps closing around me."

"What happens if the next guy you date is the one, and you live happily ever after?" Noah teases me.

See, I knew he wouldn't understand—Mr. Playboy of Manhattan.

"Anyway, I posted a photo to Instagram saying goodbye to my twenties and hello to my thirties. Someone commented on my weight, and told me that maybe if I weren't so fat that Walker wouldn't have cheated."

"Oh, Chloe." Noah stops and turns to me.

I'm trying to hold my emotions in, but the comment stung.

"They're just a troll. Ignore them."

"But what happens if they're right? Was that the reason he cheated?"

"That was *not* your fault," Noah tries to reassure me. "None of it was your fault."

"I must have done something to make him cheat, though." I don't know why it is now that these questions are haunting me. I thought I'd dealt with all of this months ago.

"He cheated because he could, not for any other reason than he thought he was a fucking god." Anger laces Noah's words. "The fact that still after all this time you don't think you're good enough kills me."

We stare at each other, caught in a moment.

"I think you are one of the most amazing women I've ever met, Chloe."

My heart thunders in my chest as he reaches out and touches my cheek, sending goosebumps over my skin.

"I wish you could be mine."

Dead.

His words have killed me.

He leans into me, and I take a step forward, and we are inches away from each other. The rest of the park has disappeared. Gone silent. All except the sound of a phone ringing. It takes a couple of beats to come back from that moment when I realize its Noah's phone.

"I should take this." He moves away from me. "Brooke, hi. How can I help you?"

Hope sinks like a lead balloon when I hear the name Brooke. She's one of the women he likes to parade on his arm at certain events.

The fact he decided to take a call from her in that moment, well, it kills me.

Was what he said all bullshit?

Was it a ploy to get into my pants now he's seen how great my boobs are?

Either way, I'm not waiting around until he's finished on the phone with another woman.

Turning on my heel, I head back to the office.

19

NOAH

I shouldn't have answered that call from Brooke, but I panicked. Especially when we were moments away from something.

Fuck! I'm a damn dick.

I had no idea Chloe's still dealing with this level of trolls. I don't get how people can be so cruel. There's nothing wrong with Chloe at all. She's a beautiful, intelligent, and curvaceous woman. It kills me that Walker has done a number on her and that she thinks his infidelity is her fault. The guy's an egomaniac who couldn't keep his dick in his pants. It stung when she accused me of only dating model-size women. It's not true, but I guess I've been relying more on convenience dating than actual dating.

I'm a thirty-five-year-old guy, maybe I should be looking at settling down. I know women have biological clocks, but men can have internal clocks too. There's something deep inside of me that's been ticking away, and I guess I didn't realize what it was until she pointed it out. Fuck! Now I'm having a midlife crisis of my own. I realize I want more from my life.

Logan and I have been working so hard to build this company and our wealth, but now we don't have anyone to share it with besides women who are looking for mutually beneficial relationships which are based more on infamy or the latest handbag, not love.

Chloe's gotten into my head. She's making me question things I've never wanted to question before. It's too early for this existential shit.

"So, did Chloe like your dick?" Anderson asks, walking into my office.

I shake my head and give him a furious glare—now is not the time. "Excuse me?"

Anderson turns and sees Logan standing there with his arms folded, looking angry. He appears to be feeling a little guilty about dropping that bomb in front of my brother. Which would be a first.

"Before you get all in my face over what you just heard… it was an accident," I state, quickly trying to calm my brother down. He doesn't look convinced as he walks over and shuts the door to my office with a quiet click.

"There's nothing on earth you can say that will make what I just heard okay."

"In Noah's defense, it was my idea," Anderson adds.

Logan just glares at him.

"Does Lenna need to be involved in this discussion? Should we be expecting a sexual harassment charge at any moment?"

Okay, okay, I get why he's upset. Now that I think about it, it was a foolish thing to do. "No. Everything's fine," I tell him through gritted teeth.

He's not convinced, I can tell by the look on his face.

"You better start from the beginning and don't miss a thing."

Anderson mouths, 'Sorry.'

"You know how my meeting was canceled this morning?" Logan nods in understanding. "Well, I came back to my office a little earlier than Chloe had planned." Logan's brow raises. "She was stuck in her sports shirt." Logan frowns as if he doesn't understand. "She was naked from the waist up."

His eyes widen. "Shit," he curses.

"Chloe was mortified," I add.

"Noah called me for some advice," Anderson tells him.

"And you told him to flash his dick," Logan answers for him.

"Yes." Anderson smiles. "The poor girl sounded humiliated. So, I thought if she felt that humiliated, she might want to quit, which would be the easy way with not wanting to face Noah again. And I know how much of an asset she is to the company. So, I thought, why doesn't Noah humiliate himself instead? That way, she wouldn't have to quit. Really you should be thanking me," he cockily answers.

"I should be thanking you for causing a sexual harassment lawsuit?" Logan's definitely angry, the tone of his voice is harsh. "Of all the things you could have done to make the situation better, you thought showing your dick was the right course of action?"

Talking about it now like this, it doesn't sound like such a good idea.

"Okay, explaining it to you out loud now..." I scratch my head. "Yes, it sounds stupid, but at that moment, it seemed like a good idea. I mean it made her laugh."

I realize what I've said when I hear Anderson and Logan burst out laughing.

"Fuck you both, you know what I mean."

"I didn't realize you were working with a micro-penis," Anderson jokes.

"Fuck you. I'm hung like a donkey." I flip him off. "Tell him, Logan."

"Dude, I have no idea how big your dick is." Logan gives me a grimace.

"We're identical everywhere else. Of course, we would be down there." *Why the hell am I defending my dick?*

"If you both are going to whip out your dicks, I'm out of here. I'm strictly a pussy kind of guy," Anderson tells us.

Damn! These guys are frustrating.

"Look, she was upset. Actually, more like devastated this morning.

Plus, it's her birthday. I just…" I rake my hands through my hair, "… I just wanted to make her feel better and less humiliated."

Logan's stance softens. "You know how stupid it was to do what you did?" he lectures me.

"Of course, I do."

"Something like this can never happen again," he warns.

"Of course, not." *I'm not an idiot.*

"Fine." His face still looks like thunder, but the redness is easing somewhat. "And you…" pointing to Anderson, "… do not tell EJ."

"Promise." Anderson crosses his heart.

"He will kill you," Logan warns me.

"I know."

"Okay, well, I have work to do. See ya, ladies." Logan turns and leaves my office. I can tell his anger has receded a little because he didn't slam the door on his way out.

"Thanks, dickhead."

"Hey, sorry, I had no idea," Anderson apologizes.

"Today is one fucked-up mess." I let out a frustrated sigh.

"Has showing your dick made it worse for you being around her?" Anderson asks.

"More happened after the dick show." Anderson sits forward. "Something else was upsetting her, so we went for a walk in Central Park."

"Awfully romantic for colleagues," Anderson states with a smirk.

"It's not like that and you know it," I defend myself again. "Stupid trolls are still attacking her online."

"Need me to contact Jackson again?" Shaking my head, I don't need to involve our security guy in this, but maybe I should keep an eye on her social media to make sure I report those fuckers.

"Nah. She was just a little upset over their cruel remarks."

"You can't be the one to save her all the time," Anderson tells me.

"You think that's what I'm doing?"

"Do I need to list all things you've done for this woman over the past couple of months?" Frowning at my best friend, I mull over his honesty. *Do I have a savior complex when it comes to Chloe?* Maybe I do.

"She's really that hot?" Anderson questions me.

"Beyond." I hang my head in my hands.

"Shit! I guess you're just going to have to fuck her." I look up at him as if he's lost his damn mind. "Get her out of your system, or you're going to drive yourself crazy wondering."

"She's the head of my marketing department. I can't do that."

"Then you're going to have to forget her."

"I can't do that either." The images of this morning are like a dirty loop constantly running in my mind. I can't turn them off. Actually, I don't want to turn them off.

"Then you're fucked."

Gee, thanks for the kind words.

There's a knock at the door, so I call, "Come in."

Chloe's beautiful face appears before me, and I suck in a breath then pause.

"Oh, hey, Anderson." She gives him a smile.

"Happy birthday, beautiful." Anderson wishes her a flirtatious birthday, then looks her up and down taking in her beautiful body. *I'm going to kill him.* "What you got in there?" He points at the white plastic bag she's holding in her hand.

"Lenna and I went to Noah's favorite Italian place for lunch. He said next time we go there to grab him something, so I did." Chloe looks embarrassed when she quickly hands the bag over to me. "You had a busy day today, so I didn't think you would have had time to eat." Her words rush out like she wants to get out of here quickly. "I'll leave you both to it." She rushes out of my office, closing the door behind her.

Anderson looks at me. "Does this happen a lot?"

"We… um…"

"You bring each other leftovers?" He raises his brow at me.

"Only if we go to this Italian place we both like."

His green eyes scrutinize me. "You're so fucked, aren't you?"

"Yeah, I am."

"You need to do something. You have to either fuck her out of your system or marry the girl."

Can't I do both? That thought catches me off guard.

Anderson abruptly stands. "You just contemplated the latter, didn't you?"

I begin to argue, but it's useless, he knows me too well. So, I try the pathetic excuse approach. "We're not getting any younger."

"You are pussy-whipped, Noah." He points his finger and scowls.

"Aren't you lonely? Don't you get sick of the fakeness of the girls you date?" I question.

Anderson's eyes widen. "That's it. I have to leave. I don't know who you are anymore." And with that, he leaves dramatically, leaving me with my thoughts and some decent Italian food.

I look over at Chloe's office and see she's typing away.

Anderson's right, I need to do something. This limbo we're finding ourselves in can't keep going on like this. Something needs to give.

20

CHLOE

"What do you mean he showed you his dick?" Ariana glares at me as we settle in my bedroom before getting ready for tonight. I've just explained to the girls about my epically humiliating morning.

"It was spectacular, wasn't it?" Stella giggles. "That man looks like he'd have a perfect dick."

"You know I shouldn't be hearing this," Lenna adds with a stern voice which makes the room pause for a moment before she bursts out laughing. "Just kidding. I'm off the clock." She raises her glass in my direction and gives me a wink. "It's none of my business."

Rolling my eyes at her, I say, "It's not like that."

"Um… it kind of is. You guys should see them around the office. Flirting. Laughing. All the young girls sending daggers her way as she walks past."

"Hey, what now?" Looking over at Lenna who's smugly sipping her champagne. "No. They don't, do they?" She nods her head. "What have I ever done to them?"

"Might be the fact that you have Noah's attention, or maybe the fact you went away with him, or perhaps the fact that he checks you out as you walk past. Every. Single. Day."

"No, he doesn't," I argue. Lenna raises a 'really' brow in my direction. "Shit."

"Hey." Lenna sits up straight. "I'm only saying. It's nothing bad. You might not have realized it, but some of the girls have started to emulate you by wearing those pencil skirts you love so much. Because those skirts seem to grab Noah's attention the most."

Say what now?

"That seems awfully single, white female of them," Ariana adds.

"Yeah, but have you seen Chloe in one of those skirts? Her ass looks phenomenal, just like a gorgeous peach," Stella muses.

"What?" she questions when we all look at her. "I'm jealous, okay? I wish I had booty instead of a pancake." She sticks her tongue out then sips her champagne. "Anyway, getting back to Noah's dick... tell us more."

"You saw Noah's dick?" Emma questions while walking into my bedroom, then pulls me into a hug. "Happy birthday, beautiful," she whispers.

"Just another awkward situation Chloe likes to find herself in," Ariana adds.

I flip her off.

"Was it good?" Emma cheekily asks.

Unfortunately, I can't hide it, my cheeks flush upon remembering it. "It was amazing."

"She's been dickmatized, hasn't she?" Ariana laughs.

"Totally. You can tell when they get one of those far away looks, their cheeks turn pink, and they start biting their lips remembering how amazing the D is," Lenna adds. "You know I'm going to be staring at his crotch from now on." She wiggles her brows at me.

"I wonder if they're twinning downstairs, too?" Emma asks. "*I volunteer,*" she yells out before bursting into laughter.

"No. I volunteer." Stella stands up.

"Me, too," Ariana adds.

"I'm off the clock, so me, too," Lenna agrees.

Fuck, my friends are funny sometimes. We all burst out laughing.

"Screw you, guys. It's going to be hard—"

"Hard," Stella squeals interrupting as the girls continue their laughter, which makes me roll my eyes.

"What I was trying to say is... it's going to be difficult not to picture what I saw today when I see him next. Which is going to be a problem because that's exactly what I didn't want to happen. Hence, why I've never done anything before even when I've wanted to." I fall back on the bed and take a seat.

"The two of you have had the longest foreplay. Six months of flirting and the odd hookup—" Ariana starts but is interrupted.

"Hang on. You've hooked up?" Lenna questions me.

Shit. I've kind of neglected to tell her some things.

"We actually ran into the twins while on holidays, months before Chloe started working with them," Stella adds.

"We met on my honeymoon," I add that little tidbit of information at the end.

Lenna sits beside me and squeezes my hand. I've told her the story of what happened with Walker.

"Why didn't you tell me?" I can see the hurt in her eyes.

"I never wanted to put you in a position where it would compromise your job."

"You silly thing." She wraps her arms around my shoulders. "If it isn't impacting the business, then I'm okay. Plus, we're friends. I'd talk to you first if it were serious. Unless it's something illegal." Lenna gives me a wink.

"Fine. The honeymoon was a disaster. I kissed him. I even propositioned him. He was a gentleman—"

"Then there was a stupid misunderstanding," Emma adds.

"I wasn't in the right headspace for anything, anyway," I tell Lenna.

"Then he saved you in Vegas," Stella adds.

"You heard the story about Walker attacking me?"

Lenna nods.

"Like a knight in shining armor he attacked Walker and saved the day," Stella excitedly fills her in.

"Shame you missed it." Emma smiles, looking over at Lenna. "But I guess Logan was doing his own knightly duties, too." Lenna blushes.

"Nothing happened." She waves her hands around in the air dramatically. "Continue, Chlo…"

"Nothing else has happened. Boring really. I'm wondering about you, though?"

"Fine. We hooked up Vegas. I was drunk, extremely drunk, thanks to you." Lenna points directly at Emma.

"You're welcome." She raises her champagne glass to Lenna.

"He'd disappeared by the time I had awakened." She lets out a heavy sigh. "I thought…"

"He had changed his mind?" I answer for her.

"Yeah." She twists her glass of champagne between her fingers. "He acted as if it never happened the next morning. I felt a little humiliated because I stupidly let hope in." Lenna looks sadly around at all us.

We've all been there before there's no doubt about that.

"What about The Hamptons? Did anything happen then?" I question her about that weekend away.

Her chocolate eyes look at me, and in an instant, I know what she's telling me. Something happened, but it hadn't ended well. Again. What the fuck is wrong with Logan? Lenna's a fucking catch.

"Screw them," Emma shouts. "I've organized a wonderful birthday present for you, Chloe. Who am I kidding, I've organized it for all of us. Follow me." Emma escorts us from my bedroom and all the way downstairs to my kitchen. "Voila." Emma waves her hand through the air displaying six gorgeous men. "You're welcome." She taps my nose with her finger and smiles.

"Ladies…" one of the gorgeous men speaks, "… we're here for your service."

"What kind of service?" Stella asks.

"Anything you want?" One of the guys winks at her, which makes her blush.

"These guys are trained professionals in massage, cocktail creation, lifting heavy things... sex." She runs her finger over the pec of one of the men. "It's my birthday present to you."

Mmm, I'm not sure how to take this gift.

"Who would like to be massaged first?" one of the buffed men asks.

All the girl's hands shoot up.

I've been primped and prodded to within an inch of my life, from make-up artists to hairdressers to stylists, courtesy of Emma and her contacts. She's hooked me up with one of the most gorgeous dresses I've ever seen or worn in my life. Honestly, I feel like a sexy fairytale princess in this dress. I was skeptical at first about the sheerness of the fabric, but now that it's on, it fits like a dream.

The bluish-gray color is something I've never worn before. The deep 'V' with the tiniest of crystals hides yet accentuates my assets without making me feel uncomfortable. Then the layers of sheer fabric hide the fact that it's a built-in jumpsuit underneath not an actual skirt. So, I don't feel like I'm flashing my butt to the world which is a good thing. I've gone for black tonight for my birthday theme. I'm going to walk into my thirties with style, grace, and dignity like a fully functional adult. Plus, men look hot in tuxedos.

I'm hosting the party at the townhouse. It's easier that way. It's also, I suppose, a house warming party too. EJ, of course, is supplying the food. I hired the amazing girls from Skye & Starr Events Management who we're using for The Hamptons' party to put together this event.

I get along well with Camryn and Kimberly. After our first meeting I asked if they could throw together a last-minute thirtieth for me, and they were thrilled to deliver, and I can't wait to see what they have planned downstairs.

Sucking in a deep breath, I push the bathroom doors open and step into my bedroom, where my girlfriends are patiently waiting.

"Oh, Chloe," Emma gasps.

"You look like an angel," Stella says.

"Seriously, Chloe..." Ariana adds, "... you look breathtaking."

"Noah's going to be impressed." Leena gives me a wink.

"Thanks, guys." Doing a twirl in my evening dress, I feel so pretty, and everyone claps.

"I think we're all looking mighty fine tonight." Emma glances around the room.

There's a knock at the door and in walks one of the hunky men from earlier. He's dressed this time in a tuxedo, holding a tray of champagne glasses.

We each take a glass.

"I just want to say something before we head on down." Raising my glass, I say, "Without you ladies, I wouldn't be where I am today. It's been a long, bumpy road these past six months, but you've all helped me find myself again." The tears begin to well in my eyes, and I blink a few times to stop them from falling over onto my cheeks.

"Do not ruin your makeup," Emma says, but her eyes are glassy too.

"All I want to say is... I love you all..." raising my glass, "... and I'm so thankful you're all in my life." My lips turn up into the biggest smile. "To the next thirty years, bitches!"

The girls all holler, and we clink our glasses together.

"Watch out, boys," Emma adds, making us laugh.

"Is it safe to come in." Whirling around, I see EJ standing in the doorway. "Happy birthday, sis."

Feeling emotional, I hurry over and pull him into a hug.

"No crying," Emma yells.

"You look beautiful." EJ looks down at me with loving eyes. "I have something for you." He pulls out a small box, which is black gift-wrapped with a gorgeous bow on top, from his pocket and hands it to me.

"You didn't have to get me anything."

EJ shrugs and doesn't reply.

Opening up the beautifully wrapped present, a black velvet box appears. Looking up at EJ. I wonder what's inside while he urges me to continue. Flicking open the black box, my world stops. *How?* I don't understand. The tears which fall down my cheeks are unstoppable. "I don't..." I'm completely lost for words and can't finish the sentence.

"I remember Mom telling you she was going to give you this ring on your thirtieth birthday like Dad gave it to Mom on hers."

Gently, I pull the gorgeous pink diamond cocktail ring out of the box and hold it up to have a closer look. Mom and Dad met in college and didn't start making serious money in his business until after we were born. The first big purchase was this ring that my mom had eyed at a jeweler on Rodeo Drive one weekend. He surprised her with it a short time later, and she wore it everywhere and for every occasion. It was always on her hand. Launching myself back into my brother's arms, I have no idea how I can thank him for such an incredible gift.

"Hey, no crying," EJ warns.

"Thanks, EJ. Thank you so much."

"I'd do anything for you, kiddo." He reaches out and wipes away my tears with his thumb.

"Shit! I've ruined my makeup."

"We can fix you up in no time," Emma tells me.

"Why am I outside?" I ask Emma.

"I have a surprise for you." She jumps up and down as a large, white peacock chair comes around the corner, covered in flowers flanked by four hunky men in tuxedos who are holding it.

"What the..." I stare at it and pull my eyebrows together. "No. Ems. No," I repeat this over and over again as they come closer.

"You should be a queen on your birthday."

I get the sentiment, but this is more than a little crazy.

"I'm going to look weird."

She waves my misgivings away as the men place the contraption on the ground. "Jump on."

"No," I state while shaking my head adamantly.

"Come on... it'll be fun. Don't be a spoilsport," Emma pushes.

"For whom?" I argue back, but Emma simply rolls her eyes. "They can't lift me."

"Please! They probably bench press two of you," Stella mentions.

Thanks, traitor.

"Get in the chair, Chloe. Arrive at your birthday like a goddamn queen." Emma pushes me toward the chair, but I'm not convinced. I step onto the platform and sit in the chair like I have any sort of choice right now. The men grab each corner and lift. My nails dig into the plush velvet, while my heart thunders in my chest.

They better not drop me—I don't need any more public humiliation today.

Music starts, it's "Firework" by Katy Perry. *Oh my God, this is so embarrassing.*

We enter via the downstairs door directly into the party, and when people see me they start hollering and clapping. I feel a bit like an idiot.

Just go with it, Chlo, your friends are trying to give you a fun birthday.

So, I push aside my embarrassment and start to wave at everyone I pass, while the men move me through downstairs and out to the back garden where they finally place me down. As they do, mini fireworks go off around me from little canisters scattered throughout the garden.

Seriously?

I sit there as my girlfriends take a million photographs of my embarrassment.

"Get closer," Emma orders the men. "Pick her up." One of them grabs hold of my body and pulls me into his arms while my friends laugh and giggle as they make me pose with them.

Thankfully, after a short time, the spectacle is over, and I can mingle with my friends.

"I'm going to kill you," I berate while pointing at Emma, who simply laughs.

Looking up, I notice Noah, but he doesn't look happy at all. There's a deep scowl, and honestly, he looks like he's clenching his fists at his sides.

I wonder, what's the matter with him? Hope it's not work.

"Happy birthday!" EJ bursts out laughing.

"You knew about this?"

"Maybe. But I was sworn to secrecy. There were some choice words directed at my manhood if I told you. I didn't want to mess with that."

"Hopefully, there are no more surprises." His eyes widen with untold secrets. "There's more?" He zips his mouth shut and chuckles.

Oh my God, what more could they possibly have planned?

Before I know it, I'm surrounded by my friends wishing me a happy birthday.

That's when I notice, out of the corner of my eye, that Logan has spotted Lenna from the back garden and starts to make his way over to where she's standing. I watch as Lenna notices too, placing her drink on the table beside her. She smiles and laughs and then makes her excuses to the people she's with and leaves. With Logan following not far behind her, they disappear around a corner toward the main entrance. *What's going on between them?*

Sneakily, I follow after them, but they're gone by the time I step out into the front courtyard.

"You just missed them." Noah's gravelly voice surprises me in the darkness. He's leaning against the brick wall playing around with his phone, a beer sits loosely in his fingers.

"Something's going on with them."

"I know," he says, then gives me a small smile.

We're alone, the party going on inside without us. Noah looks delicious as always in his tuxedo.

"Happy birthday." He leans in kissing my cheek, his soft lips making connection with my skin making it tingle. Slowly he pulls himself away.

"Thank you." For some reason, I'm feeling nervous all of a sudden. "Are you having a good night?" Hopefully, no one's caught his attention. I noticed earlier that he had a group of women surrounding him, which isn't that unusual.

"It's been interesting." Taking a sip of his beer, his plump lips wrap around the edge of the bottle, and I wish they were wrapped around something else. I watch as his Adam's apple bobs as he swallows the liquid. *How come I find that action sexy?*

"How so?"

"Your entrance."

Oh, that.

"The girls organized it as a surprise. Honestly, it was way over the top."

"Didn't think it was you."

Should I be offended by that statement?

"What? Can't I enjoy four hot guys?"

Noah raises his brow. "If that's what you're into."

"It's my birthday. They don't call it dirty thirty for nothing," I reply, placing a hand on my hip which is pushed out to the side in defiance.

Noah stares me down, contemplating his words carefully before he speaks, "Guess, I'll leave you to it." Pushing himself off the wall, he steps off toward the street.

"Noah…" Grabbing his arm, I stop him, and the next thing I know he's spinning me around and pushing me up against the wall.

"You're driving me crazy, Chloe." I swallow down a large lump that's formed in my throat. Those emerald green eyes which are staring at me flare with desire, and he says, "I…" but stops and says, "Fuck." He pushes away from me, dragging his hand through his light brown hair looking almost in agony as he paces the sidewalk, then he turns and stares at me.

"You look so fucking beautiful tonight, Chloe." The need is written across his face as he attempts to get out what he wants to say. "I…" He's stumped for words again, but then realization hits him, and he yells, "Fuck it!"

Noah grabs my face and kisses me. Strong palms cup my cheeks as his mouth does incredible things to mine. My hands grab his waist pulling him to me, feeling his hard plains against my softer curves as our kiss intensifies.

The world around me ceases to exist, while everything falls away as his kiss consumes me.

21

NOAH

S eeing Chloe being carried in by those four guys, something sank in the pit of my stomach. I knew right away what it was—jealousy. Pure and simple jealousy.

Watching her in their arms as they held her, while her friends laughed and joked while taking pictures, I wanted to step over and rip their filthy hands from her body.

She looked spectacular in a dress which is nothing but a scrap of fabric, yet strikingly elegant at the same time. My eyes zeroed in on her delicate cleavage, transporting me back to this morning, where I wanted nothing more than to motorboat the shit out of those voluptuous gems.

Instead, I had to watch as she was introduced to single man after single man, each one of them vying for her attention. Watching her laugh and talk with them, their grimy hands touching her, their filthy eyes looking over her like a prize, yeah, that's when I realized I've got it bad.

I couldn't stand it any longer, I needed some fresh air and silence. I thought it would be rude to head home. So, I hid out in the front courtyard amongst the greenery.

I wasn't expecting her to come rushing out after Logan and Lenna.

I'm glad she did, but my intention was never to make a move like I have.

Jealousy is a crazy thing when it's bubbling away under the surface waiting to rear its ugly head.

Now my lips are on hers. Her hands are gripping my hips, pulling me closer to her, pressing my hardening self against her soft curves.

She feels like heaven.

I don't want to stop.

We should stop.

Anyone could see us.

Do I care? I don't think I do. *Even if it's EJ?*

A tiny moan falls from her lips, and I don't think I would even care if EJ caught us right now even with the ass whooping he'd give me because it would be worth it for this moment with her.

"Chloe. Chloe," a female voice calls out into the night halting us.

Both of us are breathing heavily.

"Shit," Chloe curses. "I have to go. That's Stella." She pushes away from me and hightails it around the corner without a second glance. Fuck. Letting my head fall forward, it hits the solid wall. *I'm an idiot.* Giving her a couple of moments, I walk back into the party, so I can see what's happening.

"Noah." Ewan catches me off guard. *What the hell is he doing here?*

"Great to see you again." I reach out to shake his hand.

"Chloe looks wonderful tonight, doesn't she?"

Did she invite him?

Is he here for her?

Shit. I thought she wasn't interested in him.

"Yeah. She does," I answer a little distracted as I watch Chloe take a seat on her throne again, her girlfriends all around her, smiling and laughing.

"Ariana's hot." He grins, looking over to where she's standing with her friends. "Chloe mentioned I should give her a call. We've been chatting for weeks now, but tonight's the first time meeting her." He seems nervous. I never thought I'd see this burly lumber-jack of a man ever crack a sweat, but here he is looking like a wreck.

Women, they can make a grown man terrified as fuck.

"They're a wild group of friends."

"I think I'm starting to see that." His eyes are firmly transfixed on Ariana as he talks.

"Happy Birthday" starts playing, and we all join in singing.

In walk two near-naked men carrying a three-tier birthday cake with sparklers on top. A huge smile falls across Chloe's face as she sees the cake.

Or is that smile for the two men bringing it to her? Stop it.

Having a secret kiss under the cover of darkness doesn't make her mine.

When the sparklers die down, everyone gives her a round of applause. She sticks her finger out and runs it through the icing with a cheeky grin on her face. She brings her finger to her mouth, her eyes close as her plump lips wrap around her finger, sucking the sugary goodness right off of it.

Fuck me dead! That's hot.

All of a sudden, music pumps through the room loudly—stripper-like music. One of the men tells her to sit on the chair, and the other does some kind of manly twirl. Her eyes widen. She looks a little taken aback.

Realization registers on her face about what they're doing, and she smiles. She fucking smiles. Her friends are hollering as the other two men join their friends in dancing around her like she's some kind of queen and they're her offerings. She's clapping and laughing as they dance, while hands touch her, caress her, the men all vying for Chloe's attention.

Honestly, I want to walk over and punch every single damn one of these Neanderthals for touching what's clearly not theirs.

She's not yours either, Stone.

Looking over to where EJ's standing, hoping he might put a stop to this craziness, but instead he's laughing and clapping along with everyone else.

What the fuck? Turning back, I see her slapping their asses, giggling, her face fully flushed with enjoyment written all over it.

I can't watch this.

Turning, I make my way through the audience and out the front door again, sucking in a couple of deep breaths to calm myself down.

"You're leaving so soon?" Logan asks.

"Yeah. We said happy birthday, no point in staying."

My brother eyes me suspiciously. "Guessing you didn't like the half-time entertainment?" I ignore him, but he doesn't stop. "Are you jealous?"

I give him my best *don't be fucking serious* glare, which makes him laugh.

"You are. Otherwise, you wouldn't be leaving the party. Fucking hell, Chloe must have a magical pair of tits if they have made you go gaga over her."

I turn and pin my brother against the brick wall. "Don't be so fucking disrespectful." Anger fills me while Logan raises his brow and bursts out laughing. I let go of him and rake a frustrated hand through my hair.

"Don't talk, I know the spiel you're about to give me."

The laughter falls from my brother's face. "Of course, I still believe that. But... you surprised me with your reaction just then."

"You were testing me?" I'm feeling a little shocked by his confession.

"Of course. You're as bad as me when it comes to women. But when one walks into your life and knocks you on your ass, well..." He shrugs, tucking his hands into his suit pants.

"Someone knock you over?" He ignores me. "Lenna perhaps?"

He turns quickly, his eyes full of anger. "I know we have the whole twin thing happening. I can deny it till I'm blue in the face, and you will still know I'm lying." *Oh, shit, it is Lenna.* "All I'm saying is, it's complicated."

"And?"

He just shakes his head. "When I want you to know, I'll tell you."

"Are you fucking serious? After all the shit you've given me over Chloe, and now, I find out something's happening between Lenna and you, and you're telling me to butt out. You're a damn dick."

"Fine. Want to hear how I fucked up?" I'm not following. "I broke our agreement. I fraternized." I'm surprised he's confessed that to me.

"And?"

He runs his hand through his hair. "And... nothing."

My eyes narrow, I don't believe him, but I can see he's not going to tell me anything else.

He starts to walk away then stops but doesn't turn around. "If you think there's something real between you and Chloe..." he spins around and looks directly at me, "... just make sure you're certain before doing anything."

"Logan..." My brother looks defeated.

"We'll chat soon. I promise," he tells me before jumping into his car.

Have I been so wrapped up in Chloe that I've missed what's been going on with everyone else?

22

CHLOE

After the cake-cutting chaos, I lost Noah in the crowd, and before I knew it, I'm downing one too many shots and having the time of my life. Dancing, laughing, hanging with my girls, minus Emma, who's disappeared somewhere.

Even through my alcohol haze, I can't get Noah's kiss out of my mind. The way he pushed me up against the wall, the way his lips commanded attention from my own, his hard body pressed against mine. Honestly, I would have let him do anything to me in that moment and wouldn't have cared if the world was watching.

I look out amongst the crowd again double-checking, but he hasn't reappeared.

Stella catches my attention from my peripheral, a slight frown has formed on her face as she watches EJ and some redhead dancing together. I elbow her which makes her jump, an embarrassed blush tints her cheeks.

"He's not worth it." I love my brother, but I hate that he's oblivious to the crush Stella has on him. He has no idea each woman he hooks up with chips away at her heart. I get why she won't say anything—she loves her job.

I wish she could be honest with her feelings for him. *Like you are with Noah?* Okay, subconscious, you have a point there.

"My brother's an idiot."

Stella just shakes her head. "It's not his fault. He has no idea. I'm the one with the problem," she confesses. "I need to get over it and stop torturing myself."

She's right, I must admit. "Go! Hook up with one of the strippers." Pointing to a couple of them who are dancing around the room. I give her a shove. "The blond keeps eyeing you," I say while wiggling my eyebrows.

She glances over, and sure enough he's looking again, so I decide to wave him over.

"What are you doing?" Stella hisses.

"Getting you laid."

"Evening, ladies… I'm Dan," the blond man introduces himself.

"I'm Chloe, and this is Stella." He gives her a bright, white smile. "Excuse me, my phone's ringing." Waving it in the air, it's not a lie, it's actually buzzing, but Stella still scowls at me. I give her a kiss on the cheek and skip away, happy with my matchmaking skills.

Moving through the crowd, I head up to the second level to check my phone in peace. There are numerous texts from friends wishing me a happy birthday, but one makes me take a pause. It's from an old friend in LA, one of the WAGS from Walker's team. Haven't really spoken to many of them since leaving him. I knew they would have to take sides, and seeing as their partners work with Walker, they would have to be on his. I get it. It sucks, though, as some of the ladies I was really close with at the time.

Bethany: Happy Birthday, Chloe. I'm sorry I haven't been in touch. You know how close Scott and Walker are.

Chloe: It's okay, I totally understand. Thanks for the birthday wishes.

Bethany: I just wanted to check in on you to see how you are doing about the news? I can't believe how vengeful those two are.

I have no idea what she's talking about.

Chloe: I blocked the two of them ages ago, so I haven't seen anything.
Bethany: Shit. I'm sorry to be the one to tell you. But I wanted you to have a heads up in case the media bombard you over it.

My heart's racing, what is going on? My phone buzzes, so I look down and see a series of screenshots Bethany has sent through from their account announcing their engagement. I stare at the time stamp, and it's today. There's a photograph of their two hands joined with the small one of their sons together. The giant rock glistening on her finger is twice the size of the one he gave me.

The caption reads…

She said yes.

Today is a special day as it's the day we first met all those years ago. I knew it the moment I met you, Tracey, that you were the one for me. We are already a family with our little bear, but now we can make it official.

#blessed #familylife #shesaidyes #bestdayever

What the actual fuck? Years ago, I introduced them at my birthday party. *Did they have feelings for each other then?* We had only been dating for a couple of months. Fuck. I'm such a fool.

I sit on the edge of my bed and stare at the photograph, memories swirl around in my mind as I try to dissect each one of them, looking for clues of their betrayal. Tears slowly fall down my cheeks at the realization I will never know the truth about Tracey and Walker and the full extent of their affair. By the sound of this post, it's been going on for a lot longer than I thought.

My phone buzzes again.

Bethany: Sorry to give you this news on your birthday.

Chloe: No. Thank you. You're right, some low life paparazzo would have surprised me with it, and that would have been worse.

Bethany: I know we used to be close, and again, I'm so sorry that I put our relationship with Walker before yours. Scott has had enough of his antics. The whole team has. Tracey brings out the worst in him.

Chloe: You have nothing to be sorry about. Breakups are hard for friends too. The team always comes first. I get it.

Bethany: There's a group of us coming to New York soon. We really would love to catch up again. We all miss you.

This puts a smile on my face 'cause I miss those girls too.

Chloe: That sounds like fun. I miss you all too.

Bethany: That's settled. I'll let you know the dates. I hope you're having a great night outside of this. Happy birthday, CJ.

Chloe: Thanks. I'm having a fantastic night. I'm not going to let those two try and ruin it for me either.

My hands are shaking as I place my phone on the comforter. I honestly can't believe they would be so vindictive as to announce their engagement on my birthday. It's not like they didn't have any idea what that date represents. I can't believe they both hate me this much.

The tears slowly roll down my cheeks while I'm feeling a mixture of anger, disbelief, and hurt over their actions. I wish them both well because as far as I'm concerned, they both deserve each other. I'm sure Tracey feels like she's the queen of the world right about now—she got the man, the money, the life that she always aspired to. She probably thinks she's the woman who's tamed Walker Randoff. But she's wrong. Walker cares about himself and himself only. He will always be number one in his eyes. You're only welcome to stay as long as you obey his rules.

Staring out my bedroom window over the rooftops of the city and out to the many lights that make up New York City, I'm so thankful that I'm out from under Walker's spell. That the life I was persuaded into wanting isn't the life I'm now living. I lost myself being with Walker, and I don't think I would have realized how much if he hadn't fucked-up. He would have eventually fucked-up because that's what he does, but it would have been so much worse. We would have been married, possibly had kids, who knows.

A tiny shiver falls across my skin thinking about that life which could have been. I may be thirty and single, but all my choices are on my terms. I don't have to answer to anyone. I don't have to fit into someone else's ideal. I can be myself. I feel liberated. Free even. Walker and Tracey announcing their engagement has put the past to bed for me even if it took me some tears to get here.

Have I already become more mature?

Chloe Jones is walking into a new chapter of her life, and her thirties are going to be spectacular.

With that internal pep talk over and done with, I square my shoulders and strut back to my party.

The party's wound down, and most of the guests have left. I have no idea where my girls are, they have either hooked up or crashed in one of the bedrooms. I've had one too many cocktails, and the sugar has me wide awake and jittery.

Grabbing a pint of cookie dough ice cream from my fridge, I head out to the back garden. Plopping into one of the outdoor chairs, I take a deep breath and listen to the melody of horns and sirens that is New York.

This wasn't at all how I thought I would be ending my birthday—drunk, in my pajamas, eating a pint of ice cream. It screams *Bridget Jones,* not Chloe Jones.

I envisioned hot, dirty sexy to start the decade of my dirty thirties. The only thing dirty is the ice cream stain on my t-shirt.

What happened to viva le birthday, carpe diem, and all that jazz? You decided to play it safe. That little voice can be an annoying cow sometimes.

I'm not playing it safe at all, I simply didn't get any chances or offers.

What about that kiss? Yes, brain, I haven't forgotten about the kiss. *But what am I supposed to do about it?*

My eyes land on Noah's townhouse. A faint glow emanates from his bedroom window. Yes, I know it's creepy that I know which window is his bedroom. That's beside the point. He's awake. I'm awake.

Maybe we should finish what we started earlier? But he's your boss. Rolling my eyes at that stupid voice again. *But it's my birthday, and he started it by kissing me.*

I mentally stick my tongue out at myself. Glad to see not all of me has grown up.

This is why my friends shouldn't leave me alone while drunk because crazy ideas pop into my head, and there's no one around to tell me it's a stupid idea.

It is a stupid idea. You don't count, tiny voice.

Jumping up from my chair, I rush back into the kitchen, throwing the ice cream into the freezer because I'm not wasting that. With quick steps, I rush to my bedroom and grab the sluttiest dress I own.

But while I stand here staring at my wardrobe, I realize I'm not as slutty as I think I am because I'm pulling out handfuls of clothes which are all way too conservative. There has to be something in here. Anything.

What about lingerie?

Pulling out the drawers, underwear flies around everywhere, but nothing sexy is in there either. No wonder I haven't been laid in months, I've been dressing like a nun.

Then I remember Emma had a second dress option for me to wear tonight—it's behind the door. Yanking it nearly off its hinges, the gorgeously slutty red dress appears. I swiftly get changed, throw my nest of a hair up into a high ponytail, double-check my makeup, spritz myself, and grab a pair of the highest heels I own then cautiously make my way through the house hoping to not get busted by any leftover guests.

I make my way to the front door without getting caught and close it softly behind me. Then reality hits me as I look out on the street, which is doused in late-night darkness. The stench of garbage floats around, the shuffle of a homeless person passing by, the singing voices of a group of very happy people leaving a bar.

A taxi's horn pulls me from my thoughts—his place is only twenty steps.

Turning my head, looking at my destination, I think, *You can do this, Chloe. Remember viva le birthday.*

With that sentiment, I quickly yet cautiously rush down my front stairs. I don't want to trip down them and land in goodness knows what's on the sidewalk.

Anxiously, I look around trying to be inconspicuous yet totally standing out like a freak. Slowly, I walk up his front stairs and notice his brass doorbell is right there glistening under the street lights.

Do it, Chloe.

Press the bell.

Before I wimp out, I press the bell. The sound echoes through the townhouse, and I want to bolt. Let Noah think it's a couple of kids pranking him.

This is so freaking stupid. *What the hell am I thinking?*

Stupid cocktail.

Stupid viva le birthday.

This is the stupidest thing you've ever done, Chloe.

Like are you just going to proposition him on his doorstep?

What happens if he's not alone?

Oh shit! I didn't think of that.

I didn't think the reason he left my party was because he had a date with someone else planned. Fucking hell, that makes sense.

Abort, Chloe.

Abort.

Turning on my heels, I decide to head back home.

"Chloe?" His voice rumbles through me.

Dammit. Cursing fate, I blink a few times and turn back around. I'm stunned by what's standing in front of me. Looking like a delectable messy feast with his light brown hair perfectly disheveled. My eyes move further south over his muscular body. The well-defined stomach, the deep-set 'V' of his hips. Shit, he must be with someone because why would he be answering the door in his boxer briefs and have messy hair if he hasn't spent the night in bed with someone.

Damn! I'm an idiot.

"What are you doing here?" His tone is curt and cold.

Think, Chloe, think. "I don't actually know. I must be sleepwalking. Carry on." My heart's thundering in my chest, my cheeks are on fire. I need to get out of here before I die of embarrassment. Turning on my heels, I hastily make my retreat. Of course, Fate decides to pay attention and my stupid heel gets caught in a hole on the last step making my body become one with the sidewalk.

Fuck. My body jars from the effect of flesh hitting cement.

"Shit, Chloe." Noah rushes down after me. "Are you okay?"

My dignity has scurried off into the gutter beside me. I try and pull myself together, but I stumble from the pain. Fuck me dead!

"You're hurt." Noah wraps his arm around my body, helping me get up off the sidewalk. I hate to think how many germs I've contracted from that little incident.

"I'm fine. Really." Trying to push him away from me, I add, "I shouldn't have bothered you. Go back to your guest, Noah."

"What are you talking about?" He's giving me a strange look, but I take no notice because the pain is what I am dealing with right now.

Fuck. My knees hurt like a bitch.

"This..." waving my hand in front of me, "... you're in your underwear."

Like hello.

"I was in bed."

"I know, Noah. You don't have to point it out."

The fucking dick.

"Alone. Chloe," he tells me

"Oh...." Feeling less embarrassed and more like mortified, I continue, "Well, I guess I should be going. I've made enough of a fool out of myself to last me a lifetime... maybe ten lifetimes actually."

"You're hurt. Look."

Checking where he's pointing at my knees, which are black and red from my fall, I notice a trickle of blood is sliding down my knee. I'm thankful for those extra cocktails I had at the end of the night, which have helped numb the pain a little.

"So, I am. Okay. Well, see ya," I state as I start to hobble away, trying to save what little respect I have left.

"Wait." Noah jumps in front of me. "Do you have a first-aid kit?"

I don't actually know. *Do I?* I'll probably just pour some tequila or vodka on the wound.

"I have one. Let me fix you up, then walk you home."

Maybe ten minutes ago that idea would have sounded like heaven, but now after all this humiliation, I'm pretty sure I want to go back to my bedroom, jump into my pajamas, climb in my soft bed and continue eating that pint of cookie dough ice cream until there's nothing left. I might even lick the container clean.

"I don't want to be a bother," I tell him while waving him away as I try to walk around him. *Does he realize he's standing on the sidewalk in his underwear?*

Off Limits   151

"Chloe, please." He lightly grabs my arm, halting me. Concern and sincerity are written all over his face.

"Fine."

"Good. Now come here."

Huh? What the heck! Noah whisks me into his arms.

"Noah, what the—"

"Shh… just go with it," he tells me as I cling onto him.

"I'm too heavy, put me down." All these curves come with consequences like broken backs.

"Stop it. You're fine." He carries me effortlessly up his front stairs and over the threshold where I'm expecting him to release me, but he still has hold of me tightly. He kicks the front door shut with his heel then proceeds to carry me down his hallway and into his kitchen where he places me on his kitchen counter.

He starts pulling out drawers and looking in cupboards.

I watch as he disappears from the room and comes back again moments later with his first-aid kit.

23

NOAH

What the hell is Chloe doing on my doorstep looking like some kind of sinful devil? I may have fantasized about her dropping in on me like this. Usually, she'd ask for a cup of brown sugar or something even weirder, and we would end up fucking on my kitchen counter. Fuck!

As I search for the first-aid kit in the bathroom, I realize where she's sitting. Hold it together, Stone. Walking back out into the kitchen, her knees look like they have taken a beating. I notice how flushed her cheeks are, and realize she's probably embarrassed about the fall. I place the first-aid kit beside her and grab her a glass of water.

"Here," I state while handing her the glass.

"Thanks."

Our fingers touch for a millisecond, but I can feel the spark shoot right through me.

"Your knees are a mess." Pulling up a stool and sitting between her legs, I'm trying desperately not to look up her skirt.

"Seriously, Noah, you don't have to fix me up."

"I know." Pulling her heel off and moving her foot in between my legs, I rest it on the stool. A slight hitch escapes Chloe's mouth when I realize where I have placed her foot.

"Maybe you should put some pants on." She bites her bottom lip, but her eyes are definitely on my package. Letting her foot drop, I head to the laundry and grab some gray track pants then resume my position. I begin to squeeze the antiseptic cream onto the cotton ball. "Better?"

"Much."

"Don't trust yourself." I'm teasing her as I start to clean away the dirt and grit from her knees. She hisses at the contact just about every time I touch her.

"Pretty much." Her comment stops me, so I look up at her. "Don't look at me like that." Chloe grins. "There's a reason I headed over here at this time of the night."

"What was that?" Desperately trying not to get my hopes up, I distract myself with cleaning her knees to which she hisses again.

"I thought maybe we could continue where we left off after our kiss."

Looking up at her, I can see the vulnerability in her eyes. "Did you?"

She nods. "But I could be wrong." Her confidence is waning as she continues speaking.

"I wouldn't mind finishing that kiss, too." I give her a wink, and a comfortable silence falls between us as I continue with her knees. "Did you really think I would have someone here with me after kissing you at your party?"

Chloe shrugs her shoulders.

"Seriously?"

Chloe nods, and I feel hurt by her answer.

"I'd never do that to you."

Chloe doesn't say anything, so I work in silence for a while until she's cleaned up, and I apply a few Band-Aids for good measure.

"People are going to think you had a great birthday when you go into work on Monday." Trying to lighten the mood, I point at her knees.

"Guess I'll be wearing pants then." She gives me a crooked smile.

"Your ass looks good in pants. Actually, your ass looks good in anything." The words are out before I can stop them. She stills as I stand and move the first-aid items to the side. I'm stuck between her legs.

"As does yours." She raises her brow at me.

Duly noted.

We both stare at each other, the sexual tension swirls around us. I let my hand ever so lightly run up her exposed thigh, and she shivers as my fingers move higher.

Are we really doing this?

"Chloe…" Her name falls from my lips, achingly.

Her hand reaches out and pulls my hips closer, sandwiching me right between her thighs. "I want you, Noah."

Those blue eyes are swirling with desire as she stares at me, begging me to take her on the kitchen counter. And I want to, I want to so much. This is going to change things, though. Once we step over this ledge, then there's no going back.

"You sure?" I want her to have a moment so she can stop this at any time.

"Are you sure?" she questions me.

I've never been surer about anyone like I am about her in my life.

I lean in. "I've wanted you from the moment I laid eyes on you, Chloe." Her breath hitches. "But once we cross over this line…" my nose nuzzles her neck, "… we can't go back to the way we were because I will know exactly how perfect your pussy tastes."

"Fuck, Noah," Chloe curses breathlessly as her legs wrap around my hips, pulling me to her.

My teeth sink into her neck while I listen to a strangled moan fall from her lips. My mouth moves down further along her collarbone, nibbling her delicate skin. The sounds coming from her mouth have me instantly hard—I can't wait to pull more from her.

Chloe's hand finds the waistband of my track pants and slips inside, her fingers wrapping around my underwear-clad dick. Fuck! Now it's my turn to let out a groan.

"God, Noah," she pants, her hand gripping tighter around me as I close my eyes, absorbing all of her attention. If she continues the way she's going, I'm going to come in her hand.

Distract yourself, Noah.

Peeling back the material of her dress, I expose her breasts to me. Her perfect, beautiful, bouncing breasts that I've fantasized about all day are right before me.

Leaning forward, I take a nipple into my mouth. Chloe's grip intensifies around my cock, a delicious moan falls from her lips as I ever so gently bite and suck on them.

"Hmmm… Noah." Her head falls back as she enjoys my lips, her hand falls from my dick as she tries to hold herself together. I move to her other breast giving it equal attention until she's squirming underneath me. Her breath is labored, her moans growing louder with each nip.

Mental note—*Chloe loves her breasts being sucked.*

"Noah, please," she begs. Reluctantly I pull myself away from her gorgeous tits.

"Baby, not yet." Looking down at a flushed Chloe, I think there's nothing more beautiful in this world.

"Noah. It's been six months of fucking foreplay. Enough is enough," she growls. "You can either fuck me on this bench or take me somewhere else. I don't care."

Who knew Chloe could be bossy in the bedroom? I kind of like it.

"Fine." Giving in, because let's be honest, she's right, it has been six months of foreplay. "On one condition."

"Anything," she tells me while I raise a brow at her.

"Anything? That's a dangerous word to a man like me." Chloe has the balls to roll her eyes at me. "Did you just roll your eyes?" She gives me a '*fuck yes, I did, and what are you going to do about it*' smile. "You have no idea who I am in the bedroom, Chloe," I warn her.

"All I'm hearing is talk of a big game, Noah. I want to see more action." With watchful eyes, she begins to shimmy out of her dress, then kicking it off behind me, and my eyes widen at her splayed out naked in front of me.

Shakily, I pull in a breath as I take her in, every dip and curve of her magnificent body, all the way down to the 'V' between her legs which are open for me, exposing her pretty pink pussy.

My thumbs hook into the waistband of my pants, and I pull both sides down exposing myself to her. Chloe licks her lips as she eyes my dick.

"Lay back," I command. She does as I say, pressing her back against the cool marble. I watch as her chest moves up and down with each breath. Taking her knees, I open them wide as I step closer between her legs.

Her hand quickly comes out and hides her pussy. *What the?*

"You don't have to do that," she says nervously. "I know men don't like it."

Is she fucking serious right now?

"Chloe…"

She sits up on her elbows looking at me, a slight pink spreads across her cheeks.

"Real men love it. Now, let me demonstrate how much." Bending down between her legs, my fingers push apart her pink lips, and I lick her. A moan falls from her lips on contact. "Eyes on me," I demand while Chloe's eyes fall back to me as I show her that real men love eating pussy as I devour her.

"Oh my God, Noah," Chloe screams as I pull an orgasm from her with my tongue. "No more. I can't…" she trails off as she thrashes around on the counter. *She's perfect.* Wiping my lips on her thigh as I move over her, I know most women don't always like the taste of themselves. Her eyes are closed, but she has smile on her face. "You were…" Her eyes meet mine.

"Spectacular, magnificent?"

"All of them. I had no idea it could feel so…" She closes her eyes again, trailing off with a dreamy expression on her face. Then she giggles. Which isn't exactly the response I'm looking for.

She opens her eyes again and sits, meeting me in the middle. "I thought I was broken."

What is she talking about?

She giggles again. "I'm not."

I'm not really following.

She wraps her arms around me, pulling me toward her, her lips are on mine as she kisses me with abandonment, and I just go with it. Her legs wrap around my hips, pulling me closer to her sweet spot.

Reluctantly, I pull myself from her lips. "I need a condom," I tell her.

She blinks a couple of times before registering what I'm saying, then she looks between us and sees how close I am to being inside of her. "Yes. You do."

"Wrap yourself around me, I'll take you somewhere more comfortable." She does as she's told, and I rush quickly through my townhouse, up two flights of stairs with this gorgeous sexy koala wrapped around me. We make it to my bedroom where we fall onto my bed. Pulling open the bedside table, I grab a handful of wrappers and put them on top.

"Wow!" She's laying there looking around my room. "This is nice."

What's nice is if we get back to what we were doing downstairs.

"Manly." Her eyes roam around the room. "I've always wondered what your bedroom would look like," she muses, which makes me pause.

"Really?"

Chloe realizes how that sounded and starts to back-peddle but then stops. She looks up at me and smiles. "Yeah, I always hoped to be in this position here, too."

Well, that's brutally honest.

"I did, too." Lying beside her, linking our hands together, I stare up at my ceiling.

"I can see your bedroom from my hot tub," Chloe quickly confesses. Turning my head, I can see she looks mortified she's just told me. Reaching out and bringing her lips to mine, I kiss her slowly.

"I can see your hot tub from my bedroom," I whisper in her ear.

She stills. "I touched myself as you enjoyed your wine oblivious to my torment."

Chloe moves on top of me, her lips are nipping my jaw and neck as I confess my dirtiest secret to her. "What did you think about?" she asks, her lips capturing my nipple in her mouth, which almost launches me off of the bed.

I reach over and grab a condom subconsciously and place it beside us. "I thought about you touching yourself thinking about me."

Her lips move over my body. "I did," she whispers in my ear.

"Fuck, Chloe," I groan.

The sound of the foil wrapper interrupts the silence, her hands move over my dick slowly, achingly, as she rolls the condom onto me. She moves back over me while I'm looking up at her, her blonde mass of curls falling around her face.

"We wasted so much time," I tell her.

"I know," she says as she slowly sinks down on me. "What else?" she pushes for more words.

"I would fantasize about you in those pencil skirts, bent over my desk, your beautiful ass exposed. Me fucking you from behind. My fingers sinking into your skin as yours gripped the desk, my tie in your mouth, so no one could hear us."

"I like the sound of that." Chloe smiles as she rides me, my fingers digging into her ass just like I had imagined.

She winces, and I remember her banged-up knees so quickly, I turn us.

Chloe squeals, but I hardly break our rhythm. Looking down at her beneath me just like I have fantasized about, I continue, "Another time you would be on your knees under my desk, your lips wrapped around my dick as I worked. Helping me relax like a good little girl." She raises a brow at me as I push harder, her mountainous breasts bouncing with each deep thrust I make inside of her.

"I imagined something similar," she confesses. "But it was you on your knees, under my desk, with that…" she gasps as I hit the right spot inside of her, "… with that magical tongue." She groans loudly. "Fuck, Noah."

As I pump into her harder, her fingers are gripping my shoulders while she holds on tightly with each one of my thrusts.

"I wanted to fuck you on the beach under the stars when we first met." Her eyes open as she looks at me. "But I couldn't because I fell for you instead." Her eyes widen. "I wanted you more than anyone I've ever wanted in my life at that moment, but not just for sex."

"Noah…"

Damn! I've said too much.

I've pushed too hard.

So, I concentrate on fucking her instead. Keeping my stupid feelings in check. Now is not the time.

"Shit! Yes. Yes," she screams while I continue giving all of me to her. "Yes," she shouts as we both come together.

I collapse on top of her, and she nuzzles my neck with her face.

Once we catch our breath, Chloe looks up at me. "Can I have more, please?" My eyes widen in surprise. "I mean not like right now, but… um…"

Reaching out, I pull her to me so I can kiss her. "I want more, too." She lets out a little yawn and blinks a few times. "Maybe we should rest for a little bit."

She nods in agreement. I slowly pull myself from her and rush to my ensuite. By the time I come back, she's passed out. Her blonde hair is fanned out around her, the tiniest of snores are falling from her lips.

She's fucking perfect.

This is what I want. Her in my bed. Every single day.

But tomorrow will bring the reality of what we've done, and I have a feeling Chloe isn't going to feel the same way as I do.

Getting into bed, I wrap myself around her because I'll take what I can get in this moment.

24

CHLOE

Wincing, I open my eyes to the blinding light coming through the windows. My head hurts. My knees hurt. My vagina hurts.

Well, shit.

Sitting up in bed quickly and turning, I notice a very naked Noah snoring away beside me.

Last night wasn't a dream—we really did sleep together.

I look around the room for my clothes, but they're not here. *Oh, that's right, you hussy, you kicked them off downstairs.* Good one. Frantically, I look around the floor for something to put on to do my walk of shame, but Noah's a neat freak, and nothing is on the floor.

Quietly, I get out of the bed, hoping not to disturb him, and make my way over to his walk-in closet. I search through his suits to find something. I don't want to take one of his shirts, they're expensive, so I pull out one of the drawers which is full of his underwear. Maybe I can steal some boxer shorts. Finding a black cotton pair, I put them on, and then pull open another drawer and find some t-shirts, which I grab one and quietly head back out.

"Fuck!" I scream.

Noah's standing right in front of me—he doesn't look happy.

I'm not happy because he has pants on. I was hoping for one more glimpse of his mighty peen before I left, you know, for my memory's sake.

"Where the hell are you sneaking off to?"

"Um... I ... I..." He crosses his arms and taps his foot, waiting to hear my excuse.

"If you want to go... then go, Chloe." He looks really hurt as he moves past me, grabbing a t-shirt from one of his drawers.

"Noah..." I grab his arm. "Did I do something wrong?"

"No," he states, but his tone says otherwise. He rakes his hand through his hair. "I... I just thought..." He shakes his head.

"You thought what?"

"That you would want to hang out with me." The vulnerability on his face breaks me in two.

"You want to hang out with me?" With my eyebrows squeezed together, I point to myself.

"Of course."

"Oh..."

"I was hoping to take you out."

My eyes widen. "Like a date?"

"Yeah. Like on a date," he tells me.

I'm slightly confused. "Um. Sure. Okay. I got to go." Panic laces my body as I high tail it out of his bedroom.

"Chloe," Noah calls after me, but I race down the stairs and right out his front door. Noah's on my heels, though. "Chloe," he calls from his front stoop, but I ignore him running the twenty steps to my home.

I turn the doorknob and it's locked. Oh, for fuck's sake, I've left my bag at Noah's. Tears begin to fall down my cheeks. *Why am I crying?* Maybe someone will find me and let me in as I collapse beside my front door.

A little while later, Noah walks over with my dress and bag in his hands. He walks up a couple of stairs and stops when he sees me curled up against the door. I look up at the sound of his footsteps.

"Hey." My eyes are puffy from all the crying.

"You forgot these." He hands over my things.

"Thanks." I take them feeling like an utter fool. "Noah... I'm..."

He shakes his head. "You don't have to say a thing, Chlo. Hope you had a good birthday." And with that, he turns and heads back home. I'm such a bitch.

Stepping back into my home, I blink a couple of times unsure if I'm in the right place, it's so clean.

"Hello," I call out to the empty house.

"There you are." Ariana pops her head out from the kitchen, and then she gives me a hug. "Just getting in?"

"I was at Noah's."

"I know. He texted us from your phone."

"He what?"

"I was worried when I got home, and you weren't here. I had no idea where you were. There was no note."

"What did he say?"

"That you had passed out at his place. That's all. But I'm pretty sure I can read between the lines. You slept with him, right?"

Walking over to the fridge, I grab myself a bottle of water and throw it back. "Yes. Guess I can't deny it."

"Hey, what's up?" Ariana asks.

"I don't know. I'm freaking out."

"Was it not good?"

"No. It was fucking spectacular. I had so many orgasms." Ariana chuckles.

"Then what's the problem."

"He wanted to 'hang out,'" I say doing air quotes with my fingers.

"What's wrong with that?"

My eyes bug out at her statement.

What does she mean, what's wrong with that?

"Everything."

Ariana looks at me strangely. "I don't think I'm following, Chlo. You like him, don't you?" I nod my head. "Well, that's a good start.

Most men aren't asking to 'hang out' after a night together. So he must like you."

"I think he wants more."

Why is my body on fire? My skin feels like I want to crawl out of it.

"More?"

"Yes, more." For a smart woman, she really isn't getting it.

"And you don't want more?" she asks tentatively.

I pause for a moment thinking over what I want. "I don't know." Ariana nods. "Tracey and Walker got engaged last night."

"What the…" I nod in agreement. "On your birthday?"

"Yep."

"They just keep getting lower, don't they?" I slump on the sofa, and tears begin to fall. "Hey, what's going on?" Ariana sits beside me.

"What happens if I'm damaged? That Walker and Tracey have messed me up so much that I can't ever be in a healthy relationship."

"Oh, Chlo…" Ariana pulls me into her arms, trying to soothe my worries. "Is that why you're freaked out over Noah?" I nod my head. "You think he's someone special?"

I sniffle out a "Yes."

"And you think you're going to mess it up?"

"He's my boss, my landlord, and a good friend. I love my job. I love this house. I love him…" *Oh shit!* My hand flies across my mouth in realization as the words come out.

"You love him?" Ariana questions me.

Furiously I shake my head. "I didn't mean to say that. I…" Ariana doesn't seem to be convinced by my denial.

Do I love Noah Stone? No. No way in the world.

It was simply a night of good D. I'm exhausted, and I'm talking gibberish.

"You have strong feelings for him, though?" Ariana adds.

"Our lives are entwined so much."

"That's not what I asked." She pushes harder.

"He's New York's biggest playboy. He dates supermodels. I can't compete with that."

Ariana rolls her eyes. "You don't have to compete. There's no competition, you're gorgeous. You're intelligent. You are so much better than any of those women who hang off his arm."

She has to say that because she's my bestie.

"I hate that Walker's destroyed your worth. You have no idea the way Noah looks at you. Even that first time meeting him on our holiday, he looked at you like he had found a precious diamond, and he couldn't quite believe that you were interested in him. He's always been there for you, Chlo, in the background, ready for when you realize that you too had found a precious diamond of your own."

My hearts thunders in my chest at Ariana's words.

"You were never like this with Walker. Each time I saw you, bit by bit you were turning into a wannabe Stepford wife." *Really?* "Walker was changing you, molding you into what he wanted, not what was best for you."

Was he? I didn't think I'd changed that much. I thought I was just growing up.

"It was gradual. Bit by bit each time we saw you, your clothes had changed, or the way you styled your hair."

"I had no idea."

Ariana holds my hand in hers. "We never wanted to say anything because you seemed happy."

"I thought I was. Looking back, I realize I wasn't."

"Noah doesn't want to change you. He likes you for you."

Maybe she's right. "I'm a mess. This getting old shit is giving me a headache." Ariana smiles. "Hang on… did you not stay here last night?"

Slowly processing my morning, Ariana's cheeks turn bright red.

"Um… yeah. Ewan and I might have, um… got a hotel room."

I squeal and bounce up and down on the sofa, wrapping my arms around her. "I knew it. I knew it."

She rolls her eyes at me. "He's nice."

"Nice? Please tell me that man is more than nice."

"Okay, he's kind of amazing. But he lives upstate, and I'm in the city."

"Um... hello. It's like an hour away. You can rent a car. Uber it. Train it. There are ways to hang out."

"We're both so busy. When he's on a building site, he works seven days a week." I frown at my friend. "It's just not going to work, other than friends."

"What? No!" Slumping back into my chair, I was counting on them moving to the country, having little lumberjack babies and building stuff.

"It's just not the right time." She looks at me sadly.

"Well, I still have hope for you two."

"As do I for Noah and you." She's smiling at me.

Fine. I get what she's saying.

"What's going on with Emma and Anderson?" I ask changing the subject.

"I have no idea. But I didn't see them all night, and she hasn't come home. Neither has Stella or Lenna."

"Really? Everyone got lucky?"

"Looks like it." We both burst out laughing. I guess everyone had a great night after all.

"I need a shower and some fresh clothes."

"Yeah, you do," Ariana teases. "I better get going, I have a ton of work to get through."

We hug and say our goodbyes.

I think I might pour myself a nice bubble bath and relax before I pop over and apologize to Noah for freaking out on him like I did.

25

NOAH

I've fucked up with Chloe. Cursing, I pace around my townhouse. She couldn't get away from me quick enough. Seeing her devastated sitting on the ground with tears streaming down her face, it broke me.

She regrets sleeping with me. That much I can tell, but I don't want to lose her. Maybe the happily ever after I thought we might get isn't in the cards. If we can't be anything more, then I don't want to lose her friendship.

My doorbell rings. Hope bubbles to the surface, maybe just maybe, she's changed her mind, and I'm freaking out for no reason. Opening the door, I'm surprised to see Ariana on my doorstep. *But where's Chloe? Is she okay? Has something happened?* Panic laces my entire being.

"Hi, sorry to pop over on you like this. Do you have a moment?" I usher her into my home, She walks into the kitchen and awkwardly stands.

"Can I get you a drink or something?"

"No, thank you. I just wanted to talk to you about Chloe."

Oh, is this the leave my friend alone talk?

I grab myself a bottle of water and lean against the island bench waiting for it.

"Chloe has no idea I'm here," Ariana confesses. "She'd kill me if she knew, but I need to say something." Be polite, she's just protecting her friend. "Don't give up on her."

That's not at all what I was thinking she was going to say.

"Not sure if she told you, but last night, Tracey and Walker got engaged."

Say what!

"Yeah… on her birthday. They will do anything to hurt her. And as much as she's trying not to let it bother her, I think it has."

"I don't get why they won't leave her alone."

Ariana nods in agreement. "Walker likes to win. He's also a control freak. Chloe leaving him and embarrassing him so publicly kills him. He doesn't care about Tracey. She's just a pawn in some messed-up game he's playing with Chloe."

The hairs on the back of my neck stand to attention. "Do you think he's dangerous?"

Shaking her head. "I don't think so. But then again, I didn't think he would put his hands on her like he did in Vegas."

Flashes of that night hit me, my fingers crunch around the water bottle, and it makes a cracking noise as I squash it.

"You know I would do anything to keep her safe."

"I know you would." Ariana smiles. "Chloe's all a muddle this morning because she's worried that Walker's messed her up. That she won't ever be good enough for anyone."

"Fuck, I hate that man."

"Me, too," Ariana agrees. "She's scared of her feelings for you."

"Feelings?"

"Maybe I've overstepped, but I kind of assumed you have feelings for her, too."

Silence falls between us for a couple of beats.

"Of course, I have feelings for her. I'd be an idiot not to."

Ariana smiles. "She mentioned she thinks you want more, and that's why she ran this morning. Not because she doesn't feel the same way. Actually, it's just the opposite, because she does. I'm totally breaking girl code right now," Ariana warns me.

"But why for me?"

"I see the way you look at her. Like you're the luckiest man in the world to have her in your life."

Like an arrow to my heart, her words hit me at full strength because she's so right. "I am. My life's better with her in it," I confess.

Ariana's face softens. "That's what I thought. I just wanted to say… don't give up on her. She's a little confused at the moment. Give her time, it's all she needs."

"Thanks." Her words relieve me of the torment I've been suffering through this morning. "I'll wait. She's more than worth it."

"Good. Now, I better go before she notices where I am and then kills me." I walk Ariana to the door. "One more thing…" she turns around glaring at me, "… stop it with the bimbos and the phone sex in your office." How the hell does she know, but then she continues with, "Girls talk."

"I'm done with that life."

"So, the 'playboy twin of New York' has fallen?"

"I hate that nickname." I groan at her words. "I'm hers."

Ariana smiles and pats me on the arm. "Good to hear."

And with that, Ariana leaves me with my thoughts.

⁂

Flicking through the channels, my doorbell rings again. I guess that must be my late lunch. Jumping up off my couch, I grab my wallet and head to the door. Opening it, I wasn't expecting to see my delivery guy and Chloe on my doorstep.

"He wouldn't let me give it to you. He basically said he didn't believe I knew you." I open my wallet and shove bills into his hand. He mumbles some form of thanks, hands the bags to Chloe as he runs back down the stairs to his car.

"Can I come in?" she asks tentatively. I usher her into my home.

"This smells amazing," she says while she places the bags onto the kitchen counter.

"I've got plenty if you want some." Grabbing two bowls from the cupboard, I set them on the counter.

"Sure." We stand in silence as I divide up the Mongolian beef and sweet and sour pork, then the fried rice. "Were you expecting company? There's a lot of food." She nervously bites her lip. *Does she seriously think I would have another woman over after what happened between us last night?*

"I was going to drown my sorrows in Chinese."

Her eyes widen at my comment. "I'm sorry, Noah." She plays with the chopsticks nervously as she apologizes. "I just—"

"I saw Walker's Instagram." I did actually check it when Ariana left, the comments are disgusting.

"Oh…" She sounds quite surprised by my admission.

"I wish I had punched him harder in Vegas." The smile that crosses her face is contagious. "Come, sit, let's eat."

She nods and follows me into my living room. I sit on my sofa, but she hesitates for a moment wondering if she should sit beside me. I tap my palm against the soft fabric to indicate she should sit beside me. She does, and we eat in comfortable silence while watching Netflix. It's nice having her here in my home, doing nothing but relaxing.

I'm so gone for her.

"That's good Chinese." Chloe begins to clean up, but I halt her.

"Leave it." Placing her plate on the coffee table before us, she sits down again, curling her legs underneath her, keeping her eyes firmly on the television. "Chlo…" Grabbing her attention, she sucks in a deep breath before turning to me. "We need to talk."

Chloe gives me a weak smile. "I know." Nervously she wrings her hands in her lap. "About this morning… I shouldn't have run."

"You have nothing to apologize for," I state trying to reassure her.

"I panicked."

"I know."

"What happened between us…" Chloe turns away from me

thinking over her words. She's going to tell me we can't do it again, that we should just be friends, colleagues, anything but what we should be.

I'll wait, Chloe Jones. I'll wait until you're ready for us.

"Last night…" she bites her lip, "… I want more." Turning to me, she surprises the hell out of me, and I'm stunned momentarily.

"More?" Slowly processing what Chloe's saying, she nods her head.

"Is that offer of a date still on the table? Because, um… I wouldn't mind it." I can't believe the words that are coming from her lips.

"Of course, it is." My stomach somersaults as I shuffle nervously in my seat. "So, you and me?"

She nods, and a faint blush fall across her cheeks. "On one condition…" She holds up her finger at me.

Anything. I'll do anything.

"Actually, two conditions." I nod. "One, we're monogamous." *Easy. It's always been her.* "Two, we don't tell anyone at work."

My eyes widen. "What do you mean?"

"We can tell Lenna and Logan, but that's it. The young girls in the office already hate me because of you. If they know we're dating, I think they might poison my coffee."

This makes me laugh as I reach out and pull her to me. She comes willingly, straddling my lap. Pulling her lips to mine, I give her a slow and sensual kiss, letting her know exactly how much I want her.

"Fine. Strictly professional at the office. But I have a condition of my own." She raises a brow at me. "When we are out of the office, it's fair game." She grins but agrees. Good. "Oh, and another condition…. I want you in my bed every night."

"Noah…"

I shake my head. "Non-negotiable, sweetheart." Leaning forward, I capture her lips again, showing her exactly how much I will be worshipping her in my bed every single night.

"You're not playing fair," she groans, pulling away.

"I mean it, Chloe. You can go back in the morning, do what you have to do. You can have your alone time whenever you need it, but I want you with me, in my bed, at night."

Chloe sighs. "Damn you and your words, Noah. How can I say no to that?"

"You can't." I grin.

She rolls her eyes. "Fine, I'll spend my nights with you."

Now that's settled, I think we need to seal the deal on this contract.

Picking her up off the couch, she lets out a squeal as I walk her through my home and up to my bed.

26

NOAH

"There's nothing to be nervous about," I try and reassure Chloe as we walk toward Logan's office.

"What happens if he fires me?" I give her my *'over my dead body'* look. I let my hand brush hers as we walk along the corridors. She gives me a little frown—I know one of the rules is not to let people at work know about us, but I'm discreet.

"This is just a formality," I reassure her.

We reach Logan's office, and I open the door for her. Lenna's already sitting waiting for us with paperwork spread out across Logan's desk.

"Please take a seat." Logan's tone is curt. *What the fuck?* "I'm assuming you've called us here today to inform us that you're dating?" Logan starts.

"Y-Yes…" Chloe stutters.

"What the hell is your problem?" I cut all civility from this meeting with my words.

"Nothing. It's protocol. If this…" my brother waves his hand in the air between us, "… goes foul, then I need to cover your ass."

Looking over at Chloe, whose shoulders have sunk from Logan's words, I'm starting to become angry. No. He's not going to destroy what Chloe and I have because of our past. *Fuck him.*

"Maybe I should be asking you the same thing, brother." My tone is sharp and to the point. Lenna tenses beside me. Logan's eyes narrow and flare with anger at me questioning him. Lenna clears her throat and sits up straighter.

"I'm happy you two are together..." she looks between us, "... but Chlo, I need you to fill out this paperwork because of it."

Chloe nods her head and takes the paperwork and reads through it. She signs on the dotted line and gives it back to Lenna.

"Happy?" I ask my brother.

"Yes. Very."

"I'm assuming Lenna you've signed the same paperwork?"

Lenna's eyes widen, and I can see the panic written across her face over my question.

"It's not necessary, nothing is going on nor will ever go on," my brother adds.

Lenna's face cracks ever so slightly at his words. *Fuck, my brother's a dick.*

"I better go file this paperwork." Lenna stands abruptly.

"Yeah, I better get back to work, too," Chloe adds.

We watch in silence as they both leave Logan's office.

"What the fuck is the matter with you?" I glare at my brother.

"What? I'm just protecting what we've worked so hard for all our lives. I'm not going to let some woman ruin it."

"Some woman?" Standing quickly, my chair scrapes along the floor. My palms come down hard against his desk, the sound echoes through the room. "You know Chloe isn't *some woman* to me." Logan crosses his arms against his chest and leans back in his chair. *The damn cocky son of a bitch.*

"We all know you don't have a very long attention span when it comes to dating."

I'm seconds away from punching him out. My fingers are itching to form a fist and send a strike his way. "What's wrong with you?"

"I'm being the sane one here. You can't see the forest for the fucking pussy."

That's it! I launch myself at my brother and grab him by his business shirt. "Fuck you! Fuck you!" Choking him with my hands, I hear the office door swing open then slam.

"What the fuck is going on here?" Anderson pulls us apart. "You do realize you're at fucking work? Act fucking professional. Will ya!" he scolds us.

We let go of each other and straighten our suits and ties.

"Now what the hell are you two ladies fighting about? Did Logan piss in your Wheaties?" We both glare at him but stay silent. "I can sit here all day, ladies. I have nowhere I need to be." He crosses his arms as he takes a seat opposite us.

"Chloe and I are together," I tell him.

"Well, no shock there. Why are you so angry?" Pointing his question directly at Logan.

"Because he isn't seeing clearly. I'm trying to protect our business," Logan tries to defend himself.

"You think Chloe's after the business?"

"No," Logan answers. "But—"

Anderson stops him there, by holding his finger up. "There's no but. You've been on the whole Noah and Chloe ride all year. She's a brilliant employee. She's kept her distance from Noah for the sake of the business."

"How do you know all this?" I question my friend.

"Spousal privilege."

Logan and I look at each other—has Anderson lost his damn mind.

"Spousal as in married?" Logan asks the burning question.

"Yeah. Exactly that."

"Are you high?" Because it seems like he's high on something, just not sure what exactly.

"I'm a professional, unlike you two. I don't bring that shit to work."

"Who are you married to?" Logan presses.

Anderson rolls his eyes. "You're not the only one with women problems. I'm not a pussy like you two. I keep it to myself. I don't need to talk about my feelings with every single person who crosses my damn path."

"Who the fuck did you marry, dickhead?" I'm losing my patience with him.

"Emma, of course," he states as if it's glaringly obvious.

"What the fuck?" Logan and I yell.

"How? When? I didn't even know you two were seeing each other?" A million questions run through my head right at this moment.

"We weren't," he states as if that makes any sense at all.

"But how did you get married?"

"Lots of tequila and Vegas."

"As in months ago… EJ's launch… our Vegas trip?" Logan peppers him with questions.

Anderson rolls his eyes as if it's all stupid questions.

"You've kept it a secret from us?"

"What? You want to come over and braid each other's hair while we gossip about our lives?" he asks defensively.

"You're a dick. Our best mate got married and never told us. We have a right to be pissed off."

Anderson's face softens. "Honestly, I can't believe I am."

"She refusing to let go. Is she after your money?"

Anderson shoots Logan daggers. "Not every woman is a gold digger, fucker." His tone is more than curt. "Emma doesn't want any of my money. She won't take the black credit card I gave her, the new car, the exotic holidays, the diamond… actually, she took nothing."

"Then why are you still married?" I'm slightly confused by all this.

"My fucking sister told my parents."

Oh shit. Elise is the female version of her brother, the stories Anderson used to tell us about the pranks the two of them did to each other are classic. I'm surprised they never ended up in jail or dead. We don't get to see much of her as she lives in Los Angeles. She's an actress, a famous one at that.

"I didn't know she was in Vegas?" Logan questions.

"Yeah, she came late, she had some industry thing." He sighs at how Hollywood his sister is. "It's actually her fault." Of course, it is. "Emma and Elise already knew each other." Now that's a twist I didn't see coming. "Emma had no idea that Elise was my sister because she goes by Mom's maiden name as her actor name." This just gets better the more he speaks. "They, of course, began partying together like old times. A couple of tequilas and Emma and I get flirty."

Anderson shrugs his shoulders. "Anyway, we end up in Elise's penthouse partying with some friends when someone suggests they should get married. In our tequila fog, we all agree because who am I to get in the way of true love." This has Logan and I scoffing, but I also laugh internally. "Anyway, we get the marriage license from someone in the hotel. We watch the ceremony, Elise asks Emma and I to sign the paperwork as witnesses, which we did. Except—"

"No." I'm now following where this story's going.

"Yep. My sister pranked me, and the paperwork was actually for Emma and me."

"That can't be legal?" Logan adds.

"Probably wasn't, but she sent photos of Emma wearing a veil and me in my suit to my parents."

"Honestly?"

"I know. It was a good prank. It's been a while since we did a good one, and this one takes the cake. I want to be mad, but I guess I'm more impressed."

Shaking my head, I'm in shock at my friend's comment.

"What did your parents say?" I ask.

"Well, you see, this is where the prank took a sharp turn to the left." *Oh shit.*

"My mom was so happy that I had actually married someone, and someone who's beautiful, accomplished, and all the things that Emma is, that she doesn't want me to end it."

"They want you to stay married to Emma?"

Anderson nods. "So much so they threatened to disinherit me, and give it all to Elise if I divorce her."

"But you have your own money?" Logan states.

"No shit, Logan. I can read my bank statement. I don't care about their money." *Sarcastic bastard.* "They also said they would give Emma twelve million dollars if she stays married to me for the year. But there has to be no scandals."

"Can't you just give Emma the money? Twelve million is a drop in the ocean for you," Logan states.

Anderson looks over at the two of us and stays silent for a couple of beats.

"You don't want to, right?" A light bulb goes off in my head. "You like being married to Emma."

"Of course, I do. She's hot, intelligent, driven. She likes to have a good time. She's wild in bed like we're talking a freak in the sheets." *Okay, maybe too much information there.* "I can't keep up."

"Never thought I'd see the day you went monogamous." Logan chuckles.

"We're not monogamous," he states shocking us both. "Oh, no. We're allowed to sleep with other people."

"But your parents said no scandal," I add.

"No shit. But there are always loopholes in any contract. My parents stated that we couldn't be seen in public with other people, but they never said anything about in private." Giving us a knowing smile, he continues, "I shouldn't even be telling you two about this as it could get me kicked out for it." I'm all ears now, waiting for the next penny to drop. "I'm a member of an elite sex club."

My brother and I choke on his words.

"'Elite sex club'?" Logan uses air quotes.

"I mean it, guys. What I'm about to tell you can never leave this office." He's definitely serious, I can tell by the look on his face. "Or get back to Emma."

Anderson shoots daggers my way meaning 'no telling Chloe.'

"I'm a member of The Paradise Club. It's for discreet fun. Invite only."

"How did you get in?" I ask, slightly intrigued.

"I know the owner, Nate."

"And you never thought to invite us?" Logan asks.

Anderson shrugs his shoulders.

"But what does this club have to do with you and your loophole." I want to get back to the story.

"The place is secret. Only members know the location of the clubs. No paparazzi. Which means no pictures of me breaking the rules?"

"And Emma is okay with this?" I ask.

"Hell, yeah, she is."

My mind is spinning.

"So, you hook up with other people at this club. Then what? Go home together?"

"Yeah."

"You're living together?" Logan asks.

"Yeah."

"She's packed up her life and moved in with you?"

"Yep."

"Separate beds?" Logan asks.

Anderson shakes his head. "No, we have to make it believable to my parents."

"So, you're sleeping together?"

"Like I said, she's a cool chick. She understands the deal. If either of us has an itch to scratch, then we use each other."

"Unless you're at your secret club," Logan adds.

"Don't use that tone with me," Anderson bites at my brother. "It works for us. I knew you two wouldn't understand. You…" pointing at me, "… you're seconds away from proposing to Chloe." *Like fuck I am.* "And you…" he points at Logan, "… you're fucked in the head when it comes to relationships. You're going to die a lonely old man if you keep going the way you're going."

Wow. That's actually spot on.

"Hey," Logan reacts. "Least I'm not cowering to Mommy and Daddy."

Anderson stands abruptly. He appears way more menacing towering over Logan than I did.

"Emma's the best thing that's happened to me. I will not have you disrespecting her, or our relationship, you hear me?"

Looking at my brother, I notice Logan's glaring back at him.

"Good. Now can we start the fucking meeting we should have had hours ago instead of kumbaya-ing like a pack of little girls."

27

CHLOE

"Are you okay?" I ask Lenna while walking out of Logan's office after that shit show.

"I'm fine," Lenna tries to reassure me.

"Wanna grab a coffee?"

Lenna stills as we arrive at her office, and she sets her paperwork on her desk. I can see by her face as she turns and looks up at me, she's anything but fine. Her eyes glisten with unshed tears as she stoically holds them back.

"It's my turn to pay…" I state, and Lenna nods her head still unable to speak.

We link arms and head out into the sunshine. I bypass our normal coffee shop and head down the street.

"Where are we going?" Lenna asks as I pull her through the crowded Manhattan streets.

"I'm taking you to the park. So we can talk freely without running into anyone from the office."

Lenna doesn't fight me on my logic, and once we reach Central Park, I grab a coffee from one of the cafés and start walking through the treelined pathways. Silence falls between us as we savor our caffeine hit.

"I'm so happy you and Noah finally got together," Lenna starts the conversation.

"It's early days." *Definitely not getting my hopes up.* "Logan doesn't seem so happy about it, though."

"Logan's a complicated guy," Lenna tells me. "He thinks he's protecting his brother."

"Do you think Noah needs protecting from me?" Curious, I need to know what she thinks.

"No. Of course, not. Logan can't let go of what happened with his father."

That would be heartbreaking watching a loved one spiral out of control like that.

"You also can't live with a wall constantly wrapped around you."

"So, how are things between you and Logan?" I ask the burning question.

"You heard him, there's nothing going on between us. Never will. I'm sick of pining after a man who will never change. A man who doesn't want to change."

Damn! I feel for her so much. Logan does care for her, but he can't let himself fall no matter how much he wants to.

"I think I'm going to start looking for a new job."

Wait? What?

"Really?"

She nods her head, tears glisten and threaten to fall. "I can't work beside him anymore. Not after everything that's happened between us. My heart can't take it."

Love sucks.

"I get it…" linking my arm with hers, "… men suck." Lenna chuckles. "I'm going to miss you if you go, you know that? You're leaving me to fend for myself against all those young, vapid girls, who at any second will blow my boyfriend in his office." Lenna spits out her coffee and starts laughing. "Stop it! You know it's true. Seriously, can't you stay? Please. Pretty, please?"

"I would if I could," she says sadly.

I get it, I totally do.

"Urgh. Seriously, I'm hating Logan right now. How can two people look identical yet be so polar opposite?"

We continue walking through Central Park, soaking in the sunshine before heading back to the office.

⁂

"We need to talk." Noah steps into my office, shutting the door behind him looking serious.

Oh, shit this doesn't sound good.

Please don't tell me he is breaking up with me—it's only been forty-eight hours.

This could be the shortest relationship I've ever had.

He takes a seat in front of me. He's so handsome, dressed in his navy suit, wearing the tie I picked out in a lovely shade of blush which is hinting at being playfully modern yet still masculine at the same time. I liked getting dressed for work together this morning, especially, when he joined me in the shower, which nearly made us late.

I don't want to give up morning shower sex, not this soon, not when it's this good.

"How's Lenna?"

Okay, so that's not what I thought he wanted to talk about.

"Is this a conversation between colleagues or partners?" I question.

"Both. But mainly as a partner." He gives me a great big smirk.

"Fine. Your brother's a dick."

Noah's eyes widen, then he bursts out laughing, and with that, the tension eases from my shoulders.

"You're preaching to the choir, sweetheart." He gives me a saucy wink. "Lenna seems down."

I'm not prepared to break our girl code on a forty-eight-hour relationship. I need to give it a little longer before I share all my secrets with him.

"She's remained tight-lipped about what's happened between them.

So, I'm not one hundred percent sure."

"But he's broken her heart?"

"I guess as much as one's heart can break when the other person lives behind a wall."

"He wasn't always like this," Noah defends his brother. "I guess I didn't realize how much Dad's death affected him as I was consumed in my own grief." *Okay, well, now I feel bad.* "I'm working on him, but he's stubborn."

No shit, is he ever. He's let the best thing to ever happen to him walk right out that door.

"Anyway, that isn't even the most surprising news." Noah perks up. "Have you spoken to Emma about Anderson?"

Geez, Noah, I can't keep breaking girl code for you.

"Other than they've hooked up a couple of times, no nothing."

"Seriously, she hasn't told you anything else? Nothing like super important? Why?"

What the hell is he getting at?

"Should I be worried?"

"Anderson literally just dropped the biggest bombshell on us." *Oh no, this doesn't sound good.* "They're married and living together."

Say what? The world goes blank.

"Chlo… Chloe… Hey, are you there?" Noah's voice pulls me out of the blank void I fell into.

"I'm sorry, I spaced out for a second. I thought you said Anderson and Emma are married."

"I did."

"What the fuck!" My voice raises about three octaves.

"Since Vegas."

"That was months ago."

"I know," Noah adds.

"They have been married and living together for the past couple of months, and neither of them has told their friends?"

"Yep, but there's more."

"More?" *Not sure if my heart or brain desire to take any more.*

"His family is paying her to stay with him. Well, once the year is up, she will be paid," he tells me.

"What… no… Emma wouldn't do that. She's not about the money."

"I know that, and so does he. But she is about her business, and this money could take her business to the next level."

Shit. He's right. Emma's a hustler.

"I can't believe she hasn't told us." I'm shocked that she's kept this all a secret. Usually, we can't get Emma to shut up about her exploits.

"I know. I'm shocked Anderson hasn't told us before this either. He loves to dish on his latest conquest." Noah then quickly backpedals when he realizes what he's said. "Not that Emma's one of his conquests, it's just…"

Well, it makes me giggle. "I get what you're saying. I can't believe they hid this from us all."

"It's not a conventional marriage by any means."

"But we're their friends." Stabbing my finger into the desk. "We understand. We won't judge. We're supposed to be there for them."

"I know, sweetheart," Noah tries to placate me. "They had their reasons, and now I guess, we have to support them."

"I have to call an emergency meeting, you understand?" Noah frowns. "It's a girl thing." Waving my hand in his direction, I continue, "Saturday night, I won't be staying over." Noah doesn't look happy, at all. "I'm calling an emergency girls' night at my place. We have lots to discuss."

Is Noah pouting?

"Don't you dare give me that look." I stare straight at him.

"I don't like it when you're not in my bed."

Cue, melting heart and panties dampening.

"Fine. I'll sneak out and give you a blow job. Will that work?"

Noah's eyes light up, his pout has all but disappeared, and he jumps up from his chair. "I'm more than happy with that. I really want to lean over and kiss you, but I can't."

I'm biting my lip because in all honesty, I want him to. "Tonight."

Noah shakes his head. "No, lunchtime. I can't wait until tonight. You mentioned blow job, and my dick's interested now."

I'm so gone for this man.

"What do you have in mind?"

"Sooo many things." The heat in his eyes tells me exactly what's on his mind.

"Okay." Heat rises up my neck. "Guess I'll see you later."

Noah gives me a wink and exits my office. Fanning myself, I pick up my phone and send a group text.

Chloe: Urgent girls' night this Saturday night. My place.

My phone starts to ping with texts coming through.

Ariana: Everything okay?

Emma: What's going on?

Stella: I'll be there.

Lenna: You ok?

Chloe: I'm all good. Great actually.

Emma: You got Noah's D.

Stella: OMG you and Noah.

Chloe: Yes. Noah and I are together.

Ariana: Finally.

Stella: Yay.

Emma: Was it good? I mean you would hope so after all that build-up.

Lenna: Noah is totally gone for her.

Ariana: Thought so.

Chloe: Guys focus. Saturday night I'll tell you all. Now get back to work you lazy bitches.

I then get a million and one emoji's telling me to fuck off.

28

CHLOE

O ne week in with Noah, and I'm having the time of my life. We're keeping it professional at work, even though it's hard with the heated stares and clandestine touches. We haven't been able to recreate that magical first lunch break.

Noah texted me a hotel name and room number.

I felt like an escort—high class, of course. I'm sure the hotel staff thought I was.

My knuckles knock on the door, my heart rate picks up a couple of beats. Why am I nervous? Noah opens the door, his suit jacket's off, the sleeves of his business shirt are rolled up displaying his tanned, thick, corded forearms. His tie is hanging loosely around his neck.

"Miss Jones." Noah holds the door open for me.

"Mr. Stone." Are we role-playing? I hope so. Walking through the door into the luxurious hotel room, the floor-to-ceiling glass wall catches my attention as it looks over the Hudson, Central Park, and city skyline.

"You're late." His voice deepens. "I'm an important man, Miss Jones, and my time is very precious."

"I'm sorry, sir." Turning and facing him, I say, "It won't happen again."

"I'm not sure if I believe you." Those steely green eyes flare at me.

"Can I make it up to you, sir?" I'm trying to keep in character, but finding it very hard not to smile as he looks so serious.

"How do you plan on making it up to me?" His eyes zero in on my breasts.

"I'm willing to do anything, sir?"

"Anything?" He raises a brow at me.

"Yes, sir. I need this job. I can't lose it. Please?"

"You'd do anything to keep this job?"

I nod my head in agreement giving him my best doe eyes.

"No matter what I ask you to do. You'll do it?"

"Yes, sir."

Noah reaches out and caresses my face. *"Such a good girl."* He gives me a wicked smile. *"Now, get on your knees and show me just how much you need this job."*

Far out, this is hot. As I fall to my knees and shakily unzip his straining suit pants, the zip echoes through the room. His thick, hard cock presses against his briefs as his pants fall to the floor.

Slowly, I pull it out, feeling the weight of his need in my hands.

My mouth waters as I take every glorious inch of him inside.

My tongue licks the small bead of pre-cum off the tip, and a hiss falls from his lips at the first contact. His reaction spurs the inner porn star in me as I start to take him all in.

Noah's hand comes out, grabbing my jaw roughly. *"You'll look at me when my cock's in your mouth. Do you hear me, Miss Jones?"*

I hum my answer around his dick, which causes creases along his forehead as I do it. I look up at his handsome face as I try to give him the best blow job of my life because let's face it, blow jobs are difficult. They take forever, your jaw gets sore, and all men want is that false illusion of porn blow jobs.

Hats off to those women because they're the true MVPs of womanhood. I wonder if they do courses. Like what are the tricks of the trade to last longer and not get lockjaw? How do you swallow like a champion because, let's face it, who really wants to swallow that crap?

Noah's fingers begin to thread in my hair as he starts to move my head further down his dick. Pushing me to swallow him as far as I can, hitting that spot that could go either way in the gagging direction, I try to breathe through it.

Don't forget you're role-playing here.

Channel that inner porn star and take his D like a pro.

Relaxing, I let him push further, pulling moves I never knew I had.

"Fuck, Chloe." Noah breaks character as I suck for dear life. "Stop. Fucking stop," he yells at me, pushing my head away.

I fall back on my heels a little surprised at his rejection.

Did I do something wrong?

Noah's chest is heaving, a slight glisten of sweat is across his brow. "Chloe." His hand reaches out and caresses my cheek. "Fuck! I was seconds away from coming."

My frown turns upside down as I internally fist pump my inner porn star.

"I planned on coming with your pussy wrapped around me, not down your delicious throat."

Far out, he's hot.

"Now, get up off the floor, Miss Jones."

Okay, we're back to role-playing again.

Goodie.

"I'm very happy with your enthusiasm. But I need more."

Yeah, I can do more.

"See that desk." He points at the wooden desk pressed up against the window. "Go stand there with your back to me." A shiver laces my skin as I do what I'm told, swaying my hips seductively as I make my way over to the desk. "Do not turn around," Noah warns me. "Unzip your dress," he orders me.

I do as I'm told and slowly unzip my dress while giving him a saucy shimmy then pulling my dress over my hips making a show out of it. Looking out at the city below, I notice I can see Noah's reflection in the glass, and I notice he's naked.

That man is damn fine.

"*Now your bra.*"

I unclasp the lacy item dropping it beside me while watching as he slowly moves toward me in the reflection.

"*Now your panties.*" *His breath hits my skin, setting it on fire.*

I do as I'm told, kicking them to the side.

Now what? The anticipation is killing me.

My eyes dart to Noah's reflection. I watch as he moves behind me, and seconds later, I feel his skin against mine. My eyes close momentarily with delight.

"*You're on the pill, aren't you?*" *Noah whispers his question, stilling me.*

"*Noah?*" *His name is barely a whisper from my lips.*

"*I have protection with me. I just…*" *His lips press a kiss to my shoulder blade.* "*I'm all in, Chloe,*" *he confesses.*

I turn around to face him. This conversation feels like it needs to be face to face.

"*Too soon?*" *Noah's face falls a little.* "*I'm such an idiot,*" *he says as he takes a step back and begins to rake his fingers through his hair.* "*I shouldn't have said anything. I—*"

"*Noah.*" *Reaching out to him, I don't like seeing him in distress.*

"*It's fine, Chloe.*" *He shakes his head.*

"*Talk to me.*"

"*I've fallen utterly in love with you, Chloe, and it's killing me not being able to tell you. Because fuck we've only been dating for like what? Seventy-two hours.*" *I'm stunned and can't reply.* "*Shit! I knew I was going to fuck it up. You're not there yet. I get it. I… shit.*" *Noah begins to pace the room, my eyes falling to his ass, distracting me for a couple of moments. Walking over, I turn him around to me, cupping his face, and press the barest of kisses on his lips trying to calm him down as I feel like he's spiraling with insecurities.*

"*You haven't messed anything up,*" *I reassure him.* "*I didn't realize you were that far gone.*"

His eyes widen in surprise. "How could I not be, Chlo?"

Urgh, this man. Why is he so perfect?

"You've knocked me off my feet. I never thought in my life that I might get a happy ending." As soon as the words are out of his mouth, we both burst out laughing.

"I'm pretty sure you can get a happy ending anytime you want."

"You know what I mean." Wrapping his arms around me, he continues, "I can't imagine my life without you, Chloe. And, if I'm honest, I don't want to ever imagine it without you."

Oh Lord, my heart gives flight to hearts and unicorns and all those magical things.

"I know this is all so soon. I've only just convinced you to start sleeping with me."

"I'm all in, Noah." I smile. "You don't ever have to doubt that." His face lights up. "I know it took me a while, but now that I'm here with you, I'm in. The whole happily ever after thing. All of it."

"Yeah?" he hesitates.

"Yeah." I nod in agreement.

"Thank fuck." Noah kisses me with everything he has, showing me just how much he's in.

The next thing I know my ass hits the desk. Noah picks me up and places me on the cold, wooden desk, pressing himself between my legs.

"Let me ask the question again… are you on the pill?" His teeth sinking into my earlobe.

"Yes. I'm on the pill."

"So, nothing between us then?"

"Nothing," I tell him.

Little does he know he's the first man I've never used a condom with. Even though I was going to marry Walker, I never let him convince me to take away that protection. I must have known deep down inside he was never faithful.

But things with Noah are different, I want nothing between us. I want all of him.

He spreads my legs with his hips. Licking his fingers, he runs them through my slit, testing me, teasing me. Slowly, he nudges at my entrance, our eyes watching as he moves through my slickness, ever so gently pushing forward. Both of us hissing as he enters me for the first time with nothing between us.

"Fuck, Chloe," he groans. "You feel. Fuck." His eyes almost roll back in his head as I urge him further with my legs wrapped around his hips until he's sunk deep inside me. "You're mine now, Chloe Jones," Noah tells me, his hand cupping my face, as his lips claim mine, and his body takes me over and over again.

"Chlo." Ariana startles me, catching me with my dirty thoughts as I stare out at Noah's townhouse.

"Hey," I greet my friend.

"Are you feeling okay? You look flushed."

"I just ran down the stairs." This seems like a legitimate excuse to me, but I'm sure she will see straight through it.

"So, why the urgent girls' night? What's going on?"

"Not with me, but with someone else. That's all I can say right now."

She gives me a surprised look, but she knows we'll get into it as soon as the others have arrived.

Noah's organized a chef for tonight and a masseuse. I'm so lucky. He has work to do as we are about to open The Hamptons Estate in the next couple of weeks, but I did promise I would sneak across when everyone was asleep for a quickie.

Eventually, all the girls arrive. We're set up in the dining room, beautiful bouquets of flowers line the table thanks to Noah. He thinks of everything. Drinks are served along with the first course—let's all enjoy our food first before I open the can of worms.

"How's things going with Noah?" Emma asks.

"It's only been a week, but it feels like a lifetime already."

"Sounds like someone's in love," Stella teases.

"Maybe," I confess.

The table erupts, and congratulations are thrown around with a couple of glasses of champagne consumed.

"We're so happy for you," Ariana affirms.

"It's been a tough year for you. You deserve to be happy," Emma adds.

"Have you told EJ yet?" Stella asks.

"No. Not yet."

Stella doesn't look impressed. "You know he will be hurt if he knows you're hiding it from him? He wants to see you happy. You know that?"

Damn her and her voice of reason.

"Fine. Schedule us for dinner at the restaurant. Maybe that way he won't kill Noah." Stella raises an unconvinced brow. "Speaking of hiding things..." I change the subject. "That's the reason why I called this urgent girls' night tonight. Someone's been keeping a secret from all of us." The table falls silent while everyone's staring at me. "Emma..." My eyes fall on her, the tiniest bit of color drains from her cheeks.

"Noah told you, didn't he?" I nod my head in agreement. "That buffoon couldn't keep his mouth shut if he tried."

Emma rolls her eyes.

"What's going on?" Ariana asks.

I look over at Emma to continue.

"Fine." Emma puts her cutlery down, and she takes a big swig of champagne before she talks. The table is silent with anticipation for whatever Emma is about to tell them.

"Don't freak out or anything, but Anderson and I are married."

Yeah, the table totally freaks out, shouting questions at her. Which makes Emma shut down.

"Come on, guys, let her explain." I know how they feel because it's how I was days ago when I found out.

"It was a prank that went totally wrong. It's the easiest way to explain it," Emma tells the group.

"Anderson's sister is Elise Parker," I clarify.

The table erupts again overhearing the superstar's name.

"Calm down, guys." Emma tries to gain order again. "Elise and Anderson like to play pranks on each other. Don't ask me why, they're weird." She rolls her eyes. "I've known Elise for years and had no idea Anderson was her brother 'cause of the whole different surname thing. Anyway, Elise and I like to party, and Vegas used to be our town. So, when she came, we slipped into our old ways. She found out her brother and I had gotten close. She thought I was perfect for him, and then somehow concocted her evil scheme."

"This is the good bit," I explain.

"One of Elise's friends said they wanted to get married. They bought a license from the hotel or something. Someone in the group was an internet ordained minister and married these two. Elise then asked Anderson and me to sign the papers as witnesses, and because 'hello tequila' we did so blindly. Only thing is, it was our names on the marriage license, not the other people."

"What the?" Lenna gasps.

"That can't be legal?" Ariana questions.

"It is. Believe me, we tried to annul it. Except, Elise sent photos of me dressed in a veil with my arms around Anderson, and a copy of the marriage certificate to his parents."

"Why the hell would she do that?" Stella asks.

"Because they love to prank each other. And their parents are used to their craziness."

"So, why are you still married?" Lenna asks the million-dollar question.

"His family made me an offer I couldn't refuse. Plus, they would disinherit him if he divorced me."

"They can't blackmail you to stay married to their son," Ariana angry declares.

"There's a loophole, and we are both using it. It's a marriage of convenience. Everyone in New York does it. Well, the rich ones, anyway." She laughs.

"Loophole?" Lenna asks the burning question.

"Yeah. His parents will pay me twelve million dollars if I stay married to Anderson for one year. But there has to be no scandals or bad press."

"Shit! That's a lot of money. Plus, Anderson is hot," Stella admits. "I'd totally do it." Emma gives Stella a high-five.

"I don't get the loophole?" Lenna presses.

"The loophole is publicly. We can't be seen with other people, but privately we can." Emma takes a sip of her champagne feeling more comfortable about her story now it's out there in the open.

"You're sleeping with other people?" Ariana asks.

"Of course," Emma states as if it's normal.

"Are you sleeping with Anderson, too?" Lenna questions.

"We share a bed, so spooning does lead to fucking sometimes. The man is hung and knows how to use it. I'm not turning that down."

The table falls silent.

"It's like a *Bold and the Beautiful* episode." I chuckle, trying to lighten the mood as the table has suddenly fallen tense.

The chef comes in with the main course, interrupting the simmering tension between us all before disappearing back to the kitchen.

"I don't get how you sleeping with other people won't get out. He's a public figure," Lenna tells her.

"There's ways," Emma says coyly.

"Do tell," Stella pushes.

"What I am about to say cannot leave this room. Do you hear me?" Emma looks at me.

Okay, so that means no telling Noah.

I get it.

Girl code locked down in the vault.

"You remember Camryn, the gorgeous woman who organized your birthday?" Emma points to me, and I nod my head in agreement. "Well, she's married to a man who owns one of the world's most exclusive sex clubs."

We all choke on our dinner.

This is the first I'm hearing of this.

Did Anderson forget to tell Noah about this, or did Noah not tell me because of bro code?

"Sex club?" Trying to swallow my lump of steak that lodged firmly in my throat, I raise an eyebrow.

Emma quickly looks around before continuing, "I signed an NDA. I shouldn't be telling any of you," Emma pleads.

"Promise, my lips are sealed," Ariana tells her.

We all nod in agreement.

"Thank you, guys. I know I can trust you, it's just—"

"Legally, you'll be screwed," Lenna adds.

"Tell me about this club? Can I come?" Stella asks.

Emma bursts out laughing. "They would eat you alive, little one." She taps Stella on her hand.

"Have you seen Anderson hook up with other people?" Because I would cut a bitch if I saw Noah with someone else.

"No. I haven't."

"Aren't you worried you might develop feelings for Anderson if you're sleeping and living with him?" I ask.

"You're living with him?" Ariana raises her voice.

"It was part of the deal," Emma tells her. "And no, I'm not worried about developing feelings for him. I mean we're not wired like you guys. We aren't searching for a happily ever after. We both just want a happily right now."

"Why didn't you tell us?" Ariana asks the question we're all wondering.

"Honestly…" Emma plays with her food, "… I didn't want to disappoint you guys. You're my family," she confesses. "I knew you wouldn't be on board with our plan."

"We love you," I tell her, and the others join in, making her a little misty-eyed.

"I get what you're getting out of this, but I don't get what he is?" Lenna questions Emma.

"What do you mean?" Emma asks.

"He's independently wealthy outside of his family. He could easily give you the money, and it wouldn't make a dent in his personal wealth. I just don't get why he would stay married, especially with the woman living with him. In his bed night after night." Lenna's making valid points.

"His inheritance," Emma adds.

"Anderson is worth hundreds of millions of dollars without his inheritance. Do you think he needs more money?" Emma slow blinks at Lenna's comments. "You had no idea how rich he is, did you?" Emma shakes her head. "Did you not Google your husband?" She shakes her head again.

"Well, least we know you didn't marry him for his money." I'm attempting to crack a joke, but it falls on deaf ears.

"Am I an idiot?" Emma seems deflated all of a sudden.

We all rush to tell her, "No."

"Do you like being married to him?" I tentatively ask.

"It's nice coming home to someone. I've never had that before."

"Does he go out a lot?" Lenna asks.

"No, not really. Anderson's usually always home when I get in with a glass of red and dinner on the table waiting for me." As soon as the words fall from her lips, Emma gasps. "You don't think he..." She seems a little confused.

"Likes you," Ariana finishes for her.

"He wouldn't have stayed married to you if he hated you," Stella points out.

"Do you like him?" I ask because maybe there's more to this arrangement than meets the eye.

"What? No. Not like that," she quickly adds. "I like his dick. That's a thing of beauty." And there she is, the normal Emma.

"I'm not going to be able to look at him now," Stella teases. "Knowing he has a big dick." We all burst out laughing. "I need a big dick. Does he have a brother?" Emma chuckles.

"No. But if you want a big dick, sweetheart, I can find you a big dick."

"Yippee." Stella claps excitedly.

"What happened with stripper man?"

"Oh, he was fun. He's on my speed dial if I ever need him… his words." I think Stella's getting her groove back.

"Now, who's ready for dessert?"

29

NOAH

I'm so fucked. I couldn't look away. I couldn't stop watching them. She looked happy dancing around her living room with a cocktail in her hand, and a huge smile on her face. She looked free.

Shaking my head as I turn on my heel and head to bed, I can't begrudge her time with her friends. They have always been in her life, I've known that from the start—they are her squad. They were there for her over the whole Walker saga, whisking her away to New York and then onto her honeymoon, helping her rebuild her life again. It's purely selfish reasons that I want to spend every waking moment with her.

She's my drug.

I need my fix.

Finally, after most of the year being side by side, day in day out as friends and colleagues, I have her. Freely. Without barriers. Without trying to hide my feelings. Without fear. But I want more. I'm being completely irrational. She will be back in my bed again, night after night like she has every single night this week. Both of us sitting on the couch with our laptops open, working away, a nice glass of red beside us, eating take out, talking strategies and plans, finalizing things. May not be that romantic, but to me, it's kind of everything I hoped for in a relationship if I were ever going to have one.

I jump into bed, grab my glasses, and open my laptop. Might as well finish up on all the urgent shit related to The Hamptons Estate.

At some point, I must fall asleep because footsteps through my house wake me with a jolt. My bedroom light is still on, my laptop has fallen to the side, and my glasses are on my chest.

Rubbing the foggy sleep from my eyes, a silhouette of a woman stands at my door.

"Did I wake you?" she seductively purrs.

"I'm most certainly awake now." Taking in every inch of her glorious get-up, she has a Burberry trench coat on, fuck-me boots that disappear underneath it, and a deep 'V' displaying the swell of her voluptuous breasts.

"You've been working too hard. I'm here to help you relax." Chloe smirks.

God, she's cute especially when her hand misses the doorframe, and she stumbles forward a little bit, letting out a giggle. She's tipsy. She straightens herself up and goes back into character. Slowly and shakily, she saunters over to the end of the bed.

"My poor, hardworking executive. Dealing with such important things all day long. You must be exhausted."

I nod my head in agreement because yes, it is hard. I am tired. And I fucking want her so much.

"I am," I reply, playing along.

"Lucky I'm here to help you, then." She licks her lips.

Chloe unties her coat and lets it fall to the floor.

Holy hell, I was not expecting her to be buck-naked underneath.

My dick shoots to the sky against my boxers. My chest begins to hyperventilate, my heart constricts, my brain implodes from the extreme stimuli. She's so beautiful. She's sexy as fuck. I love that her confidence in the bedroom is growing. I'm excited to be reaping the benefits. I'm one lucky son of a bitch because she's all mine.

She rips off the bed cover, exposing my tented boxers. "Take them off," she demands.

Quickly, I do as I'm told, yanking them off and throwing them beside the bed.

Her eyes widen as she takes me all in. Her cheeks flush as her eyes zero in on my dick. "I don't know what I want to ride first, your dick or your face." I literally choke on her words.

Hottest thing a woman could ever say to a man as she taps her fingernail on her chin as if it really needs that much thinking.

"May I suggest—"

She cuts me off before I can finish. "No," she states, giving me a heated stare.

Chloe moves a knee to the bed, and then the other, and crawls up over my body, stopping above my dick.

She's going for the dick.

She's going to ride me like a good little cowgirl, and I'll fucking buck the shit out of her.

Chloe smiles at me and then begins to move past my dick.

Fuck yes.

Yes.

Sit on my face baby.

Yes.

She shakily stands up on my bed in her sky-high heels and takes the last couple of steps standing. Her pussy's right above me. I can see it glisten like a fucking diamond, and it's all for me. She's just as turned on as I am.

I shuffle a little to where I'm seated closer to her. I can't quite reach, my nose runs along her slit, taking in her feminine smell, but my tongue, my tongue can't get there.

I shove a couple of the throw pillows under my ass which elevates me directly to the space I need to be. My hands reach out and cup her ass, moving her into the position I need to give her what she wants. The first swipe of my tongue has her falling forward and gripping the headboard. Honestly, I want to take my time, but I can't, that first taste of her has me rabid. I feast on her like a starved man. Devouring her. Tasting her. Licking her. Sucking her.

My fingers grip into her peachy ass as my tongue assaults her pussy. Chloe's panting, her breath is labored. Her hand keeps hitting the headboard when I hit the right spot. She's just as feverish as I am.

Her legs begin to buckle the closer I get her to orgasm.

She can't stand up for much longer. I need to take her over the edge, so I can fuck her, sink my aching cock right inside her fucking delicious pussy. One last suck of her clit, and she's gone. She's screaming my name while thrashing about above my head, and her orgasm fills my mouth with her deliciousness.

When I have wrung every last bit of her pleasure out of her, I pull her down on top of me and fuck her like a wild beast. She holds onto my shoulders for dear life as I buck into her, her tits bouncing in time with each one of my hard thrusts. Fuck they're beautiful, they mesmerize me.

Chloe begins to howl as she falls backward, her hand resting on my shin, her fingernails digging into my skin. The change of angle has me hitting that spot, that bundle of nerves which are like a firecracker in a woman. The perfect spot to make her soar over and over.

I hit it. My bullseye. Right in the center. Every damn time.

She's panting. Cursing. She's practically delirious with pleasure. I want more from her. I want to wring every last bit of everything from her body. I need her to know she's mine. That I'm hers.

That no one can, or will, ever treat her the way I do.

No one can, or will, fuck her the way I do.

The thought of her fucking someone else sinks in my stomach like a lead balloon.

That thought makes me thrust into her harder, imprinting myself on her body, leaving my mark so she won't ever want anyone else.

I'm so fucked up over her.

She's turned me wild as we continue our fucking frenzy until she comes again all over my dick, her pussy clamping down around me, sending me spiraling to the edge where she takes me there over and over as I fill her up, staking my claim on her pussy over and over again, leaving my mark. These thoughts are so fucked up. I'm like a damn caveman reduced to base needs. I want her to walk around with me inside of her. I want her pussy to remember who it was that fucked it perfectly.

I want my seed filling her up until… until her belly is round.

That thought fucking halts me.

Where the fuck did that come from?

I've never wanted kids. It's just the orgasm talking. I'm high.

Then the images of a white picket fence, a shaggy dog, me at the grill, Chloe waddling around the yard with a big old belly and a little blonde kid running around her feet.

Fuck.

Shit.

No. No. No.

What the hell is going on with you, Noah Stone? You've never wanted a family, not after what you went through with your father. *Who the fuck are you?* Chloe collapses against me, and she hums her satisfaction in my ear.

My body tenses up over my wayward thoughts.

"Let me get you a towel." Gently moving her off of me, I rush into the bathroom and wash my face. Catching a glimpse of myself in the mirror, I see a man who's happy and satisfied. A man who has the world in his hand.

So why the fuck am I freaking out? Because it's only been a week, you fucktard, an inner voice tells me. *You're moving too fast. Slow the fuck down.* That voice tells me again. *She might not want kids. She may not want the white picket fence*, that same voice reiterates. It's right. *Why the hell am I getting ahead of myself? Because you're thirty-five years old, and you don't want to be a dinosaur when you have kids.*

I'm hallucinating. Good sex. No. Best sex of my life is making me crazy.

I wet a washcloth and take it back into the bedroom where Chloe is resting against the headboard with a frown on her face. She reaches out for the cloth, but I move it away.

"Let me." She doesn't fight me on it, and I ever so gently clean myself off her. Jumping back off the bed, I throw the wet cloth into the laundry shoot, grab a clean pair of boxers and a t-shirt for her. Handing her the shirt, she puts it on. She looks hot with the boots still on.

"Are you going to tell me what freaked you out just then?" Her eyes are imploring me to tell her.

"It was nothing." I've already told her I'm practically in love with her, hours after falling into bed with her. I can't tell her I'm seeing kids in our future after a week.

"I thought we promised to be honest with each other."

Urgh, she hits me with the honesty statement.

"I know. But I'm embarrassed." Maybe that will stop her from poking. She reaches out, pulling me to her, her lips meeting mine in a soothing kiss.

"Was it something dirty? Do you have a secret fetish I don't know about?"

If only.

"Yeah, something like that."

She grabs my face halting me, her eyes stare into mine. "You just lied to me." Chloe jumps up off my bed and grabs her coat, angrily tying it around her waist.

Wait, what just happened.

"I thought you were different, Noah. I thought we could tell each other anything. After everything I've been through lying is a no-deal for me." Chloe turns on her heels and exits my room.

Shit. This is serious, so I run after her down the stairs.

"Chlo… please… it wasn't anything that serious."

She whirls around, and I run into her. "Then why lie? If you can lie about the small stuff, then you can certainly lie about the big stuff." She attempts to walk away again, but I grab her by the waist pulling her back to me.

"You seriously want to know what freaked me out? Because once it's out, Chloe, I can't take it back. You will look at me differently. Maybe you might even change your mind about dating me."

I can see this gets her attention.

"It can't be that bad, Noah." Her voice is soft, but I can witness the hesitation on her face. Reaching out, I touch her face. She wants to know, and if I don't tell her, it's going to ruin what we have, and if I do tell her, it will anyway. I'm fucked either way.

"When I came inside of you..." Chloe slightly stiffens, "... all I could think about was filling you up with my seed and claiming you as mine."

"Oh." Her face relaxes. "That's kind of hot."

"Good to know." I give her a wink. "But then... things took a turn in a direction I never thought they would." Her eyes widen. "I saw pictures of us in the suburbs, with a dog, kids running around, you with a swollen belly." My stomach is turning as I tell her. Honestly, I want to throw up.

Moving away from her, I rush into the kitchen and grab myself a scotch, drinking straight from the bottle. My shoulders are heaving as my hands grip the edge of the sink.

"Noah." Her soft hands touch my feverish skin.

"Maybe it's best that you head home. Your friends are waiting for you."

I can't look at her.

I'm a fucking idiot.

Maybe I need to get some therapy. Maybe I have mommy issues or something.

Chloe's hand falls from my shoulder, and silence fills the room. The ticking of the clock echoes through the kitchen, the mechanical whirl of the fridge cooling down comes through loud and clear.

"What kind of dog was it?"

Her question surprises me. Turning my head ever so slightly I think, *Is she serious?*

She tilts her head, giving me a warm smile. "Was it a Jack Russell? Golden Retriever? English bulldog?"

"A chocolate Labrador."

"I bet we call it something ridiculous like…" she muses for a couple of moments, "… Frank. A dog needs a human name."

"I didn't get that far." I'm now staring at her in disbelief.

"Food for thought then." She smiles at me.

"You're not freaked out?"

"Oh, no, I'm freaked out." Her comment hits me like a punch to the chest.

"I should never have had said anything." Turning back to my scotch, I take another swig.

"Hey…" Her hand halts me as I swallow the shot. "You're not alone with these thoughts." This surprises me. "I've thought about us like that, and it's scared me, too."

"It's too soon."

"Yeah. Maybe to the outside world, but we have known each other for six months. We work together. We live next door to each other. We travel in kind of in the same circles. We've been interconnected from day one." This is so true. "I don't know what the future holds for us, Noah. But I think it might be good."

"You do?" I smile.

"Don't you?" She returns my question back at me.

"I'm wanting things I never thought I ever wanted, and honestly it scares the shit out of me but, in the same breath, it doesn't." Pulling her to me, I hold her tightly. "Can we forget what we think we should be doing for only being together for such a short time and just go with it."

"Yep. I mean if Emma and Anderson can get married, then we can talk about ever after, after just a week."

"They are kind of insane, aren't they? Least we're normal compared to them." Chloe chuckles.

"You think Anderson has feelings for her?" she asks.

"Maybe. I mean it's so out of character of him. But, then again, he's probably thinking I can sleep with other people, and come home to my wife and not get into trouble." As soon as the words are out of my mouth, I regret them, maybe Emma hasn't told her friends. Chloe eyes me suspiciously.

"You know, don't you?"

"Know what?" I'm panicking.

"The thing we aren't supposed to know or talk about." Shit, she does know.

"Bro code thing."

"Yeah, the girl code thing." She gives me a wink.

"We're talking about the same thing, aren't we?" I ask because I might be confused with all this innuendo.

"The loophole?" Chloe adds. *Oh, thank fuck she does know.*

"I couldn't tell you. I know we just had a whole thing about secrets and lying but…"

She shakes her head. "It wasn't your thing to tell. I don't care about other people's lies, I care about yours," she reiterates.

"What do you think about the whole thing?"

"Is it something you want to do?"

I shake my head quickly. "Hell, fucking, no. I'm not sharing you with that shit."

"Good, 'cause I will cut a bitch if they touch you." I chuckle. "I guess if it makes them happy, and it's not harming anyone, I just worry that someone's going to catch feels and—"

"I know, me, too. But they are adult enough to work it out themselves."

"True." She lays a small kiss on my cheek. "I better get going."

Pulling her in for a kiss, she lets out a sigh when we finish.

I feel the same way letting her go.

I give her ass a good slap as she walks away, which makes her giggle.

30

CHLOE

Holy shit! Noah wants marriage, kids, and suburbia with me. My mind is whirling with his confession. Deep down inside my romantic heart, I was thinking the same things, but I thought this was all too soon to have feelings like this. Maybe because we became friends first and got to know each other outside of a romantic capacity, and now we've finally gotten together, we feel like we are way further along in our relationship than we physically have been.

"You dirty little bitch." Emma catches me coming back home.

"You fucking scared me." I place my hand on my chest, trying to calm my beating heart.

"Look at you dressed like a whore. Makes me so proud." Emma places her hands across her heart.

Rolling my eyes, I continue into the living room, crashing against the armchair, and slowly start taking my whore boots off.

"You look thoroughly fucked." Emma smiles at me.

"I most certainly have been."

Emma bursts out laughing. "It's nice to see you back to your normal self again."

"He makes me happy," I confess to her. Honestly, I want to shout it from the rooftops.

"I know. I can see it. He's a keeper, Chlo. He's a good guy." Emma's confession surprises me.

"I think he's the one," I blurt out the turmoil that's been swirling around in my mind.

Emma's eyes widen, and her face lights up. "Wow. That's big."

"He told me tonight he can see us in the suburbs with a dog, white picket fence, and kids running around."

"Holy shit," Emma gasps. "What do you think about that?"

"I want it, too. I never thought I did, especially not with Walker, but with Noah…" I let the words fall away.

"You love him," Emma states.

"Yeah. I think we both love each other. It's fast, though, right?"

"You're talking to the wrong person." Emma throws her hands up. "But as long as you're both on the same page, then that's all that matters."

"Are you and Anderson on the same page?" I question her now it's just the two of us.

"Yeah, we are. Otherwise, it won't work."

"How does it work? You two living together."

"We're both very sexual people. We like exploring things outside of what normal society thinks a couple should." I'm intrigued. "We're both too busy to focus on a relationship. Most people are needy when they're in one. You have to consider their needs when you're barely able to look after your own." I get that. "I'm so focused on growing my business, I don't have time to maintain a boyfriend. I have time for pleasure, and that's about it. Hence, why I am up at one in the morning working my butt off."

Shit, I had no idea she's working such long hours.

"You have to look after yourself, too. Otherwise, you will burn out," I warn her.

"I know." She rolls her eyes. "That's why this thing with Anderson works. If we are both home at the same time and need a release, we do it. If I'm busy or he's busy, or not even in the same city, then we go and have discreet fun at the club."

"Are you jealous?"

Emma scoffs. "No. There's no feelings. We're roommates. Friends even."

"But you sleep together."

"Sweetie. I can tell the difference between love and sex. You and the others, you are having sex because you're trying to find the one. Me, I am having sex because I need the release to continue working. I don't have time for man drama. So, simple, mutually satisfying, discreet fun." When she puts it like that, I get it. "But do I like coming home to Anderson's gorgeous penthouse where we have a chef on call, cleaners, masseuse, practically anything I want at a touch of a button. That part's pretty cool."

"You said you liked coming home to him earlier."

"I've been by myself since I was fifteen. You know my family situation. So, coming home to someone who has thought about your needs, without you even having to tell them, is enjoyable. It's nice to have a conversation with someone who understands business and can point me in the right direction. Who has the right connections."

"Like a mentor?"

"Yeah. He's my business mentor. Most nights, he runs through my business from the accounts to my social media. He's a brilliant man. Don't tell him I said that, he's cocky as hell as it is."

"A year is a long time, though," I warn her.

"Trust me, Chlo. I've got this." She sounds so confident, maybe she's right. I don't understand it, but that's because I wouldn't be okay with a relationship like that. Em's happy, and that's the most important thing.

"Well, I'm happy for you."

"Thanks, babe." She smiles.

"Now, are you going to tell me more about The Paradise Club?" Emma bursts out laughing.

"I think telling EJ in a public place is a good idea." Anderson chuckles in the back of the limousine, teasing Noah, who looks a little green, if I'm being honest. I convinced Emma and Anderson to double with us. There's safety in numbers.

"We can tell him that we're married first. It might soften the blow," Emma suggests. "That's what friends are for."

"Maybe that's a good idea," Noah tells me.

"Stop it, guys. My brother isn't *that* bad." The whole car erupts with laughter. "Really? You think he's going to freak out?"

"I'm putting a hundred on that he punches Noah." Anderson chuckles.

Panic slides over my body. *They won't come to blows, will they?*

"You're such a dick," Noah growls at Anderson, which makes him laugh harder. Maybe we should start with the news that Anderson and Emma are married first. Then move onto us.

We eventually arrive at EJ's restaurant, and Stella is waiting for us.

"I thought the private room would be better for tonight." She gives me a wink.

Yes, especially if my brother's going to lose his mind over us.

Noah grabs my hand, and we weave in and out between the tables. Stella shows us to the private dining room, and we take our seats.

"Welcome, team," EJ booms into the dining room like a grenade.

He shakes the all guys' hands, gives me a kiss on the head, and kisses Emma's cheek. Once the pleasantries are over, he sits with a thud then slaps the table making everyone jump. "How the hell is everyone? It's been ages since I've seen you all."

"Emma and Anderson got married," I blurt out quickly before the waitress has a moment to pour us some drinks.

Emma looks over at me, giving me a smirk.

"What the fuck!" EJ's voice raises. "How the hell did that happen?" He looks between them. "Never thought I'd see the day you'd settle down, Ando, my man. Guess it's just you and me left for the ladies, hey Noah?" EJ turns to Noah.

"Um... er..." Noah's speechless for a couple of moments.

"No. Don't tell me you're seeing someone? Oh, for fuck's sake. She must have a magic pussy to tame you, too."

I choke on my water.

Anderson bursts out laughing, and Emma joins him.

Stella gasps, and Noah's stunned silent.

"Actually…" Noah starts. My brother's attention momentarily distracted by the beautiful waitress pouring the drinks. Noah decides to wait until she's finished and leaves the room.

"It's me. I'm the magic pussy," I blurt out before Noah even gets a chance to soften the blow.

EJ chokes on his beer. "What the fuck did you just say?" His eyes widen, his face has turned red, and his hand looks like it's about to crush the beer glass he's holding.

"Noah and I are dating."

"Like fuck you are." EJ's chair slides out, and he stands up, his furious glare is directed firmly at Noah. "I told you if you touched my sister, I would fucking kill you." He points his finger at Noah.

"I know. I tried to stay away, but I couldn't… I love her, man." The room falls silent.

Turning, I look at Noah, my heart skipping a billion beats. "I love him, too."

Noah's eyes meet mine. "Yeah." He gives me a cocky grin.

"Yeah. You and Frank." Noah's eyes widen at the private joke between us, then he smirks.

"Who the fuck is Frank?" EJ roars.

"Our dog," Noah tells him.

"You have a fucking dog, too? Next, you'll be telling me you live together."

"We kind of do." EJ rakes his hands through his hair. I think he might be having a heart attack.

"And you're fucking married." Pointing at Anderson, who holds up his hands and shrugs his shoulders. "Have I stepped into the fucking *Twilight Zone*."

"EJ." Standing, I walk over to my very confused brother. "Noah

JA LOW

means a lot to me, and I know it's going to take you time to accept us, but we're in it for the long haul."

"You are?" He looks over at Noah.

"The whole nine yards, man. I'm done."

"Fuck." Raking his hands through his hair again. "Fuck me. I never… I just… you love him?" I nod my head in agreement.

"And you love her?" He looks over at Noah.

"With my heart and soul."

Oh my God, I'm so giddy with excitement. Stella lets out an "aw" beside us.

"You break her heart, I break your fucking neck." He points to Noah.

"I won't," he tells him confidently.

"You sure you want him?" EJ asks.

"Yes."

"Fine. I guess." EJ gives me a hug and sits down, but I can tell he's slightly confused. "And you two are in love as well?" His attention now on Anderson and Emma.

"Hell, no," Emma adds quickly, while Anderson agrees.

"Then why the fuck are you two married?"

Anderson launches into the whole story about how they ended up married.

After the initial shock, EJ eventually settles down and the night ends up going really well.

"You love me. You want to kiss me," I tease Noah while everyone's busy in conversation.

"You know I want to do so much more than that. But your brother's sitting across from us, and it would be totally inappropriate to say all the things I want to do to you." My legs squirm with desire as his words direct heat right between them.

"Do you think it would be rude if we left early?"

Noah chuckles against the rim of his glass. "I think we'd give your brother a heart attack."

He's probably right.

Eventually, the night wraps up. We're waiting outside for our limousine to arrive. My arms are wrapped around Noah. He kisses the top of my head as he talks to Anderson.

"Seriously?" EJ steps outside with us. "You two make me sick." But he says it with a smile. "Okay, I see it now, but I'm still pissed that you went behind my back and hooked up with my sister," he tells Noah. "But I know you're a good guy, and I guess I'd rather her be with you than some punk-ass hipster."

Noah laughs. "Thanks. I think." They shake hands.

"I'll still kill you if you fuck this up."

That warning's very serious, so I untangle myself from Noah and reach out for EJ.

"Enough with the big brother bullshit," I warn him. "I love you. I'm happy, and that's all that matters."

He looks down at me. "I'll always be here for you. No matter what, okay?"

I know he will be.

31

CHLOE

I t's been a couple of weeks since dinner with my brother, and Noah and I are going from strength to strength. We've been flat out getting everything ready for today, which is the opening of The Hamptons Estate. We're kicking off the summer with a Friday night white party, and due to the exclusivity of the event, it's been the hottest ticket. Our advertising has gone viral, and we've sold all memberships for the summer season, which has blown the boys away. Not much else to do now except to maintain the best service in line with The Stone Group's ethos.

"Are you ready?" inquires Camryn, the event planner and the woman who is married to the sex club owner. I have so many questions, but I'm not meant to know about the club's existence, so no questions will be asked.

"I think so." Looking out over everything the boys have worked so hard on, it's come together. "And thank you so much for organizing everything, it looks so beautiful."

"My pleasure, it's what I do." Camryn smiles at me. "It's such a beautiful venue and what an idea... a member-only hotel. This is what the elites of The Hamptons need. Ridiculously rich people are always trying to find something that their friends don't have or can get. It's that one-upmanship that they thrive on." What a compliment. "I also heard that you're dating Noah?" My stomach sinks. How the hell does she know this? "Judging by the panic on your face, it's not common knowledge," she states.

"Um... no. I was trying to keep the two separate. Didn't want people to think I was given favoritism or anything."

"I totally get it." She gives me a warm smile. "I married my boss."

Wow! I had no idea.

Hang on—she married her boss.

I thought her husband ran elite sex clubs.

Does she work at them too?

"You really need to work on your poker face, I can see your mind ticking over." *Oh shit.* "Plus, I know Anderson has a big mouth. If he wasn't one of my husband's friends, I would be kicking his ass to the curb. Anderson's so annoying that you just have to love him." I totally get what she means. "All I'm saying is people talk either way. You shouldn't let the small percentage of haters stop you from being yourself. People thought I slept my way into Nate's life, that I used him and his connections to help my business. My business was booming way before he came along, and it still would have been booming if we hadn't gotten together." *I like her.* "Hope I'm not overstepping here. It's totally unprofessional." She gives me a warm smile.

"No. Thank you. I really appreciate it."

"Also. Former womanizers can reform for the right woman." She rubs her stomach giving it a pat.

"No. Are you?" She nods her head and smiles. "Oh my God, congratulations." I reach out and give her a hug.

"Thank you. I've just gone over the three-month mark. It's been hell. But I wouldn't change it for the world. The way Noah looks at you is the same way Nate looks at me. He's a man totally gone." I had no idea she noticed. "I Googled you." *Oh, no.* "I went through something very similar."

"Really?" *Who the hell would cheat on her?*

"I planned my boyfriend's engagement party to another woman?"

I choke on the gulp of water I chose at the wrong time to take. "I know, right?" She smiles. "Such a dick. Anyway, a lot of shit went down before Nate and I could get our happy ever after. Just know the gossips and trolls will leave you alone, eventually," she reiterates.

"They're the worst." It's nice talking to someone who actually understands something, not many people can.

"They are. It's hard when they infiltrate your new life. I get why you haven't gone public with Noah. Self-preservation." She's right. Noah's very high profile, and after the disaster that was Walker and all his fans, I don't want to have to deal with Noah Stone's groupies. "But honestly, they will be there whether it's now or in a year's time." *That's very true.* "Maybe it's the hormones, but I want everyone to be in love and happy," she says giddily.

I give her a hug taking in everything she's said.

"You can call me anytime, too. You've got my number."

That's so sweet of her.

"We should have you around for a barbecue one Sunday. I've got my LA friends coming to visit soon, you'd love them. They're crazy."

"Sounds great." I'm genuinely surprised.

"Okay. Go kick butt. I have shit to finish. People to yell at."

This makes me laugh as I watch her strut off in her heels.

She's way too cool.

"Hey." Noah wraps his arms around me as I stare out toward the ocean as the sun sets. The night has been so successful, the paparazzi are out in force with so many beautiful people enjoying themselves. "You did it." Noah nuzzles into my neck.

"Yeah, we did it."

Noah turns me around in his arms, his hands clasp my face. "No. You did it. This was your idea. You turned a normal hotel opening into the hottest ticket this summer. You took our business to a whole other level, Chloe." Tears well in my eyes. That's the nicest thing anyone's ever said. "Don't cry, baby." He kisses my tears away.

"I'm ready."

The sudden change of topic throws him. "Ready for what?" he asks cautiously.

"Ready to stop hiding us." His eyes widen. "I'm ready to let people at work know we're together, especially now that the hotel is launched."

"Really?" He picks me up and spins me around. "So, that means we can hold hands as we walk the red carpet at events?" I nod. "That I can kiss you at work?" I raise a brow at him. "Okay, still keeping it professional." He smiles.

The tension in my body begins to seep away. Camryn's right, people are going to talk no matter what. I shouldn't hide what Noah and I have because of some stupid, immature trolls.

"We going to make it Facebook official then?"

"Guess so." He pulls out his phone and takes a selfie with the sun setting behind us. It's the first one of us as a couple.

"#shesallmine @Chloe_JonesNYC" Noah grins as he posts it to Instagram.

Not going to lie, there's slight anxiety bubbling beneath the surface waiting for the fallout to happen. Waiting for the trolls to find my Instagram account, which is private, but still, somehow, they will find a way to get into it like they have before.

"What a brilliant day. Hotel launch. Hot couple launch, and start of summer." Noah's giddy or maybe he's slightly tipsy.

·ıⱷıⱦ·

"Go around the block again, please," Noah tells our driver as we pass our home, and the crowd of paparazzi run after us.

"How the?"

"They're vultures. You know that." Wrapping my arms around myself, it takes me back to a bad time in my life.

"I didn't think they would actually care."

"You're dating one of the 'playboy twins of New York.'" He tries to lighten the mood. "But honestly, I'm surprised, too." He opens his phone which he's had switched off for most of the weekend. We spent it relaxing in The Hamptons after working so hard on the project. As soon as he turns his phone back on, the device buzzes to life, and he looks over at me concerned. This isn't good. Noah gives the driver directions to one of his hotels. Thankfully, we're able to use the back entrance.

"Mr. Stone. Miss Jones. This way…" The hotel manager greets us at the back entrance. "We have the penthouse waiting for you, sir. We will have someone bring up your bags. Extra security has been arranged at the entrance in case they decide to come here."

That makes me feel a little relieved.

We make our way to the penthouse suite. I'm so riddled with anxiety that I can't appreciate its beauty. Taking a seat, I open my phone and begin to Google our names. Lines of gossip fill my phone screen from all the usual outlets. Then I see a video by TMZ about an interview with Walker, and curiosity gets the better of me.

My hands are shaking after watching it.

He's so angry about Noah and me.

"Babe, are you okay?" Obviously noticing the color has drained from my face, he asks me to hand over my phone to him. He watches the video, and I can see he's visibly shaken from it as well. His face turns like thunder, and he furiously starts calling people. He's shouting down his phone about extra security and that Walker has threatened us.

Walker won't do anything.

He won't want to lose the millions of dollars in sponsorship.

He was caught off guard and didn't have enough time to put his public mask on and think about things.

"He won't touch you ever again. You hear me," Noah tells me. The determined look on his face leaves no room for error. He goes back to his phone calls.

My phone lights up, it's Emma.

"What the fuck?" she screams. "That boy is fucked in the head. Where are you? Are you safe?"

"I'm with Noah at a hotel. The paparazzi are at our home, so we came here."

"Anderson and I are on our way back to the city. I've called a meeting with the gang. Text me where you are."

A couple of hours later, my girls are here as are EJ, Anderson, and Logan. The boys have gone into a separate room to talk strategies. I hate seeing the concerned faces of my friends before me.

"Guys, I'm fine. I had no idea Noah and I going public would cause so much drama. I was kind of hoping to lessen it. Obviously, I was wrong!"

"It's a cute pic," Stella adds. "Very swoony."

Emma pours champagne for everyone except Lenna who declines.

"Why are you not drinking?" Emma questions her. "You never say no to champagne.

"I just don't want any," Lenna says defensively.

Emma eyes narrow on her.

"How are things with?" I flick my thumb toward the other room.

"You have enough going on, try not to worry about me." Lenna's eyes are glassy.

Honestly, I need the distraction.

"What's going on?" Moving forward and grabbing a sandwich, I can be concerned and fill my belly.

"Nothing. It's no big deal. Don't worry about me. Really."

I frown at Lenna's response.

"We can't do much for Chloe at the moment, but maybe we can help you," Ariana says gently as tears begin to well in Lenna's eyes.

"I love my job, but I can't work there anymore." She tries to hold her tears back. "Not with him."

My heart breaks for her.

"Oh, my Lenna bug." Emma sits down and pulls her into arms. "No man is worth your tears. Especially not one so emotionally stunted like him. No offense, Chlo. You got the good twin," Emma tells me.

Thanks, I think.

"He made it obvious this weekend whatever fleeting thing we had was done and dusted. I can't turn my feelings off like that. I'm not a robot."

I want to punch Logan in the dick for being, well, a dick.

"I'm sorry, guys. Seriously, Chloe has more important things going on than my stupid crush."

"Hey, no. This is just as important," I tell her. I don't know why everyone's freaking out, to be honest. Walker said something in the heat of the moment, but he won't do anything. He won't risk the new persona he has as the doting dad and faithful fiancé.

"I can't do it anymore. I thought I was stronger, but I'm not," she tearfully tells us.

"Does it have anything to do with you not having any champagne?" Lenna flinches at Emma's question.

"No!" she yells, standing quickly.

Okay, not sure what's going on right now.

The boys walk back in after hearing the commotion, and they see a tearful Lenna standing in the middle of the room.

"Logan, Noah. I just wanted to let you know that I'm giving you my two-weeks' notice."

The room falls silent.

"Lenna." Noah steps forward. "No. We don't want you to leave," he tries to reassure her.

Logan's standing frozen with a scowl on his face.

"Say something, dickhead." Anderson elbows Logan.

"You're a good employee. We don't want you to go." But Logan's words sound so robotic, it's as if he's just going through the motions but not really feeling them.

Lenna's face turns red.

"Urgh… men," she huffs frustrated. "I have to go." She grabs her bag. "I can't be here anymore." Her eyes glare at Logan, who doesn't say a thing.

All of us girls rally around Lenna, trying to reassure her that she shouldn't leave.

"I'm sorry, Chlo. I know I should be here for you right now. But I just—"

"Shh." I pull her into my arms. "I'm fine. But please, don't leave. Something's going on, and you need us."

She shakes her head. "I know. But I have to sort this mess out myself. My life has decided to go in another direction."

Cryptic. You've just quit your job. Maybe deep down, this wasn't what she wanted.

We all say goodbye to her.

Walking back into the suite, the boys are talking amongst themselves.

"You're a dick." Emma's the first one to speak, directing it straight at Logan. "You should have begged her to stay. She was waiting for you to man up."

"If she wants to move on, then that's her choice," Logan tells her.

"Seriously, did you get dropped on the head or something as a child?" Emma yells at him.

"This has nothing to do with you," Logan advises.

"Like hell, it doesn't. I'm her friend."

Logan scoffs, which makes Emma see red. "You're a selfish bastard."

"Anderson control your wife," Logan spits at his friend.

Anderson turns to Logan, and he looks furious.

"Don't involve him. Are you not man enough to take on a woman?"

"I don't have time for this bullshit. I never thought you were one for the dramatics."

Emma's eyes go wild.

"Back the fuck off," Anderson booms putting himself between Emma and Logan. "You will show my wife some respect."

"Your fake wife."

Anderson's hand comes out at lightning speed and grabs Logan by the front of his shirt.

"Whoa, hold on." Noah jumps in wrestling Anderson from his twin.

"Emma's a part of my life. A permanent part of my life. You better get used to it."

"I don't get how you can stay with a gold digger like her," Logan spits.

"What the fuck, Logan?" Noah turns on his brother.

EJ restrains Anderson from knocking Logan out.

"I'm not a fucking gold digger," Emma screams at Logan. "I have my own shit."

"Ems…" I tug on her arm, "… leave it."

Her eyes widen at me. "You're siding with that dick after the way he's treated Lenna. Your friend. You do remember that?"

What's going on with Emma.

"I'm not siding with anyone. I don't think hurling insults at each other is working either."

Emma pulls her arm away from me. "I'm out." She reaches out, grabbing her bag.

"Me, too," Anderson agrees with her, leaving the suite with a black cloud hanging over it.

"What the hell is wrong with you?" Noah asks his brother.

"Leave me the fuck alone." He pulls himself from Noah's grip, and the boys disappear back to the other room.

"Wow! Okay. That was a little much," Stella interjects.

"Made me totally forget my shit."

"I've got whiplash over all those verbal volleys," Ariana states, looking confused.

"Something's going on with Lenna. Then Emma's outburst. Why is she so angry?" I ask the group, who all shrug with no idea.

"I'm so lost. I think Lenna's pregnant, and I think Emma's in love with Anderson. But who knows?" Stella adds.

Ariana's and my head turn instantly, giving us both whiplash at her comments.

"What?" Stella looks at us both. "What makes you say all that?"

"Oh, 'cause Lenna didn't want a glass of champagne. She's more than a little emotional, and she's quit her job because she's in love with Logan."

Seriously, how did I miss all that?

"And Emma has to be getting the feels for that hunk of a man. I mean they spend every waking moment together. Plus, they have sexy times. But she's too proud to say she likes being married to him or that she's emotionally attached. Did you not see the way those two were all over each other this weekend in The Hamptons? I mean… they can tell the world they were putting on a show for the cameras, but it so wasn't. They were drawn to each other every chance they got, especially when there were no cameras around."

Far out, I suck as a friend. I'm so caught up in my life and drama that I haven't noticed what's been going on with my friends.

"Wow! You really are on the ball," Ariana adds.

Stella shrugs.

"I'm not getting laid, so I need to do something to keep myself busy. Luckily, my friends live dramatic lives." She smiles, then sips her champagne.

32

NOAH

"What the hell just happened?" I yell at my brother.

"I don't know. They're the ones coming at me."

"Because you were being a dick."

Logan flips me off.

"I think everyone's a little touchy at the moment, and everyone's trying to protect everyone," EJ adds. "I've also known Emma for a really long time. She's no gold digger, man," he tells my brother.

"Fine," he huffs. "I was wrong there. I owe her an apology over that." Now we're getting somewhere.

"Also, you insulted a man's wife," EJ adds. "I know they have some weird, fake marriage going on, but still the way he stood up for her tonight, that didn't seem fake."

I have to agree, there's more going on there.

"Fine. I'll apologize to everyone. Happy?" Logan throws up his arms.

EJ and I look at each slightly concerned.

"You okay about the whole Lenna thing?"

The death stare he gives me tells me he's not.

"She looked so upset." A tiny glimmer of remorse flickers across my brother's face.

"Mixing business and pleasure is hard. That's why I don't do it."

"You haven't even once with Stella?" I ask the obvious question.

"No way. She's a good girl. Look at her, she has wholesome written all over her. She's marriage material, not banging material," EJ muses.

"You started off so strong then fucked it all up in the end." He looks at me confused, but I'm not touching that.

"But then there are people like Chloe and me, whose workplace romance works."

"I don't want to hear about it," EJ grumbles.

"You're the exception," Logan admits.

"What are you going to do about Lenna?"

"Nothing."

I'm shocked. "So, you're just going to let her quit?"

"She can't work with me anymore. What more can I do? I fucked it up. I fucked it all up." I've never seen my brother so defeated.

"Lenna's a valuable employee. Honestly, I don't want to lose her. There has to be another way. We have two weeks to change her mind."

"Fine," Logan sighs.

"Great. Can we get back to the bullshit that is Walker and his threat about getting Chloe back."

We've been stuck in this hotel for the past two weeks. Our friend, Jackson Connolly, from LA came out to help update the security on Chloe's and my townhouses and work. We have employed a private investigator to keep track of Walker to ensure he isn't making any trips to New York. I've watched the video over and over again, and each time it raises my anxiety.

"Walker, what do you think about the news of your ex, Chloe, dating and living with multi-millionaire hotelier, Noah Stone?" the reporter yells at Walker.

"What the fuck did you say?"

The reporter repeats his question, but this time his voice is a little shaky, especially given the daggers Walker's shooting at the camera.

"She can run, and she can hide, but I will always find her. And when I do, I'll bring her home, so we can start the life we were supposed to have had together."

The reporter is a little stunned by Walker's comments.

"But you have a fiancée and son at home."

"She's my first love. Nothing can take that away, especially not some punk-ass hotel guy. I had her first." He points at the camera, threatening me. *"She will always be mine. Mine!"*

Then he's pulled away by his football club's representative, obviously seeing his unhinged ramblings as bad publicity for the team.

She will never be yours.

You fucked it up.

You chose to think with your dick, not with your heart.

Walker's bitter because he knows what he's lost. Chloe's a goddamn diamond set amongst cubic zirconia. I'll never make that mistake. No way in the world. She's mine now, and I don't intend on ever letting her go. She's it for me. And as scary as that sounds to a commitment-phobic man like me, when it has to do with her, it feels right.

We're going to get that house in the suburbs, the dog named Frank, and the blonde kids running around between our legs. Our home is going to be filled with laughter and smiles, and I'm going to give my kids the idyllic childhood I had before everything went to shit.

"There's cake in the lunchroom," someone tells me as I walk down the corridor at work.

There's nothing to celebrate. I'm not happy that my brother wasn't able to convince Lenna to stay. In fact, he hasn't spoken to her since he asked her to stay, and she turned him down.

Lenna took the job Emma offered her—running the HR for her

fashion marketing business. Chloe's excited that Lenna's still close by, and that they can still do lunch together.

My brother's a stubborn and complicated guy. He bottles things up. Logan doesn't involve people in his business, but Chloe and her friends are all up in each other's business. Now that Lenna is part of their squad, that means those girls are all up in my brother's business, and that doesn't mesh well.

He apologized to Anderson and Emma for the way he acted, and thankfully they didn't hold it against him, which was commendable of them.

I've noticed he has withdrawn a lot since the whole Lenna thing happened. It reminds me of how he acted after dad died. I'm concerned, but like I said, he's stubborn.

Things at work have been running smoothly even though Chloe thinks the young girls in the office are flirting with me more blatantly now that they know I'm dating her. I didn't believe her at all until I overheard the girls in the lunchroom bitching about Chloe.

I soon put a stop to that kind of office gossip, and if they don't like it, then I have no qualms over firing them all, which might be a problem seeing as we don't have a new HR Director.

"Hey, babe, just dropping off some cake to you." Walking into her office, I place the plate beside her.

"Aw, thanks." Standing, she gives me a quick peck. "Who's the other slice for?"

"Logan." She raises her brows at me. "I'm worried about him."

"I know you are. But he needs to work through his feelings in his own time."

"He's stubborn, Chlo."

"I know. But if you keep backing him into a corner, that's not going to help either." *Maybe she's right.*

"I can't just sit back and see the woman, who I know my brother wants, disappear from his life."

"Aw, you old romantic, you. Maybe it's a case of… if you love it, set it free."

"It's just cake."

"If it ends up on your face, I'm going to say I told you so."

"I'll take my chances." Walking down the corridor to my brother's office, I push open his unlocked door and barrel my way in.

"Here's some cake, dickhead." He doesn't even flinch when it lands beside his work. "It's good cake." I give him a nudge, but he just grunts. "You said your goodbyes yet?"

"I've said all I've needed to say." He doesn't even look up from his work to answer me.

"Why won't you talk to me?" Never thought I'd have to plead with my own twin to tell me what's going on inside his head.

"There's nothing to talk about. We hooked up. It was a mistake. Now it's over. The end."

"Was it a mistake, though? Because you didn't feel anything or because of the business?" He doesn't answer me, which totally means it was only because of the business. "Why do you think you don't deserve love?" Now, I'm turning into a therapist.

"Love?" he raises his voice. "You think what happened between Lenna and me was love? Hardly. It was a couple of convenient fucks."

There's a gasp at Logan's door, and I turn around to see Lenna standing there, the bottle of whiskey she has in her hand drops in slow motion. She's turned and left by the time the bottle smashes over the floor.

"You just couldn't leave it alone, could you?" Logan screams at me.

How am I the bad guy here?

"Fuck. Fuck." Logan thumps his fist against his desk as he stares at the spot vacated by Lenna.

He hesitates for a couple of moments before jumping up from his desk and rushing after her.

33

CHLOE

I t's been a couple of months since the whole Walker threat happened. Noah's private eye hasn't turned up anything. It seems like it was just an angry outburst by an overzealous athlete, one that had no real consequences behind it. We've waited and waited, and nothing's happened. So, I've told Noah it's time to relent on the whole twenty-four-hour security detail, so we can stop living our lives in fear of my ex.

As much as it pained Noah, he agreed. He's relaxed enough even to go away on a business trip over the next couple of days. I told him I will be totally fine as I'm heading off to Bali tomorrow anyway with Emma to shoot that campaign, and Noah's going to meet me there next week. We are going to have our first official holiday together. Stella thinks he's going to propose, but I don't think so. Even though we have spoken about the future, it's still too soon. I wouldn't say no if he did ask, though, that's for sure.

Grabbing my phone off the side table, I pick it up.

"Hey, babe." Seeing Noah's name flash up. "Fuck, I miss you," he moans into the phone which is making my stomach do somersaults.

"I miss you, too." I really do. During the whole Walker situation, I moved all my stuff in with Noah, and I haven't moved back. I don't want to now. "How's Australia?"

Noah, Logan, Anderson, and EJ are all out there looking for the next location for The Stone Group. EJ's there because they're collaborating on this Australian project with him—his restaurant will be the hotel's in-house dining experience.

"It's great. Haven't run into anything yet that can kill me, so that's a bonus." I giggle. "It's so beautiful down here though, babe. You'd love it."

"As long as none of those huge-ass spiders attack me, then I'll be fine."

"You excited about tonight?" I'm catching up with some of the old football WAGs, Bethany, and her crew.

"Actually, I am. It will be nice to sort of put to bed that part of my life. I don't think we'll be as close as we once were, but it will be nice to clear the air. Plus, they're cashed-up. They do like their luxury holidays and have an extensive social media following, so maybe getting them to stay at one of the hotels might give us some great publicity."

"Fuck, I love you, especially when you talk business to me." His gravelly voice sends shivers down my spine.

"Nuh-uh… I don't have time for phone sex. I'm running late as it is." I bet he's pouting on the other end of the phone.

"But I'm hard," he moans.

"Then introduce your dick to your hand."

He laughs. "I can't wait till next week. Your pussy better be ready for me."

"That's my fucking sister you're talking to, dickhead. Treat her like a lady," my brother yells in the background. He's obviously walked in on a conversation he was not supposed to hear.

"Urgh," Noah groans. "My dick's shriveled up now."

"On that note… I have to run, babe. Love you."

"Love you, too."

And with that, he's gone.

I'm late. I hate being late as I rush toward the bar. I can see the group of ladies inside dressed to the nines. The doorman opens the door for me as I head on inside.

"Chloe." Bethany's the first to greet me.

Then I go around the table and say hi to everyone.

"You look amazing. New York suits you." Bethany gives me a wink.

"Thank you." I'm still unable to accept a compliment easily, but I attempt a smile.

"Can we get the elephant out of the room first," Ciara starts. "We saw Walker's TMZ interview, and we were all like what the fuck!" The other girls nod in agreement.

Okay, they're hitting me with the hard stuff straight away.

"I might need to grab a drink first." Feeling a little uncomfortable, I call over the waiter and order a margarita. "Not going to lie, the interview was troubling, but I think he was just letting off some steam." Wishing my drink would hurry up, I shrug my shoulders.

"O.M.G. I was so scared for you," Sherri adds.

"I have good security." Giving them a wink, they quickly look around the room wondering where my security is, so I keep up the ruse.

"Your new man is hot." Tiffani licks her over-inflated lips.

"He's the best. I'm lucky to have him in my life."

"He was your boss, wasn't he?" Bethany asks.

"Yeah. But it wasn't like that. We met ages ago before I got the job. So, it was a shock when I found out he was my new boss." I'm not going into great details about how I really met Noah. I don't feel all that comfortable with the group anymore. Maybe too much time has gone by, or maybe I've changed. I never thought I was the stereotypical WAG, but seeing the way they talk and dress now with fresh eyes, I really was embedded in that footballer's wife life.

I'm so happy to be out of it now.

"And he's rich," Jenny adds, giving me a wink as if that were a job well done. I don't care about Noah's money, the same way I didn't care about Walker's.

"And you have access to all those beautiful resorts. Like hello... best catch, ever. Free holidays for life. Work it, bitch," Ciara adds.

Her comment makes me feel sick to my stomach.

Finally, the waiter brings my drink over, and I quickly take a sip.

"So, what's been happening with all of you guys?" Turning the question back onto them. Thankfully, they can talk about themselves for hours because that's how long I've been stuck here talking about a whole heap of bullshit.

"Can you excuse me. I need the restroom."

"Me, too," Bethany adds. She links arms with me as we walk to the back of the bar. "You're not having fun, are you?"

Her honest question shocks me. I thought I was hiding it well.

"Of course, I am." My voice rising with the lie.

Bethany doesn't look convinced. "I know those girls are a lot, but they mean well." Feeling like a little bit of snob, I know she's right. The girls are encased in this luxurious bubble, and they're used to everyone looking like them, having the same interests. They spend their days getting plastic surgery and their nails done. That isn't me. It was never me, even when I was in that world, but for some reason, now it irritates the hell out of me.

We do our business and come out again.

"Have one more drink, and then you can make your excuses and head off." Bethany bumps my hip.

"I can't stay long anyway, I'm off to Bali tomorrow for work."

Bethany's eyes widen, and she smiles. "Good for you. Don't let those other bitches hear you say that. Their jealousy knows no bounds."

"I'd love to catch up, one on one, next time you're in town."

I like Bethany. She's different to the others. She's self-made with her own beauty salons.

"I'd like that. We might be moving out here next season."

"Wait! What?" Bethany puts her well-manicured nail up against her lips. "Like I said, they are a bunch of jealous bitches, and if they find out Scott's signed with the Patriots, they will skin me alive."

I pull her into a congratulatory hug. "I'm so happy for you."

"Thanks. We're over LA. Scott's over Walker's dramatics, too. They've gotten so bad, Chlo. He's ruining the team." This makes me sad because that team was my family for so many years.

"Well, keep me up to date with everything." She gives me a genuine smile.

"Ready to face the sheep again?" She makes me giggle as we walk back to the table.

***

"I didn't have that many drinks," I say, but my words begin to slur.

"Are you okay?" Bethany asks.

"She's just drunk, Beth. Obviously can't handle her liquor anymore," someone says.

I feel hot.

Maybe I'm coming down with a fever.

"Let's put her in an Uber and get her home. She needs to sleep it off," another voice adds.

"I don't want to be seen with her like a hot mess. Think of the press. She's already a social pariah," another voice adds.

What a bitch, whoever you are.

"What's your address?" Bethany asks, and I mumble it off. "I'll go home with her," someone adds. "I'll get her into bed. Make sure she's okay then meet up with y'all later." There's mumbling, and then I'm moving, being shoved like a pinball from one person to another until I'm shoved into an Uber.

The foul-smelling seats filter through my nose.

Then we're moving.

A hand is stroking my hair. My back.

"There, there, Chlo. You will feel better in the morning," her voice soothes me as I fall asleep.

34

NOAH

We've just sat down to dinner, and Anderson's phone begins to ring. He excuses himself to take the call but is back moments later. His face is white when he calls my name.

I know that look.

No.

Something's happened to Chloe.

No.

"Chloe's missing."

Two simple words, and my world comes crashing down, and here I am halfway across the fucking world.

No. No. No.

He has her.

That fucking bastard waited for me to be out of the country to grab her.

Fuck.

No. No.

I claw at my shirt—my collar feels like it's strangling me. I have to go. I can't be here, not when that madman has his hands on her, doing God only knows what. Fuck. She's mine. He better not have touched a hair on her head. Otherwise, I will fucking kill him and do it fucking slowly.

"Where the fuck is, she?" EJ's yells. "This can't be happening."

"I have to go. I need to get on the next flight home. We're so fucking far away. Fuck. We need to find her. He has her." I'm tearing my hair out as I speak.

"I'm organizing a private jet. We'll get her back," Logan tells me.

Stella's on the phone, tears streaming down her cheeks.

No, this can't be happening.

"Where the fuck is my sister?" EJ grabs Anderson. "Where is she?"

Picking up my phone, I try Chloe's number. Come on, baby, pick up, pick up. Her cell rings out. Shit. I try our home phone. Please, pick up, pick up. Nothing. It rings out. My heart's constricting. This can't be happening right now.

"Where is her fucking security team?" EJ screams.

Stella tries to calm him down, but he won't have any of it.

"This is your fault." He points his finger at me. "You stopped her damn security. She thought she was safe. You threw her to the fucking wolves, you bastard."

"EJ," Logan yells at him. "This isn't his fault. She wasn't in danger. For months they monitored her, and nothing happened."

"Fuck," EJ screams through the restaurant.

"We need to get out of here." I don't need someone leaking any of this to the press before we know what's going on.

"Jackson's tracing her calls, trying to pinpoint her cell phone," Anderson explains to us as we pile into the limousine and head to the hotel.

I just keep trying her phone over and over again.

Where the hell is she?

Where would he have taken her?

"They are fueling up the jet as we speak. We will be back in New York in nineteen hours," Logan tries to reassure me.

That's too long.

He could have done anything to her in that amount of time.

"It's not Walker," Anderson states, and the limousine turns silent. "One of Jackson's security men physically has eyes on him. He's in LA."

My stomach turns inside out, and I think I'm going to be physically sick.

If Walker hasn't taken her, then who the fuck has? Shit.

"Who the fuck would want to do Chloe harm?" EJ shakes in his seat. "She's a fucking good person. She has no enemies."

"They'll find her," Stella tries to reassure him.

"If Walker had her, we would know where she was and be able to get her back. But this… this is like searching for a needle in a massive haystack."

"Snap the fuck out of it," Stella yells at EJ. "Don't think like that. If you want to put negative thoughts out into the universe, then you can fuck off. Chloe doesn't need that out there. She needs us to think. She needs us to work this out to fucking save her." Stella breaks down.

EJ pulls her to him as he apologizes for his comments.

Stella's right, though. We do need to sort this out quickly because every hour that she isn't found, her chances lessen. But she's a fucking fighter, my girl. She isn't going to give up, and neither are we.

"Emma's broken into both of your apartments. Sorry, I owe you a couple of new windows."

I don't give two shits about that at this moment.

"It doesn't look like she came home last night. Nothing's been touched," Anderson relays the bad news.

"Fuck!" I scream while tears roll down my cheeks.

Where are you, baby?

Who the hell has you?

Fight for me.

I'm coming. I'm coming.

Two hours later, and we are up and on our way back to New York, all of us frantically calling anyone and everyone we know.

238

JA LOW

Ariana is talking to the police—she has a friend in the force who's helping.

Jackson has hacked Chloe's phone.

He found the messages from Bethany about drinks, and we gave her a call. She's devastated when we tell her the news. She then begins to blame herself for not being the one who took her home last night. She told us she thought it was strange that all of a sudden Chloe's drinks hit her all at once—she was acting sober then all of a sudden, her speech started to slur, she was hot, and she couldn't move. Bethany thought Chloe was a lightweight. The group decided to put Chloe in an Uber and send her home. That fucking Uber driver better not have touched her. But then Bethany tells us that Ciara went home with her.

Thank fuck she wasn't alone.

Does that mean Ciara is missing too?

We ask Bethany to find Ciara for us, which she does. While we wait for her to get back to us, Jackson begins to hack Bethany's phone. She calls us back, saying that no one can get in touch with Ciara, and she's not answering her door.

Bethany hands over Ciara's number and Jackson begins trying to hack into her phone. Maybe hers can tell us where Chloe is. An hour later Jackson is in Bethany's phone, but he doesn't find anything related to Chloe other than a text from Bethany last night asking Chloe to call her in the morning, so she knows she made her flight on time. She even set an alarm to wake up and check on her. So, she was concerned over Chloe last night.

Ariana had passed on the information about Ciara being the one to take her home. The police are off paying her a visit. Hopefully, there are clues there.

Eventually, Ariana calls back and lets us know that Ciara was found safe and sound in her hotel room. She said she left Chloe at her home at 11:20 p.m. last night. That she then jumped in an Uber and met up with some of the girls to continue partying.

The police check out her story with the Uber company, and they provide video evidence that she did indeed get into the Uber at that time.

Fuck! I'm stuck in this stupid jet halfway over the Pacific, and I can do fucking squat.

Please, baby, hang on.

I'm coming.

Hours later, Jackson calls with some news. He's been able to get into Ciara's phone, and he's found some evidence that suggests she isn't that innocent after all. She's been texting an unknown number letting them know Chloe had arrived. That she had put drugs in her drinks.

Fuck, I'm going to kill this girl.

Who the fuck drugs another woman?

It also said that she dropped her home and left the door unlocked for them.

My stomach lurches, and I rush to the bathroom where its contents fill the bowl.

No. This can't be happening.

This seriously cannot be happening.

Not when I've finally found her.

"You okay?" Logan checks in on me.

"No, I'm fucking not," I say as I'm slumped on the jet's bathroom floor.

"We're going to find her," he tries to reassure me.

"She's my everything, Logan. I was going to ask her to marry me in Bali."

Logan sits beside me. "You're going to get that chance. I promise you."

I'm not a praying man, but at this moment, I'm asking for divine intervention. I want Chloe back and unharmed.

"I can't lose her, Logan." He pulls me into his arms as I break down. If we get through this, no, when we get through this, I'm never letting Chloe out of my sight ever again. She is my everything. My heart. My soul. My future. My end.

Finally, we land in New York and head straight to my townhouse. We're going to retrace Chloe's steps until Jackson can uncover more. Arriving at the townhouses to police tape and a media frenzy, I jump out of the car and barrel toward an officer.

"Hold up there, sir. This is a crime scene," the young guy says to me.

"I know. It's my fucking girlfriend who's missing, and that's my house." Confusion falls across his face as a plainclothes detective walks over to me.

"Mr. Stone, I'm Detective Smith Johnson," the stony-faced detective greets me. "I'm a friend of Ariana's," he elaborates.

Thank God someone's on our side.

"Any news?" Hope bubbles to the surface as I await his answer.

"Let's talk inside." Pulling the police tape to the side for us, we follow in after him. "This is your house, but please sit," the detective tells us.

"Andy." Emma rushes out from the hallway.

"Baby." Anderson rushes to her, pulling her into his arms as Emma breaks down.

If I weren't so damn devastated, I'd be happy for them.

"I'm going to be real honest with you, detective. I'm going to find her no matter the cost, no matter the way."

He nods his head in understanding and leans forward so only I can hear him.

"I'm going to pretend I didn't hear what you just told me. What I don't know, I can't pull you in for. Understand? Make sure whatever you do will stand up against prosecution in a court of law." He's getting his point across. "Now, what we know at the moment is that Chloe was brought home by Ciara. There's security footage across the street showing the Uber pulling up to the sidewalk, and Ciara helping an unsteady Chloe inside. They go through the front door, and about ten minutes later, Ciara walks back out of your home by herself and into a waiting Uber."

What the fuck.

"We know she's working with someone. We have her telephone records where she texted whoever Chloe's kidnapper is, saying she put drugs in her drink and that she left the townhouse unlocked for them."

The detective's eyes widen—this is obviously news to him.

"I'll get someone to look more carefully at the bar's camera footage, checking for the moment she places the drug in her drink. We have to find the evidence to get her to talk. But this is a great lead," he tells us as he furiously types away on his phone.

"We're trying to work out who the unknown number belongs to."

The detective nods his head as he continues to type. "Do you have any enemies, Mr. Stone. You're a very powerful man in this town."

"We are honest men," Logan interrupts. "We do business by the book."

"I wasn't saying you weren't, but I've seen people seek revenge for the smallest indiscretion." He opens a notebook. "Who do you think you may have angered?"

The door opens, and in walks Ariana and Lenna, their eyes are red raw from crying, and they look exhausted as if they have canvased the streets all day.

"Lenna?" Logan says her name, which surprises him.

"I'm so sorry, Noah." She comes over and gives me a hug, which I appreciate.

"Logan." She turns to him. He stands and awkwardly pulls her into him arms. The detective's eyes follow Ariana around the room. Chloe would totally be picking up on that if she were here. *Where the hell are you?* My heart constricts in my chest, not knowing if she's safe.

"We just came back from searching Chloe's office, sorry about that," Ariana confesses to us.

"No. You do what you have to do," I tell her. "No stone should be left unturned. And?" I ask.

"Nothing. She hasn't had any suspicious emails, phone calls. Nothing."

Fuck.

"Do you think this could have been a random attack? A robbery gone wrong?" I ask the detective.

"If what you're saying about Ciara is true, then no, this was premeditated. We just don't know who it could be. Who does Ciara and Chloe have in common?"

"Walker," EJ states.

The detective writes that down.

"No. He's in LA. We checked him out. Unless he has a twin we don't know about."

"I might have my fellow officers pay him a visit anyway. He could have hired someone. You know, not to get *his* hands dirty. I've seen the TMZ interview," the detective tells us.

"Tracey!" Emma blurts out.

"No. She wouldn't," Ariana adds.

"Really? We didn't think she would get knocked up by Walker, but she did."

Why would Tracey harm Chloe? They're family. I think it's a big leap from sleeping with her best friend's fiancé to kidnapping her.

"We will check her alibi out."

"Tracey's friends with Ciara," Stella advises us. "I've just looked up their Instagram and found photos of them together."

"You fucking superstar." EJ grabs her face and kisses her. "Um. I…" He runs his hand through his hair.

"We both want Chloe home safely," Stella tells EJ, thwarting their awkwardness.

"Noah. I promise you… we *are* going to find her. And when we do, I am going to make sure whoever's behind this is put away for a very long time," the detective tries to assure me.

I'm just worried that time is running out for her.

35

CHLOE

U rgh, my head hurts, so I rub my throbbing temple. A chill slides over my body as I try and push open my heavy lids. My stomach churns, and I struggle to keep the contents down. Finally opening my eyes, I jump back in surprise as darkness surrounds me.

Where the hell am I? There's a slight slither of light coming in through a high window, highlighting the room. *Where am I?* My brain's foggy. I try and push through the fog, but it hurts.

Fear grips me as reality dawns that I'm not at home. That I'm not on my way to Bali. That I'm in a potentially dangerous position.

My first thought is to scream for help, but something inside stops me. Whoever has me must still think I'm still knocked out from whatever they gave me. My heart accelerates as I attempt to work out how to get the hell out of here.

The sounds of the waves crashing filters through into the room.

Think, Chloe, think.

You're near the ocean.

I look around my darkened cell again, which looks like I'm in some underground basement. Maybe it's a cellar. The light filtering through the tiny window is my first clue. Grabbing some old crates, I place them under the window and step on them to then peer through the tiny sliver available to me. I can see sand dunes, the crystal blue ocean, and seagrass in front of me.

Definitely on the coast somewhere.

Think, Chloe, think.

I'm trying to wrack my foggy brain.

Where's the coast that's closest to New York? Long Beach, The Hamptons, maybe I'm further south like Seaside Heights.

Urgh. I squint my eyes and try to see if I can register anything which might be familiar to me. Nothing. I try to push open the tiny window, and it gives a little letting in some fresh air. But the window is so small it's only enough for me to push my hand through, nothing more. So, it's hardly an escape route.

Claustrophobia takes over as I begin to hyperventilate.

You've got to keep it together, Chloe, to survive. You need to get home to Noah.

Fuck! Noah.

He's halfway across the world and has no idea I'm missing. *Or does he?*

I have no idea what the time is. I mean, I'm assuming I've missed my flight to Bali, so that will raise alarms. Frantically, I start searching the basement for my phone. After searching for a couple of minutes, I realize they wouldn't be stupid enough to leave my phone with me, not when they have gone to such lengths to capture me.

Slumping on the floor, I try and retrace last night's steps in my mind.

Everything was fine until I got back from the bathroom. I finished the last of my drink and declined another. Hazy memories pop back through my mind reminding me my drink tasted bitter, and I ignored it, thinking it was just the lime.

Obviously, they put something into my drink because everything went foggy after that.

Thumping my fists against the rocky floor, I try to think. *Who would do this to me?* Realization kicks in. *Is this Walker? Would he seriously kidnap me?*

I know I thought Noah's concerns seemed far-fetched. Now, not so much. Fuck! Banging my head against the brick wall, I internally scream as hopelessness surrounds me and tears begin to fall down my cheeks.

How long is he going to keep me here?

What are his plans?

Is he going to kill me?

"Noah, please find me. Please," I whisper as I collapse on the floor in a flood of tears.

I must pass out for a little while until a robotic voice bellows through the basement, waking me up.

"Wake up, bitch." The voice echoes through the room and through my brain as well. "Glad to see you're finally awake."

Now I am scared. The room must be bugged, how else can they see me.

"Had a bit of a rough night last night, Chloe?"

They know my name. I shuffle back and cling to the wall behind me as I try and work out where the hell the microphone and camera are located.

"You're such a sloppy drunk."

"Who are you?" I scream into the darkness.

The robotic voice simply laughs at my question.

"You don't need to know who I am… just yet. All will be revealed soon."

That sounds an awful lot like a threat. Then the voice is gone.

I scream my lungs out, feeling frustrated and scared at the situation I find myself in. Whoever has me is going to kill me, I can feel it in my bones. I have to get out of here. But first, I must find and rip down that fucking camera and mic. I search every single corner of the basement until I find the camera disguised as a rock and pull the fucking thing apart.

"Wrong move, Chloe." The robotic voice echoes through the room as a little doggy door opens, and a cannister is thrown inside the basement.

The room quickly becomes foggy, and then there's nothing but darkness.

36

NOAH

W e've been in New York for twenty-four hours, and we're still no closer to finding Chloe. I'm genuinely starting to panic because the longer she's missing, the less chance we'll have to find her alive. Jackson's been working day and night trying to hack the unknown number. He's getting closer, but still nothing so far. The detective has flown some of his men to LA to confront Walker and Ciara, who mysteriously hightailed it out of New York, and we're waiting for his call at any moment to tell us what's going on.

"I can't just sit here and do nothing," I scream, pacing around the living room.

"We're looking at every possibility, Noah. Jackson has a huge team working on this for us. We want to find Chloe, too, but we have nothing to go on," Anderson tells me.

"You seriously think Tracey would do this?" Because that's where everything is starting to point to.

"The night before Chloe's wedding, the underhanded venom she was shooting toward Chloe shocked me. Those two were as close as two non-blood relatives could be," Ariana explains. "So, Tracey cheating with Walker wasn't that much of a surprise. Especially the way Tracey was acting just before Chloe busted them."

"She was jealous of Chloe. It was subtle, never enough to alarm you, but enough for it to register. If that makes sense," Emma adds.

"Chloe was popular in school. She was beautiful, intelligent, friendly, and everyone loved her. She had loads of friends and was a good girl. Whereas Tracey was standoffish, aloof, and a bitch. She liked to cause trouble. She wanted people's attention, and she got off on it. Especially male," EJ adds. "Tracey had a reputation at school as a good-time girl. She used her looks and sexual skills to lure anyone she wanted. And to randy adolescent boys, she was a god. But she was trouble. She would go crazy if the guy left her for another girl. She hated to lose. She hated that she was only popular because she spread her legs. It seemed like she was always searching for more."

Now I am becoming worried.

Tracey sounds batshit crazy.

"You think she would harm, Chloe?" I'm asking the question I don't want to hear the answer to.

"Tracey hated all the girls at school except Chloe. I don't know why, but they just got on. And it wasn't because our parents were best friends and we were stuck with her. Chloe would always stick up for Tracey. She had her back no matter what because she was a loyal friend to her. I never heard any stories about Tracey screwing Chloe over like she did with Walker, but I had heard her doing it to their other friends. Tracey loved Chloe in her own weird way," EJ tells me.

"I think she snapped over what Walker said," Emma states. "I know we all freaked out over the threat we thought he was giving. But if you play it again, and listen to his words like I'm sure Tracey would have done, you can clearly hear that after everything, Walker still loves Chloe."

The room falls silent.

"Shit." Jumping up from my chair. "You're right, Ems. Fuck. What do we do?"

Suddenly, my phone rings, and it's Jackson.

"What have you got?" I put him on speaker.

"I still have no idea who the unknown number is, but the last known ping from the cell phone was in Montauk."

Everyone around me jumps into action, grabbing stuff. Looks like we're going on a road trip.

Hang in there, Chloe, we are coming for you.

"Also, Walker borrowed a plane. We've only just picked that up, and the flight log has him flying to East Hampton. He should be there now."

Fuck.

"We'll take a chopper, Noah. We'll be there in thirty minutes," Logan tells me as he rushes away with his phone to his ear.

I follow the rest of them into a town car, taking us hopefully to the heliport.

"Also, Walker has a house in Montauk. He recently purchased it last month."

Shit! I punch the seat in front of me.

"My bet is she's there. I'm sending over the address now." I hang up, and my phone beeps, and I look down at the address before me.

I'm so fucking close, baby.

Hang on.

Hang on.

We arrive at the heliport on the Hudson, and just as I'm about to jump aboard, my phone rings, and it's the detective.

"We believe it's Tracey who's kidnapped her."

"I know," I tell him. "We're on our way to get her. Walker has a house in Montauk. We think she's there."

"What the fuck. No, Noah. Give me the address, and I will send the police."

"I'll send you the address, but I'm going. I've just stepped into the helicopter. I'll be there in thirty minutes."

The detective curses down the phone at me, "Don't be fucking stupid. Let the police go in. She could be armed and dangerous. You have no idea what's going through her mind at this moment, especially if she's cornered. She kidnapped her, for fuck's sake, she could do anything."

I hesitate stepping onboard hearing the detective's warning.

"Noah. I can have a team assembled in ten minutes. They will get there before you. Send me the address."

"Fine." I pull the phone away from my ear and forward the address to him. "Do it. There will be a chopper waiting for you. Get here now." He agrees, and I hang up jumping onboard.

"What's going on?" Logan asks.

"The detective is sending local backup to the house. He's worried for Chloe's safety. He believes Tracey's unhinged and us going in there could get her killed."

Logan curses.

37

CHLOE

Fucking hell. Groaning as I try to sit up, but I can't. I move my arms because something seems to be holding them down. Then I'm drenched in freezing cold water.

"Wakey, wakey, sleeping beauty."

A shiver rolls down my body from the icy water. Shaking the droplets from my face, my eyes widen when I see who's standing in front of me with a bucket in her hand.

"Tracey?"

"That's right, bitch." Dropping the bucket to the floor, the loud clang echoes through the room. Ever so subtly, I look around me. Looks like I'm in the living room of a luxury home somewhere, and I can see the beach behind Tracey.

"Why?" It's the only question I have for her. I don't understand why she hates me so much to do this to me.

"Why? *Why?*" She manically laughs.

Then I see the sun glisten off something in her hand.

Fuck. Fuck. Fuck.

She has a gun.

No. No. No.

Testing my restraints, I try hard to get loose, but I'm tied to a chair by my arms and legs. There's no escaping. I'm at her mercy.

"Because after everything I have given Walker, he still wants you." The gun moves from her hip and is pointed directly at me.

No. No. No.

"I don't want Walker. He's all yours. I'm in love with Noah."

Tracey's eyes narrow at me. "You're in love?" she sneers. "You find it so fucking easy moving on from one guy to another. They just keep falling at your fucking feet. Wonder if I can turn Noah's head like I did Walker's." She laughs.

Oh God, the thought of her touching Noah has me Hulking out against my restraints, which makes her laugh even more.

"Sweetie, don't you remember those lessons on Shibari that I did? The art of Japanese rope bondage. You have to keep the spice in the bedroom going. I mean…" she chuckles, "… let's be serious. Men don't want to fuck good girls. Good girls are boring." She waves the silvery gun around in her hand, and honestly, it scares the living daylights out of me. "Why do you think Walker was so easy to take." She smirks.

Keep her talking, Chloe, that's what they always say in the movies.

"I always wanted to know how you did it?"

Tracey wants to gloat, she wants to tell you just how easy it was to fuck your fiancé, so you're going to let her. It will give you more time.

"You really want to know, Chloe?" She's almost glowing with glee.

"Yes."

She jumps up onto the kitchen countertop and places the gun beside her before she starts talking, "Oh, it was so easy. I mean, I was always at your place while you were at work. It started out slowly, a little flirtation here and a little flirtation there. Once I knew his schedule, I made sure I was always around when he came back to your place to freshen up. I made sure I had my skimpiest bikini on as I cleaned the pool. Pretended I was shocked he'd found me like that."

My stomach lurches, but I keep it down somehow. I gave her a key to my home, I paid her to help around the house to assist her between jobs. I didn't realize it was her plan from the start to seduce my fiancé.

"Walker loved hosting parties when you were away. It wasn't until I busted him getting blown by some football groupie that I finally had my chance." She looks smugly. "You were out of town, so I thought, why not pop over. Poor Walker must be so lonely, but I was surprised to see he wasn't sitting at home pining for you. Instead, he was living it up."

I hate both of them so much. I knew Tracey wasn't the only woman he fucked around with, but she's just confirmed it for me.

"Curiosity got the better of me and I went inside. I looked everywhere for Walker but couldn't find him. So, I went up to your bedroom and jackpot... there he was getting his dick sucked." She bursts out laughing. "You should have seen his face when I busted him. He almost shat himself."

She doubles over with laughter, she obviously thinks it's so funny. Once she's composed herself, she continues, "Tracey, Tracey, please don't tell Chloe. It was a mistake. I'll do anything to keep it between us," she says in a deep voice mimicking Walker. "That was my in."

She's fucking sick.

Is she going to tell me she blackmailed him into sleeping with her?

"I told him we weren't having the conversation there, and I opened the spare bedroom's door and locked it behind me. I told him that I wasn't going to tell you. That I understood, sometimes men need to relieve the tension, especially someone like him, who's so filled with testosterone. He needed somewhere to let it off." Tracey sadistically smiles at me. "He fell for it hook, line, and sinker," she gloats.

"I told him that it wasn't a good idea to hook up with random women at parties like this. That they could sell their stories to the press. He agreed. He was so worried you'd find out that he begged me to help him. Oh... and I did."

She's practically glowing telling me the story of how she seduced my fiancé.

Who the hell is this woman? I don't know her anymore.

"I told him he needed to find someone he could trust, who had his best interests in mind. Who was discreet. He was practically foaming at the mouth to find out who this magical unicorn was. When I proposed it was me, he was shocked and a little taken aback. He hesitated. Thought maybe I was setting him up. I pulled out my phone and called you. Do you remember that conversation?"

Yeah. I do. Fucking bitch. We chatted for about five minutes about nothing much in particular.

"What you didn't know was that as soon as you picked up the phone, his tongue was on my pussy eating me out. He was so desperate to keep the charade up that he didn't even hesitate to get down on his knees and eat his fiancé's best friend's pussy while she was on the phone to his fiancée."

I've never wanted to kill someone more in my life than I do right at this moment.

She is an evil, vindictive psychopath.

"Oh... does hearing that make you upset?" She grins. "Knowing that I had the power to make your fiancé do anything I wanted, when I wanted. Not like he was complaining. He loved it. He got off on it— the thrill of nearly getting caught. He especially liked it when I brought a friend. He couldn't get enough of that. I gave him every single depraved fantasy he ever wanted. While you just laid there and fucked him like a fucking nun."

Fuck her.

Fuck, I scream internally.

"I'm glad you fucked him. I'm glad you got what you wanted in the end. A man who wouldn't hesitate to cheat on you because he cheated on you so many fucking times." Tracey's eyes widen. "You think once I was out of the picture that you were it for him?" Now it's my turn to laugh. "Once a cheater, always a cheater," I spit back at her.

I'm bullshitting. I have no idea if he's cheated on her or not, but I suspect he has.

"Fuck you." Tracey jumps off the counter and rushes at me with the gun.

As the metal butt slams across my cheek, she yells, "Fuck you. You always thought you were better than me." She holds the gun to my face. I can feel a trickle of blood slowly falling from my nose down and over my lip. The strong iron taste hits my mouth.

"I never thought I was better than you." Looking up at her, I say, "You were my fucking sister, Tracey. I loved you."

Tracey shakes her head. "No, you didn't," she screams at me. "You took everything from me."

What is she talking about?

"Every single guy I liked…" she waves the gun in the air, "… they wanted you. They always wanted *you*," she spits at me. "Kyle, Jake, Coby… the list goes on." She's reciting my high school boyfriends. "I was good enough for them to fuck, but never good enough to be on their arm, to show off in public. That was always you."

"High school was years ago."

Why is she still harboring resentment about that?

"No," she screams, her eyes wild with fury. "You did it again. You took away the man I loved. The father of my child," Spittle hits my face as she yells at me. "You're trying to destroy my family. Walker is mine."

"I don't want him. He's all yours. I'm not trying to destroy your family. Bear is so gorgeous, you must be so proud." Tracey's face softens the tiniest bit at me bringing up her son. "He is. He loves his daddy." Her voice is almost at a whisper. "Walker's a great dad."

"Good. I'm glad. You make a beautiful family." Keep her talking about her child—that seems to be working. Tracey must forget herself for a moment, but the psycho comes back soon after, and the barrel of the gun is aimed right at me.

"Even when I've given Walker everything he could ever want, he still wants you." Her eyes glare at me as her hand shakily holds the gun. "Even when I turn a blind eye to him fucking his football groupies, he still wants you."

I shake my head. "No, he doesn't. Walker wants to hurt me because I humiliated him. He just wants revenge. He doesn't want me. He loves you. He wants you." I'm trying to reassure her, but Tracey shakes her head, not believing me.

Then we hear a twig snap, and Tracey whirls around to where the sound came from.

"Baby girl." Walker steps in from the beach as if he's just finished surfing, and his voice is soft. "What are you doing, Tracey?"

Tracey's stunned momentarily upon seeing Walker right in front of her.

"What are you doing?"

She shakes the gun at him, and he automatically holds up his hands. "Baby, I came for you. I thought you needed me. Seems like you've gotten yourself into a mess. I've come to help you." He's talking to her ever so softly as if his normal voice might spook her.

"You made me do it," she tells him. "You couldn't let her go. She's not good for you, Walker."

"Oh, baby girl. No… I don't love her. I love you, baby." Tracey's face softens instantly at his words.

"But you said in that interview that she was yours."

Walker starts laughing. "Oh, baby girl, I was trying to get under her new man's skin. I wanted him to know that I was the one who had her first. He will always be second best to me. I was just being prideful, sweetheart."

"But…" She doesn't seem convinced.

"Baby, you know she could never satisfy me like you can," he coos.

Not going to lie, his confession kind of stings.

These two are a pair of sick fucks.

"It was always you. Every night I would sneak to your cabin and fuck you instead of her. It was always you, baby." He walks closer to her, trying not to spook her, I'm guessing. Another branch cracks, and she whirls around and points the gun at me.

"Baby, go check out what that sound is." Tracey turns back to Walker and notices him reaching for one of the knives in the knife block. She hesitates, unsure of what he's doing. "I'm going to have some fun first." Tracey smiles and does as she's told and rushes out of the room. Walker's face changes as he rushes toward me. I scream, but he puts his hand over my mouth.

"I'm trying to fucking save you."

My eyes widen at his words. He moves his hands away and starts slashing at the ropes, while nervously looking over my shoulder for Tracey. "I'm so sorry, Chlo. I had no idea she's crazy," he states while he attempts to hack through the ropes.

"What the fuck are you doing?" Tracey shouts.

"I'm letting her go, Trace. It's not right what you're doing. The police are here."

Tracey lets out a primal scream as a boom goes off behind me. Something breezes past me, and I watch in slow motion as Walker stumbles back a couple of steps clutching his side. Seeing the crimson red stain on his shirt, I scream. Another loud boom erupts, and Walker clutches his lower half, he's screaming out in pain as the bullet goes through his thigh. I'm struggling to get free, feeling like a sitting duck stuck in this chair.

"Freeze. Police." The request echoes through the room. "Miss, no. Miss, put the gun down." I wiggle in my chair, not knowing if my time on earth is up. Then the sound of the gun going off again silences the room.

"Fuck," a male voice screams. "We need medical backup. Now," the man shouts. "One woman with self-inflicted gunshot wound to the head, and one male victim with two gunshot wounds."

"What about her," someone asks, and that's when I see the heroic faces of the police officers. "Ma'am, are you okay?" he asks, seeing me sitting in my seat.

I just simply nod my head.

"A woman victim with a suspected broken nose and shock." He radios the details in, then finally helps me out of my restraints. I cling onto him, my legs not feeling up to the task.

"You're safe now," he tries to reassure me.

Then Walker screams out in agony, and I rush over to where he's lying.

"Hey…" With small strokes, I touch his face, trying to calm him down as he must be in incredible pain. "You saved my life." As much as I hate him for what he's put me through, he took bullets for me, so I owe him something.

"Fuck." He rolls around in pain. "You good."

I nod my head. "Yeah."

"She's arresting. She's arresting," someone screams, and people rush behind us.

Then I realize it's Tracey they're talking about.

"Ma'am. Don't" A police officer holds me back.

The sound of sirens filter through all the commotion. Someone wraps a foil-like blanket around my shoulders and ushers me away. As I walk past, I see the pool of blood coming from Tracey's lifeless body.

Tears fall for the person I used to know, for her son who she won't ever watch grow into a man. For her mom. For the stigma of what Tracey did today and for the loss of her child.

But, I'm not sorry that the monster who took over Tracey is now gone. Because it could have so easily been me lying lifeless in a pool of blood.

38

NOAH

We arrive at the address, there are police and ambulances lined up in the street. They have roped off the area. Just as we step up to the police tape, we see a body being taken from the house.

No. No. I'm too late. No.

I stumble as I get closer.

"Sir, this man's partner is the woman who was kidnapped. He needs to see her," Emma states.

The policeman radios ahead.

"Only immediate family," the police officer adds.

"That's me," EJ shouts. "I'm her brother, and this is her fiancé." He places his hand on my shoulder.

"Just you two then." They tell us to go, and we rush toward the chaos.

"Chloe, Chloe," I scream at the top of my lungs.

Please be safe, please be safe.

"She's over there." A policewoman points to the open doors of the ambulance. A figure wrapped in a foil blanket is holding hands with someone screaming on a stretcher. I see her blonde hair peeking out from the top of her blanket.

"Chloe," I scream as my jelly-like legs try and help propel my body forward.

She turns her head, and I see her bloodied face. "Noah." Her eyes light up seeing me. "Noah…" She jumps out of the ambulance and begins to run toward me. We meet halfway, and I wrap her in my arms. I've never felt such relief as I do right now. We're both sobbing as I wrap my arms tightly around her.

"I thought I was never going to see you again."

"Me, too," she confesses. "It was close, Noah. It was so close, too close." She bursts into tears.

"You're safe." EJ rushes over.

Chloe lets go of me to rush to her brother.

"Fuck, little one. You gave us a scare." He looks down at his bruised and battered sister. Chloe reaches back out to me, pulling me to her side.

"Walker saved me." She turns looking over at the man on the stretcher, and my stomach fills with acid. "He took a bullet. Actually, he took two for me." Chloe looks up at me. "He tried to free me, Noah."

I hate that fucker so much, but right now, I can't thank him enough for saving my girl.

"I can't leave him, he needs me." Her words are like a sucker punch to my chest.

What in the hell?

"Miss…" the paramedic interrupts, "… he's out of it now. They will be taking him straight into surgery. He's safe," she reassures Chloe. "We're ready to take you, though," she says while opening the ambulance doors for her.

"You sure he's okay?" Hesitating, Chloe asks again.

Calm down Noah, she's been through a traumatic experience. Now is not the time for your jealousy.

The paramedic nods. "Okay." Taking the paramedics hands and jumping into the ambulance, another medic tells her to lie on the stretcher so she can check her over.

"I'm coming with you," I tell her.

"Me, too," EJ adds.

"Fine." The paramedics think it over for a couple of moments while we bundle ourselves into the back and both take a seat beside her. We sit silently while the paramedics look her over, checking her out.

"Are you in any pain, miss?"

"Just my nose."

"What happened?"

"She hit me in the face with the butt of the gun."

EJ and I both suck in a shaky breath hearing her words.

"Anything else happen? That we should know about."

Chloe's silent for a couple of beats as she thinks it over. "I'm not sure what I was given at the bar, but it was some kind of drug." The paramedic writes down this information. "And I'm not sure when, but when I was locked up in the basement, she put something in the room, and I passed out."

Far out.

<hr>

"Why can't I see her?" Frantically I'm pacing in the hospital waiting room.

"They're checking her over, and the police have questions." Logan tries to calm me down.

"I should be with her." Panic grips it's talons into my skin and starts to tear me apart being so far away from her.

"I know. But they're just doing their job," Logan advises me. Everyone's in the waiting room. We haven't slept in God only knows how long.

"Team." The detective walks out of her room. "Great outcome." He smiles. "She seems to be holding up well."

"I need to see her."

He nods his head. "You will in a moment, we're just finishing up our questions." Putting his notepad back into his pocket. "My officers tell me Tracey committed suicide when they surrounded her after she shot Mr. Randoff, twice."

"Did she see it?" The detective shakes his head.

"Thankfully, she did not witness it. But she did see Mr. Randoff get shot which seems to have upset her."

"She said he saved her," I add.

"When he's out of surgery, I will get his side of the story. But yes, that's what Miss Jones is saying."

"Is he going to survive?"

"Yes, Mr. Stone, he will, but I think his football career is over."

Wow! That's not going to go down well. Tracey really did fuck up everyone's lives.

"And what about Ciara and her part in all this?" She's the one who set this in motion.

"As that is an ongoing matter, I can't discuss that investigation further with you at this time. But thank you for your help in finding what we need to take it to court." *Guess that's good news.* "Mr. Stone, you're free to go in, but one at a time," he tells the others in the waiting room.

"Go," EJ tells me. "She's safe now. I can wait."

I rush into Chloe's hospital room.

"She's sleeping," the nurse tells me.

"But she's okay?" She gives me a warm smile and nods.

"Thankfully her nose isn't broken just badly bruised. We've taken some samples of her blood to test for toxins to work out what they drugged her with. She'll be happy to see you when she wakes."

I must fall asleep at some point and wake up to fingers in my hair.

"Hey," she says.

Looking up, all I can see is her bruised face.

"Hey," she says again, groggily.

"I was so scared, Chlo."

Tears begin to fall down her cheeks. "I didn't think I would ever see you again," she tells me. "But I wasn't ready to go, not when I'd only just found you."

"I'm sorry I wasn't here for you. I'm sorry I didn't fight harder about security. I should have pushed you harder. I won't make that mistake again."

Chloe shushes me. "This is not your fault, do you hear me?" She's adamant, I can tell. "Tracey was a very sick woman. She would have found a way." Giving me a small smile, she says, "I can't believe she's dead."

"How do you feel about that?" I can see the war that's plaguing her mind is not a good one.

"She was family." Her hand twists in mine. "But when she pointed that gun at me, there was no hesitation. I could tell she would have pulled the trigger." Hearing the trauma she's gone through is killing me. "I'm just finding it hard to rectify the two personalities as the same one."

"Walker's surgery went well." This perks her up, which is hard to witness, but I know she loves me, and he did save her.

"Hey…" She places a finger under my chin. "I love you." She gives me a smile. "It was you I was thinking about through it all. It was you I wanted to come home to. You have nothing to worry about with Walker."

"I know, baby. I'm sorry. I… just…"

She shakes her head. "Walker has made our lives hell. I get it."

"I want to hate him, but I can't. I can't find it in me anymore to hate him because he saved you. He saved the love of my life."

"Kiss me," Chloe demands.

You don't have to ask me twice. It feels like heaven tasting her after so long. She hums against my lips. God, I've missed her so much. Standing beside her, I stroke her hair. "I love you, Chlo."

"I love you, too." She smiles up at me. "I want that white picket fence, Noah. In the suburbs. With a dog named Frank."

"Really, Miss Jones?"

She nods her head, enthusiastically. "I want you, Noah Stone. Forever and ever."

"You're wish is my command, Chloe Jones."

39

CHLOE

I t's been months since that fateful day, and slowly over time and a
hell of a lot of therapy, the nightmares are not as bad as they once
were. PTSD is what the counselor tells me I have. And it's understand-
able after the traumatic experience I've been through. But having the
world's greatest man right by my side, I know I can get through
anything with his support.

Life gets put into perspective when you see it flash before your
eyes, and you're moments away from the outcome being the end. As
Noah said, life's too short to hold onto grudges, especially when
Walker saved my life.

I know, what a turn-around, right?

At first, it was hard going back to my normal life, especially with
the nightmares. One particular night I reached out to Walker in a
moment of desperation, and he too was having the same nightmare. I
told Noah that I'd been in touch with Walker. At first, I could see me
reaching out to Walker had really hurt Noah, and I totally understand
why. My therapist thought it would be a good idea if the three of us did
a session together. It took a lot of convincing on my part to get the two
of them in a room, but once Noah heard our stories of that day, he
understood that he couldn't give me what Walker could. So, from that

day, things changed between the three of us. It's been a long road to recovery, but we're all thriving.

Walker has had to grow up a lot since the incident. His football career ended because of the bullet wound in his thigh and stomach. He got a new job as a sports newscaster as well as a high school football coach in upstate New York. I know, small world. But I can't begrudge him the chance to start over because he's changed. Matured. Realized he isn't the god he always thought he was.

After the incident, he spent a long time in the hospital and then in physiotherapy. He lost all his ride or die friends. His whole life was gone in an instant. It's hard to kick a man when he's hit rock bottom. But it was the custody case over Bear that really brought Walker fully into our lives.

Tracey's mom filed for full custody of Bear while Walker was in the hospital. She advised that Walker was not the biological father of Tracey's baby. *I know, insane right?* Even from the grave, Tracey seems to be able to fuck with everyone's life.

Walker spiraled when the DNA results came back, and it showed that he was indeed not Bear's father. EJ even flew out to LA to stand beside him during the case because he had no one else on his side.

Walker was a dick, but he loved that little boy, and to have your child taken away from you is the lowest of blows.

Tracey was a monster.

I don't know what happened to the girl I used to know.

Did her hunger for fame and fortune finally corrupt her?

Did I really make her life miserable, or was she always this evil?

So, after the case, we kind of adopted Walker into our menagerie of a group. Believe me, we're all surprised at the turn of events. None, more so than me.

Once we convinced Walker to leave the West Coast and move back to the East Coast where his family is, Noah suggested that maybe Walker and I should have separate counseling over our relationship because saving my life really doesn't null and void the vile stuff he did to me.

I'm glad Noah pushed me to go because, in all honesty, it was cathartic. We both realized how unsuited we were for each other, that I hadn't really dealt with the death of my family, and he hadn't dealt with the fact his father was a womanizing athlete who treated his mom like shit, and that he had turned out just like him.

Both of us truly moved on after the experience.

They may never be best friends, but Noah has welcomed Walker into our little circle. I think the season tickets helped break the ice between them. I know it's strange to be happy about what Tracey did to us because it was so traumatizing, but the aftermath of it all has turned into such a blessing. I can't deny that I don't think I would be at peace like I am now if it hadn't have happened.

I have so much to be thankful for—life's looking pretty damn sweet.

One Year Later

I don't want to get up, but we are hosting Christmas Eve in our new home in Greenwich, Connecticut. I love our place out here, it's so perfect. We've just finished the renovations and brought the sprawling estate into the twenty-first century but still kept all the original features, thanks to Ariana's amazing work. And the best thing is, it has a white picket fence.

I feel hot breath on my face—utterly unsavory breath at that.

"Clean your teeth, Noah," I mumble, pushing him away, but my fingers sink into fur instead.

Instantly I'm awake, turning to look at what's woken me, and I'm greeted by a little chocolate Labrador with a bright red bow. He gives me a bark as he realizes he has my attention.

Oh my God, he's the cutest thing. Picking him up and squishing him against me, he tries to bite my fingers with his sharp puppy teeth. I don't care if they are like razor blades against my skin, I totally love it.

"His name is Frank." Noah walks into our bedroom, announcing happily.

"You." Looking over at Noah, tears fall down my cheeks.

Noah gives me a huge smile. "Did you check his bow?" he asks.

Shaking my head, I undo the bright red bow and a large diamond ring falls onto the bed, and when I look up, Noah's on one knee.

"From the moment I met you, on your honeymoon..." he gives me a smirk, "... you had my heart, Miss Jones. I tried to fight it, but I couldn't. The pull between us was too much."

I can't stop the tears, but the puppy licks them away.

"Then there was the day my world stopped. The day I thought I had lost the love of my life. I made a promise to the person upstairs that if I got you back, I would love you with all my heart, forever."

Far out, I love this man.

"So, I'm making good on that deal with the man upstairs today. Chloe Jones, will you be my forever?"

"Yes. Yes. Yes."

THE END

ABOUT THE AUTHOR

JA Low lives in outback Australia. When she's not writing steamy scenes and admiring hot cowboys, she's tending to her husband and two sons, and dreaming up the next epic romance.

Facebook: www.facebook.com/jalowbooks
Twitter: www.twitter.com/jalowbooks
Instagram: www.instagram.com/jalowbooks
Pinterest: www.pinterest.com/jalowbooks
Website: www.jalowbooks.com
Goodreads: https://www.goodreads.com/author/show/14918059.
J_A_Low

Come join JA Low's Block
for awesome giveaways, sneak peak at WIP, exclusive content and
much more.
www.facebook.com/groups/1682783088643205/

THE DIRTY TEXAS BOX SET

Five full length novels and Five Novellas included in the set.

One band. Five dirty talking rock stars and the women that bring them to their knees.

This collection includes:

Suddenly Dirty

He was everything she wasn't looking for.

She was everything he wasn't ready for.

A workplace romance with your celebrity hall pass.

Suddenly Together

She was everything he always wanted.

He was everything she could never have.

A best friend to lover's romance with the one man who's off limits.

Suddenly Bound

He was everything she could never have.

She was everything he couldn't possess.

An opposites attract romance with family loyalty tested to its limits.

Suddenly Trouble

She was everything he wasn't allowed to have.

He was everything she couldn't have.

A brother's best friend romance with a twist.

Suddenly Broken

He was everything she wasn't looking for.

She was everything he wasn't ready for.

A friend's with benefits romance that takes a wild ride.

One little taste can't hurt; can it?

If you like your rock stars dirty talking, alpha's with hearts of gold this series is for you.

The Dirty Texas Box Set

LOVE IN COLOUR

I will not kill my boss.

I will not kill my boss.

I will not kill my boss.

This is the mantra I tell myself every day.

Because I know I won't survive jail and orange clashes with my strawberry blonde hair.

It's just for the summer, Emily, it will fly by.

Lie. Time has stopped. He is probably controlling it to torture me.

You are working in the South of France.

At least there is wine and cheese.

He is the artist of our generation.

Before he became a washed up has-been whose ego is bruised, and now he's self-destructing with wine and women.

He's hot.

Okay, well I have nothing.

The man looks like Michelangelo carved him with his bare hands. And that French accent, those soft lips, and that giant um...never mind. It's still connected to him and no amount of magnificence can take away that it's connected to the biggest jerk in history.

So, I tell myself again. I will not kill my boss.

Love in Colour

BRATVA JEWELS SERIES

Sapphire

An unconventional love is tested to its limits.

Mateo is used to being in the spotlight, he craves it in everything he does . . . except when it comes to his love life - that is firmly in the closet.

Tomas shuns the spotlight, the one he was born into, he wants nothing to do with it or his high-flying family who now reject him for his choices in love.

But Tomas' and Mateo's carefully constructed lives are turned inside out when they discover a beautiful, battered woman on their doorstep. The woman with the sapphire eyes has no memory of who she is or how she got there. She doesn't know about the Bratva Jewels - the Russian mafia's most desired escorts - or how her story intersects with theirs. Can Tomas and Mateo help her remember before the men who are after her find her first?

Sapphire - Book 1

BRATVA JEWELS SERIES

Diamond

Round 2 with the Devil begins.

Grace thought she had left the nightmare of the Bratva Jewels behind her. Her days spent as one of the Russian Mafia's most desired escorts were some of the darkest of her life, but she was safe now. Or so she thought.

When Russian mobster Dmitri seeks revenge, he gets it, and Grace knows she must call on every ounce of inner strength she has to withstand what he has in store for her. What she didn't expect was to meet someone like Maxim . . .

Maxim is one of the Bratva's most skilled, and most feared, assassins. But his relationship to the Bratva is a complicated one. And when he meets Grace, suddenly everything becomes clear.

Diamond - Book 2

FATE'S PLAN

Lilly Simpson's life hasn't turned out the way she planned, especially her fiancé. She's on the first plane out of Africa and back home to a family she's missed the last couple of years.

But what she wasn't expecting when she arrived home was a hot, naked, Italian man in her living room, instead of her sister.

Guess I should stop staring at his …

Luca Fiorenzo has lived by his family's rules all his life. Until the person he was supposed to spend forever with betrays him. So to hell with the rules.

But what he wasn't expecting when he booked a cottage in the middle of nowhere Scotland was a cute, awkward brunette, who just wouldn't stop looking at his ....

Guess I should put my pants on then.

Fate's Plan - Novella

Made in the USA
Columbia, SC
30 June 2024